"What the hell was that?"

Kate watched in helpless horror as the train station erupted in gunfire and what looked like small explosions. She dialed in. "M-One, this is Primary. What's your sitrep?"

"Upon entry, the team ran into a pair of hostiles on the way out with the target. The standoff distracted them long enough so that a backup pair was able to ambush, terminating M-Four. We have recovered the target, and she is on her way up now with M-Two. M-Three and M-Five are also withdrawing, and I expect them to arrive shortly."

"Okay, listen up." This was the part she hated. "When the target is aboard, you give your people ninety seconds to arrive and if they're not there, you withdraw."

"Say again, Primary?"

"The rest of your team has ninety seconds from when the target arrives to get to the evacuation vehicle. If they don't make it, you leave them behind. Acknowledge."

There was silence, then the team leader replied, "Affirmative."

Other titles in this series:

ROOM 59

THE
FINISH
LINE

CLIFF RYDER

A GOLD EAGLE BOOK FROM
WORLDWIDE®

TORONTO • NEW YORK • LONDON
AMSTERDAM • PARIS • SYDNEY • HAMBURG
STOCKHOLM • ATHENS • TOKYO • MILAN
MADRID • WARSAW • BUDAPEST • AUCKLAND

Recycling programs
for this product may
not exist in your area.

First edition January 2009

ISBN-13: 978-0-373-63269-5
ISBN-10:   0-373-63269-X

THE FINISH LINE

Special thanks and acknowledgment to
Jonathan Morgan for his contribution to this work.

Printed in U.S.A.

THE
FINISH
LINE

As he watched the nude, writhing, sable-haired woman rock back and forth above him, Harry Vaughn could scarcely believe his luck. Ah, the fringe benefits of being a radical environmentalist, he thought, trying to hold out as long as possible, to prolong their lovemaking until the very last second.

Her long locks falling over her face in a black curtain, Marlene leaned over and kissed him hard, nipping his lip in the process and making an animalistic growl rise in Harry's throat. Pulling back, she laid a slender finger against his lips. In the dark hours of the fog-shrouded London evening, they had to be quiet, lest they wake any of the other half-dozen mates of his cell crammed into the flat they had rented at Edgar House.

He felt the familiar pressure in his loins, and clenched his pelvic muscles, gritting his teeth as his hands cupped her breasts. While Marlene wasn't quite as well endowed as Harry would have liked, she had a coiled intensity that more than made up for what she may have been lacking. He'd certainly seen it before. It was the certainty that they might be arrested or even killed at any moment while preparing for and carrying out their mission. With that knowledge came the belief that every moment of freedom was precious, and should be enjoyed to the fullest before they went out to spread a plague through London's city streets. Harry himself had likened them to modern-day samurai, exhorting his comrades to fear neither the police nor death itself, as long as the mission was completed. That Japan's medieval warriors were often totally subservient to the state was a fact he was careful to omit during his carefully honed speeches.

Although his rhetoric was sometimes greeted with amused scorn, Marlene hadn't scoffed or sneered, just regarded him with those smoldering, dark brown eyes that had made his groin tighten as he had returned her steady gaze on the first day they had met. As the elder statesman of the group, which had formed under the loose auspices of the leaderless Earth Liberation Front, he had sat back and watched as the younger men, filled with their self-important nattering, had tried to gain her affections ever since she and her brother had joined their cell about two months ago. The lucky ones had escaped with only their egos bruised. One young man had been so embarrassed after his failure that he had quit the group entirely.

Harry had simply bided his time, waiting for the right moment. It had come three weeks earlier, when she had visited the room where he stayed alone, by virtue of being the leader, in the early hours of the morning. She had come by every few days since, and they had kept their relationship private by mutual consent, not wanting the others to labor under the dividing sting of jealousy. The mission was all that mattered.

He heard Marlene's ragged breath quicken as she leaned back again, her slim body settling on his thighs, and he increased the tempo of his thrusts, exulting in the small stabs of her nails on his skin as she rode him toward climax. Their coupling grew more rhythmic and frenzied as Harry, unable to contain himself any longer, bucked and arched beneath her, wanting her to come, as well. Even with the condom she'd insisted on, she made him climax faster than any other woman ever had.

Throwing her head back, Marlene's breath hissed out between her teeth as her body shook in a long, shuddering spasm, completely lost in her own pleasure. At the same time, Harry felt that familiar white light explode behind his eyes as he also trembled in release. With one final jerk, Marlene leaned forward to collapse on him, her chest heaving.

"Goddamn, that was amazing." Harry kept his voice to a whisper as he stroked her hair. He had been with many women in his thirty-eight years. The eco terrorist gig had always been a magnet for women—whether they were somewhat naive university students newly committed to the cause, or older women slumming while providing funds to fuel their low self-image. There was just something about the outsider, the rebel, that drew them like cats to clotted cream. Fortunately, both of us usually end up purring afterward, he thought.

She rolled off him with practiced economy and burrowed under the sheets, one hand snaking out to the cluttered nightstand to grab a crumpled cigarette packet. "Bloody hell," she said.

She tossed the empty pack on the floor, eliciting a frown from Harry. Unlike the more radical members of their group, he knew the value of a shower, and liked to keep his quarters neat, one of the last byproducts of a stint in the army in the late eighties before he'd gone AWOL and dropped off the government's radar completely.

He turned to her, resting his head on an elbow-propped hand. "I wish you wouldn't do that."

"Tell you what—I'll pick it up if you be a dear and run to the corner to get another pack, love." Her sultry voice never failed to send pleasurable shivers down his spine.

"First you shag a man till he can barely stand, then you want to send me out into the cold night air just so you can have a fag." He laughed quietly.

She ran a hand beneath the sheet and up his leg, her nails sending tremors of delight through him. "If you hurry, maybe it'll get your blood pumping again—and I'll still be here in this nice warm bed, waiting for you."

Harry leaned over and kissed her, relishing her eager response to him. "You drive a hard bargain, lass."

"Hopefully it won't be the only thing that's hard in a bit," she teased.

Rolling out of bed, Harry strolled to the bathroom, where he disposed of the condom in the toilet and wiped himself down with a warm washcloth. After toweling himself off and brushing his teeth, he dressed in the bedroom, pulled on boxers, pants, a T-shirt and a rugby shirt. He felt Marlene's eyes on him all the while. When he finished, he turned back and leaned over her, kissing her one last time, his hand stealing below the sheet to cup a last feel of her breast.

"Mmm, minty." She arched into him, her fingers caressing his stubbled cheek.

"You wait up for me now, eh?" he said.

"I won't move a muscle until you return. Then we'll see if you can move me again like you just did."

"Count on it." With a wink, Harry walked out of the bedroom, closing the door behind him.

The room opened into a narrow hallway with two other wooden doors along the left wall, and an ancient staircase leading down on the right. Other than the high-pitched, nasal whistle of Aron's snoring, the rest of the flat was dead silent.

Harry crept past the closed doors, one of which opened slightly as he passed. With a grin, he eased it closed—that was where Marlene had come from in the first place, where she slept with Raynie. Staying close to the side of the staircase to avoid the creaky boards, he tiptoed down to the ground floor, and, after slipping into his battered jacket and equally worn pair of Doc Martens, he ghosted out the front door into a world of white.

Wyvil Road was wreathed in evening fog, the thick mist cooling his face as he walked toward South Lambeth Road. It was so heavy he could barely make out the small dead end where truck drivers often parked for a smoke or a cup of tea on their break between runs. Squinting, he made out a high-sided delivery van, its engine off, tucked into the small alcove. With a shrug, he continued toward the main road.

Harry had been protesting a bit too much back in the bedroom. He actually preferred walking around when the detestable city was quiet and still, not filled with the frantic scurrying of the hundreds of thousands of people running to and fro through their mindless, media-saturated lives. He knew the majority didn't give a tinker's cuss about what they were doing to the planet they were slowly trampling over, choking into polluted, smoggy submission and overdeveloping into extinction.

And if the planet itself cannot strike back, then it must have help, Harry thought.

As he turned the corner and strolled down Lambeth, Harry mused about the stroke of providence that had brought Marlene and her brother into their little circle. Not only had their devotion to the cause been fervent and absolute, raising the at-the-time flagging morale of the cell, but they had also been instrumental in moving the plan forward, helping to obtain the high-quality anthrax spores the cell planned to use to contaminate the British Museum, the Tate Gallery and several other large public areas where many groups of people attended. Harry, always pragmatic, had reserved a healthy dose of suspicion about them and the fact they had come to the Wyvil Road flat at such an opportune time, but his careful surveillance on the two had turned up nothing. When away from the rest of the cell, they carried out whatever duties they had been assigned, usually taking the Vauxhall Tube to scout out the various assigned targets. The two were dedicated members—and one an absolutely great shag. With another dozen as committed as them, Harry knew he could bring London to its knees. But for now, he'd have to settle for sowing contagious havoc throughout the city. Unlike those stupid gits who had tried to drive car bombs into the capital of England last year, his plan would succeed.

At the corner of Wheatsheaf and Lambeth, Harry ducked into a tuck shop and picked up two packs of cigarettes: an expensive pack of Gitanes Blondes for her, and Marlboros for himself. Although aware of the irony of smoking while trying to save the planet, he preferred to think of it as suffering along with the Earth instead. Resisting the urge to light up on the way back, he decided to wait until after the second round. The thought made him quicken his step, however, and he was almost trotting as he retraced his steps back to the flat.

Coming up the walk, he stepped on a rock that twisted under his foot, splintering apart with an odd scraping noise. Stifling a curse, Harry stopped and looked down at the sidewalk. In front of him was something that looked like a loose red brick that might have come from one of a dozen buildings or walkways in the neighborhood. But this one hadn't turned his ankle like a real brick would have, and it hadn't made the solid impact against the walk it should have when he'd stepped on it.

Squatting, Harry looked at the ersatz brick without picking it up, a sinking feeling growing in his stomach by the second. As he suspected, it was made of some kind of Styrofoam, and he spotted the round tube of a camera lens in its center.

The bastards are on to us.

Rising as if he didn't have a care in the world, Harry's brain churned through the possibilities open to him. Chief among them was that he could simply keep walking, continue down the street and get the hell out of the city. Glancing up at the first-story window, he shook his head. He couldn't abandon Marlene and the rest to get nicked.

Climbing the steps, Harry fumbled with the lock,

already going over the necessary actions. Don't stop moving, get upstairs, get everybody up and out the back way. He knew the high improbability that the back way would be clear, but it was the only chance they had. If they hit us before, it's everyone for themselves. Even Marlene. He knew she was the real reason he was even going back inside.

Wrestling with the lock, he wrenched the door open and slipped inside, resisting the urge to slam it. Instead, he shut it with a soft click and shot the bolt, then whirled around to head for the staircase—only to stop dead before he could take a single step.

Standing in front of Harry was a person dressed from head to toe in some kind of matte-black, close-fitting uniform, with a web harness across his chest covered with equipment. The intruder's face was completely covered by a sinister-looking mask that completely hid his features. The smell of burned gunpowder and blood was thick in the hallway. Harry absorbed all of that in a split second, but his attention was drawn to the smoking, silenced pistol aimed directly at his face.

"Where's the girl?" the masked figure whispered.

Harry frowned in feigned confusion. "I have no idea who you're talking about."

The pistol's muzzle dipped and coughed, and Harry's left leg buckled as the bullet smashed into his kneecap. He dropped to the floor, gritting his teeth as he clutched his ruined leg. Who the hell is this bloke? No copper, that's sure.

"Last chance for you to limp out of here rather than be carried out. Where is she?"

Through his tears, Harry couldn't help glancing up at the staircase, but he was determined to give her as much time to get away as possible. "Bugger off!" he barked, then opened his mouth to shout a warning. As if in slow motion, he saw the pistol's muzzle in front of his face, the round hole looking large enough for him to fall into. Then his world flashed apart in a burst of orange-and-red fire, and Harry knew nothing more.

"Team Two, hold your position!" In the white panel van parked in the turnoff north of Wyvil Road, Midnight Team member David Southerland wiped sweat from his brow and squinted at the suddenly underpowered forward-looking infrared system he had been using to watch the front door of the eco terrorists' flat.

The five-man squad had been watching the flat for the past six hours, preparing to infiltrate the house and capture or eliminate the occupants, all wanted for conspiracy to commit terrorist acts against a sovereign government. Once their undercover agent had confirmed the presence of both biological weapons and homemade explosives in the house, Room 59, the global, top secret intelligence agency that had been tracking this cell for the past several weeks, had called in a Midnight Team, their own special-weapons-and-tactics division.

David was ready to move, but at the moment he was caught between closing the trap and trying to figure out what had just occurred. He and his partner in the van had just watched their target crouch down on the sidewalk, as if he had spotted something, but they couldn't be sure. Even with the fourth-generation thermal vision scope he was using, he couldn't make out the fine details necessary to confirm if their surveillance had been spotted.

"Jesus, M-Two, I told you, we've got a two-man hit team that just entered the back door. We need to get in there before they rabbit," one of the other operatives said.

The voice of their leader came on. "I ordered radio silence unless anyone spots a target leaving. Anyone else speaks out of line, and they'll answer for it."

"What do you think just happened?" Next to David, the newest member of the squad, a green recruit named Tara McNeil, lowered the infrared binoculars she had also been using to scan the house.

"I can't tell, but get your MASC on—we'll be going green any second. Team Two, any activity on your side?" he asked over the radio.

"Nothing coming or going since we took our position, M-Two."

David thought he heard the other half of the back-door team, the member who'd been dressed down earlier, mutter, "At this rate, they'll die of old age before we get to them."

David ignored the comment as their leader spoke again. "Nothing on the rooftops. However, one of our targets has been eliminated. My scope picked out two figures in the hall, and two flashes of what was undoubtedly a firearm just now. Move in and take the house," he ordered.

David flushed as their team leader pointed out what he should have seen in the first place. "Damn it!" He switched channels with a practiced flick of his eyes. "Vole, there are hostiles inbound, repeat, hostiles inbound on your position." The plan had been to "capture" their inside man, in case his cover needed to be maintained. Now that, along with everything else, was in jeopardy.

Switching back to his team's channel, David issued orders. "Team Two, take the back entrance. We have the front. Everyone make sure your seals are secure—there are biologicals in there."

A chorus of affirmatives answered as David pulled on his Multi-Aspect Sensor Covering, or MASC for short. He'd always hated the acronym, but loved the full-head protective helmet with its integrated visual sensor suite, enhanced audio pickups, flash defense system, voice mask and networked heads-up display and communications unit. Along with their night-black uniforms under Dragon Skin flexible ballistic armor covering their limbs and torso, they looked like soldiers of the future, which, David supposed, they were.

He scrambled out of the van, with Tara right behind him. The fog was dissipating and the narrow street was deserted as they ran across and up the stairs to the door. With David covering her, he motioned for Tara to try the handle. She did and found it locked.

M-One's calm voice sounded in David's ear on the secure, laser-beam comm channel. "The door is blocked by a body on the inside. Suggest using the left window—that room appears to be empty."

David switched over to thermal and saw M-One was correct—a still-warm body lay against the lower half of the door, while the room to their left appeared to be empty. Sudden motion in the hallway beyond caught his eye, and he glanced back to see a glowing red-and-orange-and-white human form step out from another room on the other side of the house, leveling something at the door.

"Cover!" David shouted and ducked away as a silenced submachine gun loosed several rounds inside the flat, a long burst of bullets perforated the door and sprayed shards of wood into the street. David looked at his HUD to check Tara's status, along with the rest of his team, and was relieved to see that they were all uninjured.

More suppressed gunfire could be heard in the building from several weapons. "Team One, this is Team Two, be advised we have encountered multiple shooters upon rear entry."

"Affirmative. M-One, clear the hallway, if possible. We're going in through the side," David said.

"Roger." On the roof of the building across the street, David glanced back to see a hunched form poke out a long-barreled, suppressed XM110 rifle and place a trio of 7.62 mm bullets through the center of the door. David wasn't worried about being hit by friendly fire, even at this close range. Their team leader's weapon was wired into his HUD, and the Friend-Or-Foe imaging program meant he could not shoot his fellow team members unless he took the rifle off-line.

"Follow me!" David readied his silenced TDI Kriss Super V .45-caliber submachine gun in one hand and stepped onto the railing on the left side of the steps, bracing his free hand against the side of the building. Pointing the gun at the window, he triggered a short burst, shattering the glass and its wooden frame. As soon as the larger pieces stopped falling, he leaped to the windowsill, knocking out shards of glass with the butt of his weapon.

"Team One, where are you? Hostiles are advancing toward your position. They're almost on you," M-Five radioed.

"Almost there." Clearing the last of the glass from the window, David slipped inside, finding himself inside a kitchen. His thermal vision picked out several figures, each outlined in shades of red, orange and yellow, jockeying for position on the other side of the wall, their automatic weapons spitting flame as they shot down the hallway. David was about to give them a huge surprise when a smoking canister flew through the doorway that led into the kitchen, landing almost at his feet.

"Flash-bang!" he shouted. Snatching the weapon even as he knew it could go off at any second, David tossed it back into the hallway and turned away. The grenade had barely disappeared when it detonated with a thunderous explosion and bright flash of light.

The sound dampeners on David's MASC neutralized the potential damage to his ears, and the light-sensitive photofilm layer in his goggles had darkened at the first millisecond of the light burst, keeping his vision clear. Behind him, Tara had just come in through the window, and was moving into a position.

"Wait a—" was all he got out before the hallway lit up again with automatic-weapons fire, stitching her high across the chest as several rounds burst through the wall and impacted on her body armor. Caught by surprise, Tara still stayed upright and returned fire through the doorway, laying down a diagonal line of Le Mas .45-caliber SPLP blended-metal bullets from right to left.

"M-Three is hit, M-Three is hit!" David rose to check her, but Tara shrugged him off.

"I'm fine, let's clear the hallway." As if nothing had happened, she moved to the left side of the doorway and scanned the hallway again.

"Team Two, we are inside the perimeter to the left of the hallway. What's your status?"

"Hostiles on ground level are both down. We are proceeding with caution—shit!"

David heard more gunfire. "Report!"

"Taking fire from the first story."

"We'll clear the front hall and meet you near the stairway."

"Affirmative, but watch yourselves. We're pulling flash-bangs."

"Copy that, we got a glimpse of them already."

Cody's voice broke in. "All teams, all teams, local police are en route to target area. We are pulling out in sixty seconds, copy."

"Copy that, M-One. We are clearing the area and will recover anyone still inside. You heard the man—let's sweep and clear," David ordered.

One last thermal scan revealed no one moving inside the hallway. With Tara on his right, David crept to the left and immediately covered the hall's front half, sweeping from right to left with his weapon. Crouching low, he waved Tara ahead, then slipped in behind her. A dead man in civilian clothes lay sprawled at the foot of the stairs, his face blown away. David spotted the Team Two members taking cover under the staircase, bullet holes pocking the plaster and woodwork around them.

David tightened his grip on his Kriss gun. "Team Two, we're inside. Go for flash-bang."

He watched the two grenades arc up onto the first-floor landing, then go off with twin explosions. Right after detonation, Team Two pounded up the stairway, sweeping the landing with their laser-sighted weapons. David and Tara followed, watching their six while also backing up the lead team.

"All teams, I have movement on the roof, repeat, movement on the roof. Hostiles are evacuating on top," M-One reported.

While he had said that, the two teams had split up, searching and clearing every room on the floor. David and Tara had booted in a door only to find unmoving bodies, already dead from multiple bullet wounds to the head and torso. One of the victims was their own operative, his chest a red smear of blood. Coming out, they met up with the second team, who also shook their heads. Whatever had happened here, they had missed it.

"Proceeding to the roof," David radioed as he pointed above them. At the end of the hallway they found a ladder and trapdoor. A quick scan showed no one lying in wait for them. David wasted no time in scaling it, readying his weapon before entering the room.

The dark third floor was filled with cobwebs, piles of timber and stacks of drywall. Checking all around, David spotted a square of light at the other end of the room. Once Tara joined him, he cautiously approached the far end, making sure their opponents hadn't set up any surprises. At the next ladder, he looked up, now aware of faint sirens in the distance.

"Crap, the police are on their way." Turning off his

thermal vision, he climbed up and poked his Kriss out the trapdoor leading to the roof, panning the weapon all around. The small camera lens mounted on the right-side Picatinny rail gave him a good view of the rooftop without exposing him to enemy fire. He saw one black-clad body on the tarred surface a few yards away, a crimson pool spreading from his head.

"M-One, I have one hostile terminated on the roof. We are moving to secure, over."

"Affirmative, hostiles have left across the buildings, three down. Recover the body, and I will meet you on the south side for exfiltration."

"Shit, nearly get our faces blown off, and for what— a couple dead tree huggers and some dead shooters who weren't even supposed to be here? We don't even know who these guys are. I dunno about you all, but I'm seriously starting to rethink the benefits of this job." M-Four, the loudmouth who had been riding David's back earlier that morning, kept grousing as they grabbed the dead shooter's body and hauled it to the back of the flat. Now they heard shouts and doors slamming as other people checked into the commotion in their pre-viously quiet neighborhood.

As they maneuvered the dead body over the knee-high parapet, something spanged off the edge. The four Midnight Team members ducked for cover, each one taking a quadrant and searching for a target.

"Who's shooting from where?" David asked.

"From the west." Tara pointed with her weapon along the row of three-story buildings. David looked over to see a black-suited figure two roofs over sketch a jaunty salute before disappearing from sight.

David saw red. "Regroup with M-One. I'm going after them," he told the others.

Tara stopped and stared at him. "What? Pursuing is not in our orders. We already have a body for intel—"

David was already shucking his gear, leaving only his vest, pistol and MASC on. "The three of you rendezvous with M-One. I'll meet up with you in a few minutes. Now go!"

Without waiting for a reply, he took off, hearing a muttered "When did the golden boy's testicles drop?" from M-Four. Reaching to the edge of the roof, David leaped out over the narrow alley between the two buildings and hit the top of the second one. He tucked into a shoulder roll, and came up still moving, heading for where he had last seen the mystery shooter disappear.

2

This is why I need to get out of the office more, Kate Cochran thought as she sipped champagne from a crystal flute.

Sheathed in a red stretch satin designer dress, she stood in the middle of at least one hundred law-enforcement officials from across Europe who had gathered in Dublin, Ireland, for the Second European Congress on Fighting Organized Crime in Partnership. They had convened in the main wing of the Irish Museum of Modern Art, housed in the converted Royal Hospital Kilmainham.

It was founded and built by James Butler of Kilkenny Castle, also the duke of Ormonde and viceroy to King Charles II. The classically designed building, consisting of three major wings surrounding a large outdoor courtyard, was originally completed in 1684 to serve as a home for old, ill and disabled soldiers. Over the centuries, the building had played many roles, including the residence and headquarters of the commander in chief

of the army, as well as the headquarters of the Garda,
Ireland's public police force, until it was converted into
the art museum in 1991. While the clean stone walls and
colonnade had remained on the outside, the interior
halls had all been updated with modern amenities, including a staircase in the main hall that seemed to float
in midair, and gleaming, black marble flooring. The
hall's inner wall was made of floor-to-ceiling windows
that revealed the immaculate courtyard, with its neat
grass lawns and graveled pathways, all shrouded in the
light, misty rain coming down outside.

All in all, a rather strange place for a law-enforcement conference, Kate thought. Even though Room 59,
the covert-ops agency she ran, was so secret she
couldn't even acknowledge its existence to the rest of
the conference attendees, Kate knew the best way to
gather intelligence was often to go on-site and get it
face-to-face. She had been planning a visit to Europe
and the various Room 59 department heads on the con-
tinent for some time—which meant as soon as her demanding schedule permitted. Although with the
incredible technology at her fingertips, she could—and
did—meet with her coworkers in virtual reality, Kate
preferred seeing real people and places whenever
possible. When the conference came to her attention,
she put it on her schedule and refused to move it,
figuring she was due for a vacation, even a working one.
Her overseers at the International Intelligence Agency
had grudgingly agreed, and she had been off before
they could change their minds.

"Ms. Massen?"

Kate hesitated a fraction of a second before turning
to see a silver-haired, middle-aged man in a sleek,

spotless tuxedo standing next to her. Since her position as director of operations was as shrouded in secrecy as the agency itself, she could never go anywhere, even on what would be normal business like this conference, as herself. For events like this, she relied on her cover identity as Donna Massen, a midlevel employee with the U.S. State Department, as its sprawling bureaucracy could easily hide an extra employee or two.

"I just wanted to thank you for your comments on the potential alliance of law-enforcement agencies with private security companies. I feel that there is much potential business—and crime stopping—to be done if both sides can only come together." The man's words had that perfect British diction, and sent a slight shiver up her spine. After all, Kate did so like educated men.

She nodded, careful not to dislodge her glossy chestnut hair, which had been done up in an elegant French twist. "I'm afraid that you have me at a disadvantage, sir. So many people here to try to remember, you know." That wasn't really the case—she knew exactly who he was—but she often found it very useful to give the person she was speaking to the idea that he or she had gained a slight advantage in the conversation.

"Please excuse me, we met briefly at yesterday's reception. I'm Terrence Weatherby, vice president of marketing for Mercury Security."

Kate extended a slender hand. "Yes, now I remember. A pleasure to see you again. I hope your company's name isn't a reference to its godlike capabilities."

Terrence chuckled and raised his drink glass before replying. "Actually, when we went global in '99, we wanted to take on a name that implied quick, efficient service for our clientele. So far, I think we've delivered."

"Of course." Kate kept her professional smile pasted on her face, but her eyes looked past Weatherby to catch the gaze of a tall, lean, mustached man talking to a pair of energetic young women who worked for Interpol. As soon as their eyes met, she made a small, innocuous gesture with her hand, and he nodded just enough to show that the message was received. Although it was possible that Weatherby had sought her out to compliment her comments at the conference earlier, Kate never believed in coincidence. Most likely getting a feel for their potential competition, she thought as she turned her attention back to the conversation at hand. "So, Mr. Weatherby, just how do you see government intelligence agencies and PMCs working together?"

It was the opening he had been waiting for, and Kate reminded herself that when it all came down to it, he was a salesman. But at least he had a pleasant, butter-soft speaking voice. "Please, call me Terrence. I won't bore you with a long, drawn-out pitch, but allow me to pique your interest with a few possibilities, as there are some legal issues that would need to be addressed, as well, before moving forward…."

He briefly outlined several potential alliances that did sound very good on the surface—intelligence sharing, team building on both sides to augment each other's forces and the relaxation of controls that would make it easier for a formal government agency to use a PMC for deniable missions.

Kate broke in at that point. "Isn't that a bit dangerous? After all, what incentive would your men have to not roll over on the hiring government to save their own skins if they were caught?" She sipped her champagne again, enjoying the mild look of discomfort that flitted across the Englishman's face. Kate didn't have much respect for most private military companies, considering only a handful of well-established ones to meet her very high standard in terms of integrity and trustworthiness.

"Well, it is our hope that would never come to pass, but in the unfortunate event of a member or team being captured, we would mount a rescue operation as quickly as possible in order to extract them before any information could be gained," Weatherby said.

"Very noble of you." Kate knew she was pushing it, but at the moment she almost didn't care. She reined herself in, however, and turned the conversation to safer ground. "Your company has been focusing almost exclusively on Third World countries, Africa and the like. I'm surprised that we don't hear more from you in more lucrative places—like Iraq."

Terrence's smile grew even tauter. "I hope you'll pardon me for being rather blunt, but once the initial fireworks were over, it certainly seemed as if the fix was in, so to speak. The American PMCs picked up so many contracts, and the rest of us were left to fight over the scraps. Then there was all that nasty business with one of the more prominent contractors, and the environment turned even less receptive. We did a cost-benefit analysis, and realized that our talents could be put to better use elsewhere."

And with even less oversight from watchdog groups, I'll bet, Kate thought. "Well, you know what they say in business and politics—it's not always what you do so much as who you know. Still, you make some very interesting suggestions, and I'd like to get some talking points on strategic alliances to show to my superiors." Kate briefly turned up the wattage on her smile, and resisted the urge to bat her eyelids. "Here's my card."

Weatherby took it and slipped it into his jacket pocket. "That would be wonderful, but I was rather hoping, if you're staying here past the conference, that we might discuss this further over dinner tomorrow evening."

Hmm, is he hitting on me, or is this purely business? Kate drained her flute slowly, taking a couple of seconds to reappraise the man in this new light. Yes, her estimate of his age was accurate, but he was slim, fit and regal looking. She shook her head with a rueful expression. You're not a field agent, you're the director of Room 59. Your job duties do not entail dallying with PMC executives at conferences like this. Placing her empty glass on a passing waiter's tray, she shook his hand again. "I'm afraid that tomorrow morning I'm heading to London for several days."

Weatherby smiled, revealing perfect, even white teeth that had to have benefited from years of the very best dentistry. "Then it would seem that fate is crossing our paths, Ms. Massen, since my company's head office is in London, as well, and I would greatly enjoy the opportunity to see you again and continue this conversation." He offered her a card, a thin sheet of clear, flexible plastic with his name and contact information holographically imprinted on it.

Kate took it and tucked it into her beaded clutch purse. "I'll have to look at my schedule and see what might be arranged, but I cannot promise anything." She looked around for the man she had seen earlier, but he was nowhere in sight. However, a stunning woman with sleek black hair, flawless olive skin and dressed in a shimmering silver evening gown walked toward Kate, leaving turning heads of both men and women in her wake. From the corner of her eye, Kate noticed Weatherby stiffen as she approached.

"Excuse me, I'm sorry to interrupt, but are you Donna Massen, with the U.S. State Department?" The newcomer was British, as well, her contralto voice making Weatherby's honeyed tones sound like those of a rough East Ender.

"I am," Kate replied.

"I have a message for you." The woman, whose face would have looked perfectly at home on the covers of the highest fashion magazines, turned to Kate's companion. "If you'll excuse us, Terrence."

The PMC representative cleared his throat as if he had just remembered how to breathe. "Of course, Samantha. You're looking well."

The barest smile flickered across the woman's face. "And you, as well. This way, Ms. Massen, if you please." The willowy woman, several inches taller than Kate, led her through the crowd, leaving Weatherby to head to the bar.

Kate regarded her new escort with curiosity. "Professional acquaintance?"

The woman who had extricated Kate was Samantha Rhys-Jones, the head of Room 59's UK division. "I knew Terrence back in his Royal Army days, before he retired, figuring there was more money in private security. When his own business failed, he must have signed on with Mercury. So, what were you two talking about?"

"Oh, dinner in London, among other things. Why, is there anything I should know about him?"

Samantha turned her head to regard her superior. "He claims to be decent in bed, if that's what you're after. I wouldn't know—the last time our paths had crossed, he'd expressed interest, until I rebuffed him—rather forcefully."

"I hope you didn't leave any permanent damage." Kate looked back to Weatherby, who had just tossed his drink back and was signaling for another.

"Only if you count his pride, I suppose." Samantha turned her laser-sharp, brown-eyed gaze on Kate. "You can't be serious about him."

"Of course not. But I'll keep track of him myself if I have to. Apparently they're headquartered in London. But I doubt anything will come of it, so thanks for getting me out of there."

"It wasn't a ploy—I really do have a message for you." Samantha snared two glasses of champagne from a passing waiter's tray with elegant ease. "A Midnight Team operation went down in South London approximately twenty-six minutes ago. Unfortunately, the targets were not eliminated as planned—the team encountered another hit team on-site and had to engage them instead."

"Another team? What was the outcome?" Kate asked.

"The main targets were terminated before or as our team arrived, as far as we can tell, but the other shooters got away. One of our operatives was taken out, as well. We're still trying to determine what happened."

Kate's mouth tightened. "South London, you said?" Off the other woman's nod, she continued. "I assume you're going back to head the investigation?"

Samantha nodded. "I took the liberty of booking us both on a ten-thirty flight this evening. You'll have just enough time to pack, but as for rest—"

Kate held up her hand. "Don't worry about it—an

airplane seat is practically like a second home to me. Just let me update Jake, and I'll have him meet us there." She scratched the nape of her neck. "Besides, it will be like heaven to take this damn wig off anyway."

3

David slowed as he approached the edge of the building, his enhanced hearing picking up both the noises of his quarry and their conversation as they ran.

"What the hell was that? We're lucky we only lost three guys to whoever those guys were, and then you go and pull a goddamn stupid stunt like that? It's bad enough I have to report this to HQ, and I'm seriously considering bringing you up on insubordination charges once we get back—"

"Jesus, would you put a sock in it, you sound like my grandmother. They were just as surprised as we were. They got lucky is all. Besides, they had some nuts going head-to-head with us. And as for our deaders, well, I never liked them all that much anyway. Besides, we got the job done—"

"Not all of it, jackass. In case you'd forgotten, she's still alive, which makes this even worse—"

They missed someone? David crouched at the roof's

edge and listened as the two arguing men clattered down the stairs of the fire escape and hit the alley. A soft beeping indicated that his superior was trying to contact him, but David ignored the insistent tone, trying to hear more. As soon as they were on the street, he swung over the side and followed them, his HK USP Tactical .45-caliber pistol out. He stepped carefully to minimize any noise.

"Yeah, yeah, we'll find her. That little bitch is crappin' her pants and on the run. We'll take her down in no time."

"Says the guy who can barely keep his own e-mail account open. Don't forget, she's a hacker, and a damn good one, if she and her brother really got what we wanted. That fuckin' prick, trying to jack up the price on us—you should have seen the look on his face just before I double-tapped him. It was almost worth all this trouble…." The first man's voice trailed off.

David was coming down the first-floor steps when he heard an engine turn over. Looking down the narrow, grimy alleyway, he saw the headlights of a boxy SUV flare to life.

Leveling his pistol, David stepped to the end of the first-floor fire-escape landing and aimed at the driver's side of the windshield. The Range Rover sped forward just as he fired three shots. A trio of pockmarks appeared in the glass, but it didn't break as he had expected. Instead the SUV zoomed forward to pass below him.

Shoving his pistol into its holster, David grabbed the railing with both hands and vaulted over the side, tucking his feet under him to break his fall when he landed on the moving vehicle. He had practiced the maneuver during his Midnight Team training dozens of times, and pulled it off flawlessly, landing on the metal roof with a thud. As soon as he hit, he dropped to his knees. The built-in pads on his armor easily absorbed the impact as he grabbed on to the sides of the vehicle. The roof was more solid than he had expected, and he realized that it was armored, as well. *If they can't shoot me, then they'll have to come out and get me.*

The Range Rover picked up speed as it shot out of the alley, swerving in a hard right turn onto Wyvil Road—away from the rest of David's team. He opened a channel to his leader. "M-One, this is M-Two. I'm tracking the hostiles, who are heading west on Wyvil—" David braced himself as the SUV ran over the curb and shot onto a larger avenue, heading north. "Make that north on Wandsworth Road."

"So nice of you to report in, M-Two. I've got you on our tracker—are you on the roof of the target vehicle?" M-One asked angrily.

"Affirmative—" David broke off as a man popped up from the passenger-side window, aiming a silenced pistol at him. Without time to draw his own weapon, he lunged toward the man and grabbed the gun just as it went off. The bullet disappeared into the night air. Holding the weapon away from him with one hand, David tried to maintain a grip on the roof with his other, but couldn't do both at the same time. The pistol slowly inched back down toward his head, the other man using his superior leverage with both hands to force it against his helmet. David let go of the roof and grabbed the man's other arm, but his opponent twisted out over the street, pulling David's upper body off the roof. Feeling himself slipping further, David lashed out with his left arm, grabbing the shooter's shoulder and pulling him down with him as he slid precariously close to the road.

"Whoa!" The man leaned back as David's weight

forced him half out of the window. Dropping his pistol, he grabbed the door frame with one hand while trying to remove David's hand with the other. The driver yelled something, but David couldn't make it out. He tried to grab the window frame, as well, but the other man knocked his hand away, then clamped on to his fingers and pried them from his own black-suited shoulder. David tried to hold on, but felt each digit being loosened one at a time. He flailed frantically with his other hand, stealing a glance at the rough London pavement flashing by below, and not wanting to get any closer than he already was.

Before he could regain his grip on the other man, David's hand was torn away, and he flew from the Range Rover as it took another right turn. He landed on the street with a breath-stealing impact, rolling, bouncing and skidding to a halt at the side of the road. He had just begun to clear the stars from his eyes and get some air back into his lungs when a tire screeched to a stop only inches from his head. He heard doors popping open above him, and then strong hands were under his arms, hoisting him to his feet.

"Let's go, tough guy, you already fucked up the op enough, don't you think?" David caught M-Four's mocking words as he was unceremoniously stuffed into the back corner of the van, right next to the dead body they'd hauled back. Everyone else was in position. M-One was in the driver's seat, and hadn't even taken his eyes off the road as they'd collected David. But as David examined his battered body, he met the team leader's eyes in the rearview mirror, and got a very clear message—we'll discuss this later. Beside M-One, looking back with a concerned expression on her face, was Tara. M-Four, the loudmouth, had removed his MASC to reveal a lean, fox-faced man with a shock of ginger hair and a smattering of freckles.

Their final member, M-Five, rose from his position at the communication console to tend to David. "M-Four, take over here," he said.

The other man did so with a contemptuous snort. "Sure, make sure the hard charger hasn't hurt himself any more."

"M-Four, that's enough." M-One's voice was as calm as if he was ordering dinner, but it commanded immediate respect from the rest. "Monitor the police channels. It's bad enough we're exposed like this, but we might as well follow through now. Coming up on South Lambeth Road. M-Three, watch for cross traffic, particularly cops."

The windshield was blocked out by the dark face of M-Five bending over him. "Saw you take that flyer off the SUV. Ballsiest move I've seen in a long time, but none too bright." The tall South African undid the clasps on David's body armor as he spoke. "Take your gear off and let's get a look at you."

The van swayed as M-Five worked, and everyone heard the blast of car horns outside. "Too close," M-One commented. "Now heading east on Fentiman Road. They'll either try to lose us in the neighborhood streets, or else take their chances on Clapham—"

"Watch your left!" Tara pointed, and the van jogged to the right just in time to avoid a truck that filled the windshield, passing close enough to knock the flexible side mirror out of alignment.

"Thanks. Passing Meadow Road. They're heading to Clapham for sure."

M-Five ran his hands along David's ribs, pressing

gently and listening for any exclamation of pain or indrawn breath. Although his joints ached from the drubbing they'd taken during his roll on the street, David said he felt fine overall. "That Dragon Skin is some tough stuff."

"Yeah, and the MASC did its job, as well." M-Five shone a light into each of David's eyes. "I don't see any immediate signs of a concussion, but I'm gonna keep you under watch for the next twenty-four hours," he said.

M-Four spoke up from the console, shoving earphones off his head. "The bobbies are cordoning off Wyvil Road at both ends, and expanding their net to include the surrounding blocks. Due to reports of explosions in the house, a bomb squad is being called in. Looks like we got out just in time."

"Good. The more time they spend there, the less time they have to look for us." M-One glanced both ways as they sped toward a busy intersection. "We're coming up to Clapham, folks, so hang on—this next bit's liable to get bumpy."

David had shrugged off the team medic's attentions and sat up just in time to see them roar into the intersection. Still hard on the SUV's tail, the van shot out into the main thoroughfare, forcing cars to screech to a stop on both sides of them and attracting much more attention than anyone inside was comfortable with.

"Damn it, we've got company," Tara said.

David looked out the one-way rear window to see a motorcycle officer hit his lights and siren and give chase.

"Can't be helped now. If we're blocked for any reason, you all know what to do," M-One said.

Since Midnight Teams were brought in only as a

final resort for specific missions, they weren't supposed
to attract attention in any way, even in what would nom-
inally be a friendly country. If they were stranded, their
orders were to escape and evade capture by any means
necessary, up to and including deadly force. David
grimaced as he realized what this chase meant—the
longer it went on, the higher the risk of their being
caught, and that simply couldn't happen. And if I hadn't
gone racing into it, we might have kept this more low
profile—the way we're supposed to operate, he admonished himself.

"Looks like we've got them." M-One alternated
between keeping an eye on the SUV and watching the
motorcycle officer slowly gain behind them. "The
traffic on Clapham is slower than usual—must be something blocking the road ahead."

The van slowed just enough to keep ahead of the pa-
trolman. M-Four looked up from the radio console,
headphones half on his head. "If we don't do something
soon, he's gonna call in reinforcements, assuming he
hasn't already."

The van's speed decreased further. "As long as it's
not the Specialist Crime Directorate, we should be all
right. If the SCD shows up, we disappear. Almost
there…brace yourselves!" M-One slammed on the
van's brakes, making it skid to a stop. The pursuing mo-
torcyclist, caught off guard, was unable to stop in time
and slammed into the van's rear door hard enough to
send the rider sailing over the handlebars and thump
into the door himself. He fell to the street, his bike
toppling on top of him.

"Damn, that had to hurt." David turned his attention
forward again, where M-One was issuing orders.

Ahead, he saw a large truck that had apparently jack-knifed in the road, blocking both lanes of traffic on their side, and slowing the cars and motorbikes going in the opposite direction. Although yellow-vested officers were directing traffic, it seemed that they hadn't been told about or noticed the slow-speed chase was approaching them.

"All right, we're coming to a stop. On my command, Team Two will exit the side door and approach the SUV, pistols out but covered. Try to take them alive if possible, but defend yourselves and the civilians. Okay, here we go—"

With a screech of rubber, the SUV suddenly lurched out of its lane, wheels spinning for purchase as it rose onto the sidewalk, clipping a light post and scattering sparse passersby in all directions.

"Son of a bitch!" M-One shouted.

The Range Rover barreled completely off the road and into Kennington Park, tearing up grass and dirt. M-One followed, edging onto the sidewalk and into the park, ignoring the whistle blasts of the London bobbies, who had definitely noticed this unusual activity.

With a wide-open space, the SUV opened up and accelerated away from the van, but M-One tried to stay with it as much as possible. A man leaned out of the SUV passenger's window again and pointed a submachine gun at the pursuing van. M-One jinked the steering wheel back and forth, trying to break up their silhouette to present less of a target. Short bursts sprayed from the submachine gun, the slugs pinging against the van's bullet-resistant glass and shattering one headlight.

"Everyone hold on!" M-One floored the accelerator,

and the van sped forward, close enough to almost tap the bumper of the Range Rover. Suddenly the SUV swerved to the right and decelerated, causing the van to pull alongside. The driver slammed his vehicle into the van, making the higher-center-of-gravity vehicle slew to the side, with everyone aboard swaying and grabbing at the sides to keep their seats.

"Damn it, we're in a clear area—can't we take them out?" M-Four asked.

"In case you hadn't noticed, that's exactly what I've been trying to do, but they got the idea first." M-One had wrestled the van back under control, narrowly avoiding a tree as they raced through the darkened park. Fortunately there was hardly anyone out at this time of night, just a few couples who gave the fast-moving vehicles a wide berth.

"If you're gonna do something, now's the time, before they get back on the roads!" David said.

"I'm open to suggestions." M-One grunted as he tried to catch up with their target again. "We're not fast enough to catch them, and trying to spin them only resulted in our nose getting slapped."

David shook his head. "Can't shoot them down, either. That windshield shrugged off my .45s like nothing. Tires are probably run-flat, too."

"We're running out of space and time, people." M-One swerved to avoid another of the many trees dotting the park, his night vision glowing green in the darkness. The small dot of light reflecting off the windshield gave David an idea.

"Are they running lights out, too?"

"Yeah." Tara glanced back. "What're you thinking?"

David grabbed a minigrenade, matched it with a

barrel adapter and inserted it into the muzzle of his gun. "If we can't bull them over with brute force, we can dazzle them with brilliance." Staying on his knees, he moved to the van's sliding side door. "Stabilize me."

M-Five's eyes widened in recognition as he grasped what David was up to, and he grabbed his teammate's web harness to secure him.

"Open the door, M-One."

The night air rushed in as the side door slowly rolled back. "You're clear ahead, but you've only got a hundred meters—don't hit anything but the ground," M-One said.

"Affirmative." David reset the grenade's fuse and eyeballed the range between the two rocking, swaying vehicles as best as he could. The fence delineating the outer perimeter of the park rushed at them. "Fire in the hole!" Squeezing the trigger, he watched the explosive arc over the SUV and disappear into the darkness. It came down almost where he wanted—a few yards in front of the speeding Range Rover. At the last second, David shielded his eyes and turned away.

Even so, he caught the flash of the detonating flare grenade, its burst of brilliant phosphorus lighting up the open area like a miniwhite sun. David stared at the ground near the SUV, hearing its engine whine and feeling dirt spatter on his arms and chest as their quarry spun out of control, crossing in front of the Midnight Team's van. With a loud crash, they caromed off a large tree and into a small wood-sided building that looked as if it might hold groundskeeping equipment. The SUV broke through the front wall in a splintering crash of wood and glass, coming to a halt wedged firmly in the middle of the structure.

M-One braked the van to a stop about twenty yards

away. "Team One, take the right. Team Two go left." He grabbed his XM110 and slid out the driver's-side window. "I'll cover. Move out—you've got twenty seconds to apprehend them."

The four other Midnight Team members hit the ground running, submachine guns out and ready. David and Tara used the century-old trees as cover, leapfrogging toward their objective. There was no movement or sound from the ruined building.

When they were about five yards away, David hailed the other team. "Team One in position."

"Team Two in position."

"M-One in position. Execute."

David and Tara rose as one and took a step toward the SUV when it burst into flames, spraying the remains of its shattered windows everywhere. David immediately ducked back down as the shock wave of the explosion washed over him.

"You got anything on scope?" he asked Tara, who was scanning the surrounding area with her MASC.

"Negative."

"How about you, Team Two?"

"If they got by us, they were freakin' invisible," M-Four replied.

"All teams, fall back to the van." David heard the two-tone scream of the approaching British police sirens. "We're leaving," M-One ordered.

Still alert in case their opponents were crazy enough to double back, David and Tara skirted the trees as they headed to the van. Jumping aboard, M-One closed the doors and drove out the back way, turning left onto the road that bordered the north side of the park and driving away casually as the rest of the team members removed their armor and changed into civilian clothes.

Driving until they well away from the park, M-One pulled into the parking lot of a car-washing facility and looked around. "M-Four, open that garage door."

David ignored the dark stare as M-Four, a guy named Robert Muldowney, shoved past him on his way out. Instead, he worked his way up to the space between the two front seats. "Sir?"

"Yes?" M-One's eyes never left the nearby road.

"The other team, they hadn't finished their job when they left."

That remark earned him a raised eyebrow. "Explain."

"When I followed them—" Against orders, David thought but didn't say "—I overheard them talking about a woman, and how she had escaped the ambush. One of the men said something about *if she got what they wanted.* She was some kind of computer hacker—"

The rattle of metal against metal interrupted him as M-Four pushed the garage door up, revealing a large interior with hoses and other cleaning equipment. M-One drove inside. "Soap it down and get every scrap of paint off," he ordered.

David scrambled outside and grabbed a wand as M-Four turned the washing system on. As soon as the soapy water hit the van's dark gray paint, it began to flake and slough off in large sheets, dissolving into a sludgy mess that dribbled toward the drain. Underneath was a pristine white coat. Inside, M-One hit a button, and the license plate rotated to a completely new number.

David smiled, humming the James Bond theme under his breath. Sometimes the old ways are still the best ways, he thought. He examined the fender damage caused by the SUV's graze, making sure that no paint traces from the other vehicle had been left over in the wash. Five minutes later, they had completely transformed the van. He also knew they wouldn't show up on any street cameras, since M-One had activated a scrambler that would knock out any recording devices in a one-block radius. Anyone using a digital camera at the time was out of luck.

Their leader pulled the van back out, and David and M-Four cleaned up, making sure that all of the paint was washed down the drain, and leaving the tools exactly where they had found them. M-Four closed and locked the door.

Tara beat David back to the side door. "M-One wants to see you up front."

"Yeah, time to face the music. Sorry to make you lose your seat."

"Don't worry about it." She held up a funny-looking piece of foam with what looked like a black piece of plastic inside. "I need to play with this at the console anyway. Recovered it from outside the house—figured the other team put it there for surveillance."

"Nice going, rook—ah, M-Three." David flushed, all too aware that he hadn't been nearly as proficient in executing the mission as their newest teammate. He clapped her on the shoulder and headed up to the front of the van.

"Now that we're undercover again—" M-One's gray eyes flashed at David, letting the other man know he was still accountable for the breach of orders earlier "tell me everything you heard—every single word."

4

The woman shivered in the chill evening air as she watched the bustling activity around Wyvil Road. The entire area had been secured by police tape, with the street blocked off at both ends by Metropolitan Police Service vehicles and uniformed, armed officers bustling everywhere. Beyond the cordon, media vans swarmed, with perfectly pressed and coiffed reporters jockeying for the best shots and interviews as they scrambled to get on the air. The woman made sure to avoid the roving cameras at all costs.

For the moment, she was safe enough among the crowd of people peering and peeking, everyday, ordinary folk looking for a bit of excitement, their voices overlapping as they tried to find out what was going on:

"Do you know what happened?"

"Probably a drug deal gone wrong. Wankers most likely lit each other up…."

"I saw some of the lodgers around…they seemed like nice enough people…."

"Dear God, what is that smell? Someone been trudging around in the sewers?"

At that last bit, she moved a couple meters away, all too aware that she was the one most likely causing the odor the last person had complained about. Even as she stood there, watching the chaotic scene, a part of her mind repeated that she needed to move, needed to get the hell out of there, just casually turn around and walk away, another spectator who had grown bored with watching the police and was heading for home. But she stayed, waiting to see the proof with her own eyes.

Waiting for the bodies to be removed from the scene.

It had seemed like only moments ago—had it really been an hour?—when she had finished with Harry and sent him on his errand, hiding the few cigarettes left in the pack because, well, by the time he got back, she'd be gone from his life forever.

As soon as she'd heard the front door close, Marlene had slipped out of the bed, grabbed her clothes and run to the bathroom, cleaning up and getting dressed in under three minutes. Pulling her long hair back in a ponytail, she had grabbed her laptop and case, trotted to the door and opened it to reveal her brother about to knock, an impish grin on his face as he sniffed the air.

"You two getting cozy in here?"

"Don't be gross. Are we done?"

He held up a matching, soft-sided computer case and patted his front jeans pocket. "I finished the final run downstairs while you were—taking care of business. We're out of here." He nudged her as they walked to the stairs. "Next time we do a run like this, we need to find a group with a hot woman as the leader. Maybe a blonde."

"I'll be sure to put that on my list. Now come on." She had been about to put her foot on the first step when she heard a noise from downstairs—a noise that shouldn't have been made in the first place.

Who's up at this hour? she wondered. None of the cell members should have been moving around—the sedative she had added to their dinner of vegetarian curry would have ensured that. And Harry had been taken care of by her personally. So who's left?

"What's the holdup?" Ray peered around her, trying to see into the gloom of the ground floor.

"I heard something—like a footstep," she whispered.

He frowned. "Probably just the crappy old house settling. Here—" he pressed the flash drive into her hand "—I'll go have a look. Hang back until I call you."

She waited on the landing as he crept down the stairs. He had only taken a few steps when the noise sounded again, a bit louder this time. "Hey, who's down there? Gabe? Aron?"

Marlene peered around him, trying to see in the dimness, her heart suddenly pounding in her chest. She wanted to call Ray back up, tell him not to go down there, but before she could, a black-clad arm extended out from the archway leading to the back hall, with something even darker extending from its fist.

The sneeze of the silenced pistol made her choke on her warning. The gun coughed again, making Ray gasp as each bullet impacted his body. He sagged, clutching the railing, then slid down the rest of the staircase to land in a messy heap on the floor. The arm pointed down at his face, and fired the pistol twice more.

Marlene clapped her hands over her face to keep from screaming. She was frozen with terror, unable to comprehend what she had just seen. The arm moved forward, with a night-clad figure materializing in the dim hallway below her, his face covered in a strange mask with large, eerie goggles over his eyes. The shooter checked her brother's body, then looked up the stairway as he lifted one foot to begin the climb. The motion shocked the breath from her body, but then the strange, masked head looked down the hall as it and Marlene heard the same noise—a key turning in the lock of the front door.

Leading with the pistol, the intruder stalked down the hallway. Only when he was out of sight did Marlene move, creeping back to the door without making a sound and slipping into the bedroom. After the door was closed and locked, she remembered at last to suck in a breath. She heard a strange, muffled thump from downstairs, and realized what it probably was—Harry had just been shot.

Oh, my god. Marlene went to the window overlooking the street and moved the heavy, dusty curtain back to peek out the window, hearing footsteps pound up the front steps.

The only thought in her mind now was escape. She had no doubt that Ray was dead—his killer was too much of a pro to not make sure of it. She looked around, frantically searching for and discarding options. The windows had been painted shut long ago, and certain death waited outside the door. Her gaze settled on the laundry chute, flashing back to a playful wrestling match Harry had had with her a few days ago as he had threatened to stuff her down it. At the time, it had been in jest, but now it was her only way out. She opened the trapdoor and peered into the square black hole. No one used it anymore, but she was pretty sure it wasn't blocked by anything. At least she hoped it wasn't. The only thing worse than facing the killers out there would be having them find her, trapped and helpless, halfway down.

Hopping up onto the ledge, she inserted her legs into the chute and braced herself against the sides, clutching at the trapdoor to make sure it closed after her. Taking a deep breath, she let go, holding the padded laptop case above her head. The fall was claustrophobic and brief—total blackness for a moment, and then she landed in a pile of stiff, moldy sheets she and her brother had seen the last time they had been down in the basement.

Rolling out, she stood and threw the cloth to one side, wiping away grime as she made sure that the laptop case was still secure, then slung it over her shoulder. "So it did work." She looked up at the square, then jerked back as she heard more firearms going off on the floor above her. Holes suddenly punched through the side of the chute, raining plaster and pieces of wood down on her. Time to get the hell out of here, she thought as she heard a deafening bang from upstairs.

Running to the opposite corner of the basement, brushing webs out of her face—the spiders are just as bad over here as in the States—she pushed aside a grubby, damp tarpaulin, revealing an old, wet and stained manhole cover, left over from one of the innumerable sewer updates during the past century. Taking a small halogen headlamp from a pocket on the computer case, Marlene levered the cover off, nearly wrenching her arms out of their sockets, and disappeared into the small, dank tunnel below, making sure to pull the cover back over the hole before she left.

She splashed through the muck as fast as she dared, the small light only illuminating a few yards ahead of her. The air was hot and moist, and she tried to breathe through her mouth as much as possible. Sounds of night creatures were all around her, with the squeaking and scurrying of rats through the muck, and the buzz of the strange insects that made their home in the filthy surroundings. Although she had watched her brother get gunned down without a sound, she nearly lost it when a large, multilegged insect dropped onto her head. Brushing it off with a stifled scream, she hurled it against the wall and kept moving.

Marlene pushed aside all other thoughts, like whether or not the masked killers were coming after her, and concentrated on the twists and turns in the tunnel that would take her to her ultimate destination and out of this hellhole. Only once did she pause, at an intersection that led to another, cleaner tunnel leading off to the north-northwest that she and Ray had used often during the past few weeks. Brushing away tears, she turned down the smaller, grimier tunnel that led to the northeast.

After several more minutes of trudging through the ankle-deep sludgy water, she saw her goal—a street drain in a seldom-used alley behind an abandoned Pakistani take-away restaurant. She and Ray had made sure the grate could be opened the previous week. Trying to hold back her sobs, she reached the iron grating and shoved it up and out of the way, set the computer case on the ground, then hauled herself up. She gulped in the stale, fried-food smell of the restaurant Dumpster nearby as if it was fresh country air. After replacing the grate, she washed her feet off as best as she could in a nearby puddle of water, but was still all too aware of the stench she had picked up on her journey.

The first thing was to change her appearance. Scanning the street of the run-down neighborhood, she spotted what she needed at the corner—a youth hostel next to a twenty-four-hour shop providing supplies for weary travelers. A quick visit to the latter got her a change of clothes, and payment for a common room ensured the use of a bathroom with a toilet stall for some privacy. Marlene got out her Swiss Army knife, opened the scissors attachment and went to work.

Ten minutes later, her long hair had been cut to a short, spiky bob, and she was dressed in clothes that belonged on the body of a woman a decade younger than her, but were suitable for today's London—striped black-and-white leggings under a denim miniskirt, an off-the-shoulder, tight-fitting T-shirt and a hoodie sweatshirt to go over the top of that. A ball cap completed her disguise, very useful for keeping her face out of sight of the ever-present cameras. The only thing they couldn't replace were her shoes, so she rinsed them out in the dirty sink and put them back on, doing her best to ignore the squelching noises they made with each step.

After leaving the hostel, her initial thought was to get to the Tube and figure out a way out of the city at least, and the country if possible. But her steps had led her back to the house on Wyvil Road, and now she smothered a gasp as two white-sheeted forms were carried out on stretchers to waiting ambulances. They were followed by two more, then two more.

Marlene knew that no one she cared about had

survived the ambush. Bye, Ray. Bye, Harry. She patted the pocket of her skirt, which held the flash drive that her brother had given her, and walked away from the commotion down the fog-shrouded street.

5

In the backseat of a limousine, Kate resisted the urge to add drops to her parched eyes, blinking to remoisten them. Although the trip from Dublin to London had only taken a little over an hour, the warm, dry air at the airport and on the plane, not to mention the accelerated pace at which she had left her hotel and raced to make the flight, had left her more tired than she cared to admit.

Next to her, Samantha looked flawless, as usual. Kate resisted the urge to sneak disdainful looks at her out of the corner of her eye—the unflappable Brit wouldn't even notice, and it would only make her feel more unkempt. Damn jet lag, she thought. I should have known catching the red-eye over the pond wouldn't help me all that much.

Even worse, the man sitting across from her also looked disturbingly bright-eyed and alert at this late hour. Still clad in the tuxedo he had worn to the party, Jacob Marrs was her Room 59–assigned bodyguard. He kept an eye on her pretty much anytime she left the house. At first, Kate had protested the very idea, stating that since the agency she worked for was so ultrasecret, who would even know that she worked for them or what she did? The board members of the IIA had insisted, however, and now she could hardly imagine a time when Jake's solid, imposing presence hadn't been nearby. Even now, with the gorgeous Samantha hardly an arm's length away, he gave her no more attention than he would any other person who wasn't a threat on his radar. He had checked their driver's identity six ways from Sunday, scanned the limousine for bugs, bombs and anything else out of the ordinary, and only when he had been satisfied had he let the two women get in and made the signal for them to be on their way. Once on the relatively quiet city streets, his alertness hadn't wavered for an instant, as he constantly surveyed the areas they passed through, watching for the slightest anomaly or anything that seemed out of place.

Without looking up from her PDA, Kate decided to test him. "How did marking Mr. Weatherby's car go?"

"The car was marked within ten minutes of your giving me the signal, and an operative is watching his every move as we speak. If there is no overt activity on his part that is out of the ordinary in the next twenty-four hours, standard operating procedure will reduce surveillance to intermittent unless otherwise ordered." His eyes flicked to hers for a second before resuming his sweep. "I would have searched his car more thoroughly, but I had to make sure to keep you in sight before you left the party."

Samantha nodded in approval. "You weren't kidding when you said he was good."

"Better than good." Kate met his gaze and flashed a brief smile.

Jake didn't stop his study of their surroundings as he spoke. "Don't get the chance to do a lot of fieldwork, other than making sure Kate can do her job without interference, so it's a nice change of pace to stretch my legs and get my hands dirty, so to speak. Besides, while I can't speak for her, six months of accompanying either Kate or Mindy on shopping trips or runs to the grocery store can make a person long for something a bit more—exciting—to break the routine."

"Spoken like a true man of action." Samantha leaned forward. "I've perused your dossier, Mr. Marrs—it's quite impressive. If there's time while you're here—and with Kate's permission, of course—I wouldn't mind utilizing your extensive training with some of my field agents. I'd imagine you would have a lot to teach them, particularly in the area of executive protection."

Jake rubbed his chin. "Well, the Room 59 training is pretty extensive, but I might be able give them a few specialized pointers. Let me know if you had any specific areas in mind, and once we're settled into the op base— and if I'm not needed elsewhere—I'll see what I can do."

The chirp of a satellite phone interrupted the conversation, and Samantha reached for hers and flipped it open. "Excuse me. Hello?"

She listened for a moment. "Yes…yes, I had been informed of the situation as of two hours ago…. Actually, our agency director from the States is sitting next to me at the moment…. Yes, I think that would be best…. Let me conference my phone to her computer, and you can brief us all directly. If I may?" Samantha nodded at Kate's slim laptop.

"Of course, I've already activated the Bluetooth program, so you shouldn't have any problem," Kate said.

Samantha plugged in, and moments later, she, Kate and Jacob all heard the ambient noises and breathing from the caller. Samantha cleared her throat. "Go ahead, M-One."

The man on the other end wasted no time. "Thank you, Directors. Initial surveillance on target for Operation Firewall commenced at 1620 hours, using the data gained by our operative who had infiltrated the group. Subjects were observed and logged for the next six hours and ten minutes, noting numbers, unusual activity, et cetera. The file of surveillance activity is being uploaded to our network for review as I speak. At 2030 hours, Team Two members noticed a pair of unfamiliar men entering the back of the house, and soon afterward, gunfire was seen in the location through thermal imaging. After attempting to alert the operative inside, both teams converged on the location and engaged the hostiles to attempt to draw them away from terminating the subjects. Although my team performed their objective with exemplary ability, killing two of the hostiles, all but one of the subjects were killed before the teams were able to get to them. Remaining hostiles were sighted on the roof, and the teams were ordered to pursue if possible. One member, at considerable risk to himself, tried to stop the hostiles, and learned that they were still searching for the surviving subject, who had apparently escaped the house through unknown means. After recovering one of the hostile's bodies, we pursued the survivors through the city, but lost them at Kennington Park. However, they were on foot when they escaped. We have also recovered a surveillance device that the hostiles used, and are analyzing it for data. That file has also been uploaded for analysis."

"What was your impression of the hostile force?" Kate asked.

"A professional group, they assaulted the location from two areas to maximize surprise, and were able to do it practically under our very noses. Their operation was quick, well-timed and ruthless. We did not have any advance notice, even from our inside operative, so whatever surveillance they had done on the location had been prior to our watch. They were definitely ex-military, and they were well armed with state-of-the-art submachine guns, flash-bang grenades and optical technology that almost rivaled our own. We'll provide a full report once we've had the chance to examine the body before forensics."

"Why did you decide to pursue the unknown hostiles when they left the target area?" Samantha's tone wasn't accusatory, just inquiring.

"The presence of the hostiles, along with their tactics and armament, suggested that they were either a unit from another intelligence agency or a private group hired to eliminate the subjects for a yet-unknown reason. I made the decision to attempt to follow and apprehend to learn what their true motives were, and if possible, whom they worked for if they were a government unit, or who hired them if they were private operators."

"So one subject is still alive and somewhere in the city, correct?" Kate asked.

"To the best of our knowledge, that is correct. However, we cannot confirm that information at this time."

Kate had already brought up a London street map on her laptop. "Perhaps when we reach the site, we'll be able to discern what might have happened. Based on your observations, why do you think the other team was there?" she asked.

"While it may have been a simple sweep and termination, M-Two overheard two of the hostiles talking, and believes that they need to recover something from the surviving subject. What that is, however, we do not know at this time. What are your orders?"

Kate exchanged glances with Samantha. "We'll need to alert all operatives in the city and surrounding area to be on the lookout for this subject, as soon as we figure out exactly who it is. Matching the bodies with the live count should give us a face, if not a name," Kate said.

The beautiful Brit nodded. "If we're going to be going up against another strike team, it may be wise to keep the Midnight Team on active status for the time being. Since they've already come up against these people, they would know what to expect and be better prepared to stop them if they're encountered again," Samantha said.

Kate noticed Jake's raised eyebrow at this idea, but didn't address it. "M-One."

"Ma'am?"

"Take your team to the nearest safehouse and prepare your report. Once there, contact Primary, and a forensic team will meet you there and go over what you've collected."

"Affirmative. M-Team out." The spec-ops leader cut the connection.

Samantha took her phone back. "And excellent timing, since we've just arrived."

Kate glanced out the window to see a London street a few blocks from the Thames that ordinarily would have looked like any other lane, except for the profusion of police cars and other unmarked cars she figured were from MI-5, the government department pledged to protect the United Kingdom from external threats. A few onlookers still milled around, but there didn't seem to be much of a crowd now, which was just the way Kate liked it. A few diehard media vans were parked down the street, and she made a note to keep an eye on them in case they decided to come too close.

Samantha had the limousine drop them off about two blocks away, and Kate drew up alongside the other woman as they walked down the sidewalk toward the house on Wyvil Road. "How much trouble do you think we'll have getting on-site?"

"It depends—this will be under MI-5 jurisdiction, and while I have good relations with anyone in the field, it has been a while. Let's see who's in charge and what the situation is."

This is always the tricky part, Kate mused as they approached the crime scene. Room 59 had incredibly broad jurisdictional powers, granted by a consortium of allied nations around the planet to fight any and all threats to the free world. At the same time, however, they had been created to operate behind the scenes, taking care of matters deemed too sensitive for the public intelligence agencies to handle. As such, there were many times when Room 59 operatives would be operating in a country without even advising the home agencies, not only for plausible deniability, but also due to the fact that negotiating every layer of bureaucratic oversight and permission took time, often a luxury the operative didn't have. Because of this, it was always best to work below the radar whenever possible—

except when a team found itself in the middle of a high-profile firefight, like earlier this evening. Then Room 59 operatives did what Kate and Samantha were about to do—walk in and see what they could find out. But before that…

"Jake?" Kate asked.

"Yes?"

"Why don't you hang back even farther and see if you can find out anything around the back. Above all—"

"Don't get caught. Yes, I do remember the drill, thanks. Page me if you need anything." The tall, ex-army man slowed down, his black tuxedo jacket helping him fade into the shadows between the streetlights. When Kate glanced back a moment later, he had disappeared.

Kate adjusted her earpiece just as Samantha got the attention of the ranking MI-5 agent in charge, a craggy-faced, brown-bearded bear of a man in a tailored suit.

"I'm Officer Kryden. Can I help you?"

Samantha showed her cover identification. "Samantha Rhys-Jones, consultant with MI-6. I understand that you might have information concerning a known terrorist suspect involved in the incident here?"

"We're still sorting through everything to make sense of what happened. What's the sister service's interest, if I may?" Kryden asked, employing the casual name for MI-6.

"One of the tenants living here was involved in a smuggling ring that may have trafficked in biological weapons, including bringing them inside the country."

Instead of replying, his searching gaze fell on Kate. "And you are?"

Kate quickly produced her own identification. "Donna Massen, U.S. State Department. I'm here primarily in an observer capacity. However, we believe that one or two of the tenants may have been U.S. citizens." Kate touched a hand to the back of her head, thankful she had decided to maintain her disguise for the time being.

"I'm sorry, ma'am, but as of right now, this scene has been classified for authorized personnel only. If this is part of an ongoing investigation with the sister service, then once I've verified it, I can discuss particulars with Ms. Rhys-Jones here only."

"Of course, Officer. I appreciate your candor and understand the need for confidentiality. If you don't mind, Ms. Rhys-Jones, I'll just wait by the corner." Just then an officer brought a piece of evidence to Kryden, who turned away to examine it. Kate caught Samantha's arm and brushed her wig back, revealing the earpiece. Samantha nodded and unpinned her own hair, letting it fall and cover her ears—and her own inserted earpiece.

Kate turned and headed up the street, walking slowly, scanning the front of the house, which looked like a war zone amid what should have been the normally placid street. The left front window had been shattered, though there was little glass on the ground, indicating that someone had come in from outside. The main door, centered in the middle of the building, had also taken heavy damage, with several bullet holes in it. Adjusting her glasses, Kate took several pictures of the building, using the tiny camera built into her spectacles. She also got a picture of the MI-5 officer in charge. After all, one never could tell when it might come in handy. As she worked, Kate also kept an ear cocked on Samantha and Kryden a few yards away.

The wireless earpieces that the Room 59 directors wore had been modified by agency technicians to transmit over short distances without the aid of a designated cell phone, although adding one could extend the range significantly. With the appropriate hairstyle, they made excellent eavesdropping devices. Even so, Kate held her breath as she saw Kryden on his cell, talking and nodding. He hung up and turned back to Samantha, his voice as clear as if he was standing right next to Kate.

"Sorry about that. However, everything seems to be in order. Here's what we know at present—"

Kate listened to the officer's succinct presentation of what they figured had happened, which pretty much matched what the Midnight Team leader had told them—two separate teams of shooters converging on the house, killing everyone they'd found inside. A blood trail led out the back door to an alley down the street, where the police had found three .45-caliber shell casings, but no evidence of anyone being injured there. The department was tying this in to a car chase that terminated in Kennington Park, where one vehicle was destroyed, along with the groundskeeper's lodge it had smashed into.

The MI-5 officers were looking at camera footage from various points around the area to get any kind of description of the parties or the vehicle that escaped released to the public. They also had the body of one of the shooters, and would be examining it as well. Kryden figured that the terror alert might be raised, since they had discovered what looked like biological weapons inside. "It's a miracle none got released, what with all the destruction that went on in there—bloody war zone, looks like."

"So it doesn't look like any of the bioweapons were taken?" Samantha asked.

"Not that we can tell. Of course, it's not like they left an itemized inventory sheet. But the room where they were storing it looked relatively untouched, compared to the rest of the place."

"Would you happen to have pictures of the victims, both the tenants and the shooters? It's possible that they may have connections outside the country, especially if biological warfare is involved. We'd like to cross-check any identification you find against our files, and see what we come up with."

"Right, I can e-mail you photos of the faces and names, if that helps."

"That would be splendid. Please keep me informed as to what you discover, and I'll be sure to do the same."

"Sure. Now, if you'll excuse me, I need to finish getting the scene processed," Kryden said.

"Of course, thank you very much for your time, Officer. I'll be in touch," Samantha said. She shook his hand, then turned and walked back to Kate. "I assume you got all of that?"

Kate nodded. "So if the second team wasn't after the bioterror weapons, why did they assault the place and kill everybody in the first place? And what part does our mysterious missing person play in all of this?"

"Good questions all. Come on, it's a bit chilly to be standing around out here when we could be discussing this in the car. Where's your shadow?"

Kate scanned the street, but didn't see any sign of her bodyguard. "I sent him off to poke around out back, see what he might come up with. No doubt he was still able to keep an eye on me at the same time."

"You're absolutely right." Jake materialized out of an alley next to them. "I didn't find much. Your boys had both entryways sealed up tight—I expect they aren't going to miss much."

Samantha smiled. "I expect they won't."

"However, I'm afraid they aren't going to find this." He brought out a small, handkerchief-wrapped bundle from underneath his jacket. "I overheard one of the techs say the vehicle that had been parked in the alley had turned right onto Wandsworth, so I ambled down to see what I could find, and came up with this in a pile of garbage near the curb."

He unwrapped enough of the object to reveal the slide and muzzle of a semiautomatic pistol. "It's a Walther P-99, DAO model. At least two shells fired."

"Well, let's get it back to Primary and see if we can trace it." Kate dialed a number on her cell as she got into the limousine. "I'll rouse the troops and have them take a look at the London city surveillance system, particularly in this area. Time for everybody to go to work."

6

Anthony Savage felt the weight of his surname pressing down on him as he led the remaining members of his team through the London streets, always making sure to keep them moving away from the cock-up that had occurred in Wyvil Road earlier that evening. Along the way, he barely resisted the overpowering urge to punch someone or something.

Who the fuck were those guys? They busted in like they owned the place and were there to kick everybody's ass, no matter who you were. And that sniper? If Tommy hadn't spotted him—and immediately become his primary target—they'd all be lying on that rooftop beside him. Our own surveillance didn't spot dick. Where did they come from? And where the hell did Mags disappear to? She had to be inside when we came in—we saw her go in the door.

"Boss, we need to take a breather—his leg has started up again." Behind him, the surviving two members of his team followed, Charlie's face pale as he leaned on Liam, his free hand clamped on his thigh.

"Right, just let me procure transportation." Anthony had already commandeered one car, driven them all several miles, then ditched it, not wanting to keep a stolen vehicle for any longer than necessary.

"Yeah, and try to make sure it's a four-door this time, will ya? I thought we were gonna kill him getting in the last one," Liam said.

"You just keep your goddamn eyes open." Their team leader scanned the street, looking for an opportunity. He found it in a tan, five-year-old Volkswagon Eurovan with no alarm. Less than a minute later, they were cruising down the street toward their safehouse on the outskirts of the city.

Once they had pulled up to the curb of the small semidetached house on the south edge of Chelsea, Anthony dispatched Liam to get rid of the van, and helped his wounded teammate into the house.

"How you doin'?"

"I've been fuckin' better, that's for sure." Charlie McCaplan groaned as he maneuvered himself across the step and into the tiny foyer. "I've been trying to figure out who the hell kicked us in the bollocks over there, ya know—keep my mind off the pain."

Anthony helped him down the hallway to one of the small bedrooms. "Yeah? Come up with anything?"

"Fuck, no. They weren't Brit intelligence—they would have announced themselves before bustin' caps all over our asses. These guys were on the same mission we were—search and destroy. Lucky we came in when we did, or the whole mission would have been shot to hell even quicker. As it was, I expect we were lucky to come out of it with only the losses we did take. By rights, it could have been all of us."

Anthony only partially suppressed his shudder at the thought—not at dying, but at the idea of not completing his mission. Since he'd started with the company four years earlier, he had gone out in the field at least a dozen times, and always had accomplished whatever had been asked of him. This was the first time that a mission he'd led had been a complete, unqualified failure, and that idea was already starting to gnaw on his innards. Anthony Savage hated failure, no matter what the reason for it, but he had bigger fish to fry instead of concentrating on what had gone wrong. There'd be time for mission evaluation later.

"Friction can be overcome through a variety of methods," he muttered under his breath as he helped make Charlie comfortable and checked the hastily applied pressure bandage on his thigh.

"Eh…whazzat?"

"Nothing, mate. You just lie back and relax, and the extraction team'll get you out of here and into a comfy private hospital bed quicker than you can blink. You need another hit?"

"Naw, I'll be fine. You just requisition me a couple o' pretty nurses while I take it easy, and everythin'll be…just fine."

"That's my boy. Stay cool, and we'll take care of you." Anthony did care about the men under his command, and wanted to see them come out of each mission in one piece, and with no new holes, either. He strode out to the living room, taking out his cell phone. He went to the sofa and grabbed a large aluminum briefcase from the floor at its side and set it on the table. He hit speed dial, then concentrated on the case, flipping up its catches and opening it, revealing a small monitor, keypad and several switches and LED readouts. As the phone rang, he powered the unit up, waiting for it to run through its self-diagnostic.

"Yes?" The voice on the other end was male and otherwise toneless. Anthony had never met his handler; the company preferred it that way. He knew why—if they ever hung him out in the wind, they thought he'd never be able to find and kill the guy who had given the orders. Anthony knew they were wrong—anyone could be found—but he let them go on believing that. So far, so good, but he was aware that this could change when the right opportunity came up—or the wrong one, like this mission so far.

"This is Precision Team One. There's been a problem," Anthony said.

"Explain," his handler said.

"Executed on target as planned, but encountered another team of spooks on-site. Completed tertiary and half of the secondary mission. However, one of the targets escaped."

"How?"

"That has not been ascertained yet, sir."

"And the primary objective?"

"Has not been obtained at this time."

"Casualties?"

"Two down, one wounded but mobile. We were unable to extract the bodies."

"Understood. Do you have a vector on the primary target?"

Anthony's eyes flicked to the screen, which showed a bird's-eye view of London. Underneath was a small action bar that was three-quarters full, indicating the long-range tracker was almost finished with its initial sweep of the area. "We're working on it now."

"I'm sending a BOLO general directive to all field agents in the area. If one of them gets to her first, then that's that."

"I understand." More competition, is what it is. His handler was sending a Be On the Look Out alert to all agents in the city. If anyone else happened to spot her first and bring her in, then Anthony's team would be out of luck—no hazardous-duty pay, and no overtime for the entire job. And the boys—those who were still alive—wouldn't be too thrilled about that.

"And you know what to do," his handler said.

"Yes, sir." Complete the mission ASAP. "I would like to request replacements for my three members, positions two, four and five."

"They're being mobilized immediately, and will be at your position within the hour. Get that program, above all else."

"Yes, sir."

The connection was broken just as the scanner beeped, signaling that it had finished its search of the area. Anthony leaned forward, mouth curving up in a mirthless smile, and rubbed his broad, rough hands together in anticipation of sweet payback. "All right, sweetheart, where the fuck are you?"

7

It's times like this, David mused, when I feel like even more of a fifth wheel than usual.

Around him, everyone was absorbed in their own tasks. Cody had gone into the second bedroom to make his report. Tara had taken apart the false brick and camera and was poking around its innards, seeing what data she could extract from it. The other two team members, Kanelo, their gregarious South African medic, and Robert, the pugnacious Welshman, were talking to each other in low voices. Leaving David as the odd man out.

He settled for fieldstripping and cleaning his weapons, making sure every part was clean, clear and ready for action. While he did that—his time spent in Marine recon ensured that any time he held a weapon for more than an hour, it got cleaned and reassembled so that he was sure it was working properly—he went over the mission, examining everyone's role and seeing how he could have executed better. After all, he was sure Cody was going to ask him that very same question later on, and he wanted to be ready with an answer.

It was hard enough coming into a team as a rookie, but so far David had been shown up by the first woman on a Midnight Team not once, but twice. Tara's composure when she had taken the burst on her chest armor, as well as her foresight in recovering the hidden camera at the entrance, had earned her high marks from their team leader and the others. David's impetuous move to pursue the hostiles, while gaining them useful intelligence, had also earned him the label of team cowboy, which was as much a curse as a nickname.

David knew cowboys were simultaneously admired and distrusted for their penchant to bend or break the rules of the espionage game. While they could be very effective in the field, they were also dangerous for the rest of the team, since they were often the only ones to survive their antics unscathed. That had inadvertently been the case with his last Marine recon team. The squad had been out on patrol when a shaped IED had detonated near the lead vehicle, flipping it and blocking the road. As the other members had moved up to assist, insurgents had completed the ambush by attacking with RPGs and AK-47s. In the ensuing firefight, each one of the other squad members was either killed or wounded so severely he would never fight again. David came through the entire ambush without a scratch, and was awarded the Silver Star for intrepid gallantry and courage under fire when he not only carried two of the wounded to safety, but also held off the insurgents until reinforcements arrived. After his second tour was over, he had been slated for Iraq, but had come to the attention of the folks at Room 59 first.

It was a different game, played with a whole new rulebook, one that, he had to admit, he was still learning at times. Although Midnight Teams had huge latitude in carrying out their missions—when they were on an assignment, only a director could alter their mission or recall them—they also had to maintain even more of a low profile than the standard operative. Each operation had to be accomplished with a minimum of fuss, muss and public visibility. And I suppose chasing an SUV through a public park qualifies as exactly what we don't want, he thought.

"Hey, I think I've got something." Tara's voice broke his musings. David reassembled his HK pistol before getting up and going over to her improvised desk, crowding around it with the other two men.

The brick had been cut away, and the small digital camera now lay in several pieces on the desk. A tiny memory chip was loaded in Tara's universal reader, which could access almost anything, even proprietary chips that weren't on the open market. Lost in her work, Tara looked up with a start. "Jeez, I didn't expect all of you to come galloping over."

"Well, since we're here, what do you have?" Kanelo gently prodded.

"Well, there wasn't a lot—they must have been replacing it daily, but it did activate whenever it detected movement, and kept going for about a minute after the scene cleared. But take a look at this."

She brought up a snippet of video showing a tall, lean, bearded man walking up the steps arm in arm with a shorter woman with long, dark hair. They talked and laughed, and at the top step both looked around furtively before sharing a lingering kiss.

"Yeah, so? That's the head bloke we were supposed to bring back alive, as I recall." Robert snorted his disgust. "Until those other bastards came in and bollixed up the whole op. Ruined a perfectly good smash-and-grab, they did. Dunno who the skirt is."

David leaned in for a closer look. "I think that's what Tara's pointing out—the woman. I don't know about you guys, but I don't remember seeing a dark-haired, female body anywhere on the premises."

"Hey, a couple of those tree-hugging hippies had long hair, so they all look alike to me," Robert said. The remark earned the wiry Welshman a cuff on the shoulder from Kanelo.

"Stop spouting *kek,* you dumb bastard, and pay attention." Instead of biting the tall black man's head off—like he most assuredly would have done if David had said something like that—Robert just shrugged and turned his attention back to the screen.

"Tara, please rewind it to where she's almost facing the camera." David leaned in for a closer look. "No, she's completely unfamiliar. I think you've just found our missing piece. Why don't you isolate that and send it to Primary for further analysis?"

"Right."

Cody came out of the back room just as his cell chirped. "M-One…Key word is 'isolate'…. Go ahead…. You're outside?… Great, we'll pop the garage door so you can pick up the package, just give us a minute." Catching Robert's gaze, he nodded at the door leading out to the garage. The smaller man slipped out. "When you see it open, come on in." He snapped the phone closed. "What's happening out here?"

"We isolated a photo of the missing terrorist group member." Tara waved him over. "Here she is."

Cody glanced at the monitor. "Okay, how are we gonna find her?"

David replied without taking his gaze off the woman's face. "With London's city surveillance program, now that we have a face, its possible they can pick up her trail from the house. Primary's biometrics program should be able to read her and track her down, even if she's tried to disguise herself."

"Except I got one question." Kanelo stood apart from the rest, fingers stroking his chin. "Just how did she get out of the building? All of us were there watching with thermal vision as we fought the other strike team. At no point did anyone sound off about another living heat source—they were either dead or shooters. She couldn't have hidden inside, so she must have left via another route."

"Over, under, around or through," David muttered as he stared at the screen.

Robert, who had come back from the garage, frowned. "The tech boyos have the package. What's he mumbling about over there?"

David didn't rise to the bait; he was still engrossed in the picture on the screen. "It's something we learned during recon training. There's four ways into or out of any situation. Over, under, around or through. Through wasn't an option, since we locked the ground floor down. Over wasn't possible, since everyone was on the roof at one point or another. She didn't go around us, either, unless she was able to turn invisible, which leaves—"

"Under." Tara's fingers blurred over the keys on her laptop. "I'll send this out to Primary and suggest that they find a map of the current sewer system in a three-block radius from the house. If the techs can get the data downloads of the cameras in the surrounding area, maybe we'll get lucky and spot her."

Robert's gaze flicked to Cody. "Hey, boss, you think it could be worth going back to the house and checking the basement level, see what we can find out there?"

The team leader thought about it for a few seconds, then shook his head. "Our profile is already too high as it is, and it's possible that nothing will be gained by snooping around a place we already shot up once. We'll let the eggheads at HQ run with this ball for a while, see what their super Cray mainframes can come up with. Good work, everybody. David, I'd like a word with you in the next room." He turned and walked back down the hall.

With a heavy heart, David followed him into the back bedroom. It was sparsely furnished, with a small table and chair, and a cot in the corner. Cody didn't say anything at first, just motioned the other man toward the chair.

David didn't move. "If it's all right with you, I'll stand, sir."

"Fine by me." Cody walked over to the chair and plopped himself down, rubbing a hand over his face. "Tell me what happened at the house today."

That was the question David had been dreading ever since they had returned. Nothing to do now but face the consequences. He stiffened against the wall, straightened his arms down at his sides, and stared at a point above his commander's head. "Sir, I disobeyed a direct order and compromised the security of the mission and my teammates."

"And in doing so, you learned valuable information that we wouldn't have known otherwise. However, I have to balance whether the risk taken was worth the reward. It is possible that we may have found out that the woman existed through other means, either on our own or through Room 59's other people. What is certain is that you forced us to expose ourselves and our vehicle to the enemy when we had to pick you up in the street. By rights I should have left you there to make your way back to the safehouse—and avoid the authorities—on your own. But that kind of lesson would carry too high a price if you had failed."

"I wouldn't have failed, sir."

"No, I don't believe you would have." Cody rose from the chair to pace the length of the small room. "Why was there a delay at the start of the operation?"

"Sir, I did not have all of the available evidence regarding the status of the house, and therefore made the decision to hold until I had gained a clearer picture of what was happening."

"By the time we had that picture, the hostiles were already inside and taking out our targets."

"Yes, sir. However, I did not want our team to rush in without assessing the situation and having a solid plan of action. I gave the order to engage the hostile team when I felt confident we could do so with the maximum chance of success."

"Our success rested on taking the people in that house alive, not dead. You and your other team members have to execute the primary mission and handle any other friction that comes up, regardless of what it is or how incomplete your data is."

Cody stopped at the window and clasped his hands behind his back. "I read your file, including your psych profile, before I agreed to take you on." He continued despite David's surprised look. "Unlike the armed forces, directors allow Midnight Team leaders more flexibility in assembling our units. I don't believe you're a cowboy—your actions in Afghanistan and your plan to stop those shooters in the park tell me that. And yet you jeopardized not only yourself, but your entire team by pursuing unknown hostiles against orders. So how do I reconcile that—do I have a very good operative in my squad who is prone to only occasional lapses in judgment?"

"Sir, you have an operative who will do whatever is required to get the job done—" David could have left it at that. It would probably have satisfied his leader. But he didn't want to leave anything in the air between them, even if that meant he would be reassigned. "Even if that means reinterpreting the directives of the mission at times."

"Or my orders?" Cody asked.

"Sir, at the time I responded in what I felt was the appropriate manner for the situation. I chose to follow the hostile team myself because—because I would not order another team member to do something that I wouldn't do myself."

Cody turned on his heel and came right up to David's face. "Is that the real reason you went off hotdogging by yourself? Or do you think you're just that much better than the rest of us? That you don't need a team to accomplish a mission?"

"Sir, I do not believe that. I rely on my other team members as much as I know they rely on me to get the job done."

"Do you, now? I wish I could believe that. But I don't know if I can. I'm sure your other teammates are thinking the same thing. For these units to be successful, each member has to know—without a shadow of doubt—that when they're going into a room, the person on their left will terminate every hostile on their left, and the person on their right will terminate every hostile on their right, without fail or deviation from their proper course of action. When doubt creeps in about a member, everything changes. They look at you differently, they act and react differently, and those different reactions—the ones that aren't in their training—are what gets hostages, them or you killed. In our line of work, there can be no hesitation, no doubt about any of us, especially about each other. If there is, then that member has to leave the team. I can't make it any clearer than that."

David had not moved an inch during his leader's words. "Sir, I understand."

Cody pulled back a bit. "If we weren't still on duty, I would have ordered you to stand down already. As it is, replacing you now with another team member increases the chances for more friction during the operation, so you're staying for now. When you have the chance, I'd advise you to give some serious thought to what you're doing here and whether this is right for you. That's all."

"Thank you, sir." David resisted the urge to salute, but instead walked to the door and opened it.

"David?"

He paused, half expecting Cody to change his mind and deactivate him. He turned back. "Sir?"

"For what it's worth, I think this is the right place for you. I just don't know if you believe that. Think about it—and that is an order."

David nodded. "Thank you, sir." He walked out into the living room slowly, aware of, but not meeting, the stares of the other team members.

"Hey, you all right?" Tara asked, ignoring the dark looks of the other two men.

"Hmm? Yeah, fine, thanks. I just—I'm gonna head out to the garage."

It was a lame answer, but the only reasonable one he could give. David walked down the short hallway, now fully aware of their stares boring into his back, and hating every second of it. Stepping into the single-car garage, he closed the door and leaned against it.

What am I doing here? At that moment, he felt trapped—by his situation, by the team, by the room itself. Normally David would have handled things by going for a long run, the mindless, repetitive exercise clearing his brain of everything else and allowing him to attack the problem with a clear head. But they had to stay put, ready to move out on a moment's notice. And that was the real problem.

David knew that Cody had done what he needed to do—address the breach in the team's operating procedure as soon as possible. However, their meeting had also intensified David's already growing feeling of doubt in himself, and he knew that could be even more crippling to a spec-ops member. Once he started doubting himself, the fear of screwing up, of putting another team member's life in jeopardy through his actions, could balloon until he became paralyzed into inaction, not wanting to do anything because it might hurt someone.

That's the risk that we live with every single time we go out, he admonished himself. Taking a deep breath to try to clear his head, David immediately realized his mistake. Although they had wrapped the body of the dead hostile, the enclosed space still smelled of him, still stank of blood and shit, even over the bleach cleanser the techs had used to destroy any evidence of his being there in the first place. The combination of odors was nauseating. He walked over to where the corpse had been placed and squatted down, seeing the lifeless form in his mind's eye as if it were still lying there, wrapped in the sheet they had stripped off the bed.

What if that wasn't a hostile lying there? What if it was one of my own? And what if he died because of my mistake? Those were the questions that David couldn't answer to his satisfaction as he stared at the empty concrete, seeing a sudden, terrible vision of his team members lying in front of him, their sightless eyes accusing him of the worst crime of all—failing them.

8

Kate stood on a raised platform at the end of a large room, amid what looked like barely contained chaos. A half-dozen men and women swirled around her, analyzing data on wirelessly networked laptop computers, the low mutter of conversations providing a steady backdrop of noise in the space. On the opposite wall, a huge monitor showed the progress in the case on several different windows—a shot of the house on Wyvil Road, various views of the streets around the area as seen through the London city cameras and even a shot of their forensic team in London as it examined the recovered body.

All of it was real, yet in a sense none of it was real, for Kate was viewing the entire scene through a pair of virtual-reality glasses and attached headset, which enabled her to move about the room simply by looking at where she wanted to go. If she wanted a screen brought closer to her, she merely had to stare at its upper two corners, and it would automatically magnify

for her. She could instantly see what any one person currently on duty was working on, or bring up all of their
screens at once in front of her. Using the sensitive microphone that curved down her smooth jawline, she
could instruct and guide the men and women who risked
their lives on a daily basis to keep the rest of the world
safe, dictate after-ops reports to an autotranscriber, co-
ordinate meetings between directors and operatives
around the world and basically keep tabs on any mission
she chose to follow.

And that was often the hard part, choosing which
ones were the most vital. Room 59 operations were
going on in every corner of the world, as befitting its
mandate. Some operations were easily handled by personnel below her. Intelligence-gathering, or even the extraction of a double agent, if planned properly, often
happened with her knowing only two things: when it
had started and when it was finished. Blown ops,
however, like the Wyvil Road incident, always garnered
her immediate attention. Although she had every bit of
confidence in the people under her, Kate fully agreed
with the maxim of No Plan Survives Contact With The
Enemy. She had simply updated it. Her maxim was No
Plan Survives Implementation Intact, despite all of their
efforts to the contrary.

At the moment, she was reviewing the Midnight
Team's first-person videos of the operation. Another
feature of the MASC units all members wore was that
everything they saw was transmitted back to Room 59's
virtual headquarters, where it could be reviewed for
after-action reports, as well as future training simula-
tions. There was nothing like using the real thing to test
operatives to see how they would fare. *We'll definitely*

have to run this one, although I'm a bit concerned as to how these guys got past our operative and the team's surveillance in the first place, she thought.

Using the glasses, she could fast-forward or rewind the action, zoom in on anything the team member saw during the op or even work up the footage into a three-dimension re-creation of the entire mission, including every action that person took in it. At the moment she was staring at a close-up view of the pavement as a team member—M-Two, she confirmed—was dumped off a moving vehicle to land on the street. Gutsy but damn reckless, she thought, her lips pursing in disapproval. I'll be very interested in seeing that AA report.

A soft chime interrupted her thoughts. "Yes."

"Director, this is Dr. Samuelson, forensics."

"Go ahead, Doctor."

"I just wanted to let you know about the body we've been examining over here. It's going to take a bit longer to confirm an identity than we first estimated. There is evidence of extensive facial surgery, as well as the fact that his fingerprints have been removed."

"Removed?"

"Correct. We're trying to establish a match using middle phalanx prints, but I don't know if AFIS or other international databases will be able to provide a solid match based on that. We're running the target's current appearance through the databases now, as well as attempting to reconstruct what he looked like presurgery. I will advise you when we have any further information."

"Thank you, Doctor." She had just disconnected when another chime went off. "Yes, Samantha?"

"Do you have a minute? I'd like to discuss the Midnight Team's AA report."

Kate scanned the virtual room around her, ensuring that nothing needed immediate attention. "Sure. Come on in."

She sensed a presence, and turned to see Samantha's avatar sitting beside her, looking every bit as polished as she did in the flesh. "Hope I didn't startle you," Samantha said.

"No, although it is a bit unnerving to be on the receiving end when someone pops in." Kate lowered her voice and leaned over. "I have to confess that I enjoy the effect it has on others when I do it, however." Samantha's conspiratorial grin and nod confirmed that Kate wasn't the only one who thought this way. "However, back to business. Secure channel."

There was a brief blur around them, and the rest of the room took on a slightly hazy look. While Kate still had access to everything in the room, the communication wasn't two-way anymore. The rest of the operatives had been effectively blocked from this conversation. Normally Kate tried to keep as open a forum as possible—after all, the men and women working there had been recruited and cleared at the highest levels of intelligence work—but there were many aspects that had to be kept compartmentalized. Discussing failures in carrying out a mission was certainly one of them, at least until the problem could be identified—if there was indeed one—then corrected.

Upon seeing Samantha's grim expression, Kate didn't even bother with formalities. "I take it you've been reviewing the operation recordings?"

"Yes, and I'm not pleased with what I saw, particularly concerning the failure to achieve certain mission components."

Kate had been expecting this sort of response from Samantha ever since she'd begun examining the records. While she had very high standards for each mission's completion, she could also look at the bigger picture and take a win where she could get it. Samantha held her personnel—and herself—to almost impossible standards, and was very hard on anyone who didn't measure up, sometimes critically so. It was one reason that while the UK branch of Room 59 had one of the highest success rates, it also had the highest dropout rate in the entire agency. Kate didn't have anything against pushing the operatives hard—indeed, she was one of the leading proponents of tip-top training and near-constant evaluation. But to her, this mission had rapidly fallen outside normal parameters, and because of that—and the fact that the main priorities had been accomplished—she was willing to cut the Midnight Team some slack.

With a disarming smile, she tried to get the conversation headed into more positive territory. "The planned attack on London was foiled, and the bioweapons were recovered, so I'd say the primary and secondary objectives were achieved—not exactly a failure," Kate said. Her eyes flicked to the screen, where M-Two floated in midair, frozen in the act of being hoisted into the company van. "But please, continue."

Samantha's left eyebrow arched up in disbelief. "Perhaps. However, I dislike other people doing our work for us in such a—blatant manner. The third aspect of the mission was to capture the subjects alive, which was rendered impossible by their termination. Overall, I am concerned about the control that this team's leader is exerting over his members."

The British director paused for a moment, as if picking her next words carefully, something Kate had rarely, if ever, seen her do. "We're supposed to be getting the best of the best from the world's armed forces and intelligence agencies, yet we have a Midnight Team member going off on his own—against orders—to perform unsupported reconnaissance and engagement of the hostile team. Besides the increased risk to the rest of the team, this also eliminates any chance of disengaging from the encounter and attempting to establish surveillance at a later time."

Kate nodded. "I agree with that assessment. However, I think the last thing anyone, particularly them, expected was to find another strike team in the exact same location, going after the exact same people. We try to plan for ambushes, insurgents, just about anything that can go wrong. But considering what they came up against and how they acquitted themselves, I'm not ready to throw the book at them just yet."

"The fact that a team of hostiles was able to get to the target in the first place brings up other security and surveillance issues that I will address in my final report and recommendations. However, the more important question, in light of this new evidence, is whether we deactivate the team at this point and let a regular operative take over this investigation," Samantha said.

Kate steepled her fingers. "Correct me if I'm wrong, but weren't you the one who suggested keeping them activated in the first place?"

Another woman might have taken the comment as sarcastic, but Samantha just gave Kate a look that told the director that she knew she was being bullshitted. "Of course you're right, but that was before I saw how the op had gone down. If I'd had this information before, I would have advised pulling them immediately."

"Samantha, you know that I dislike switching teams in midop. One of our intelligence operatives would have to pick up the trail cold, and if they ran into this team, they would be at a distinct disadvantage."

"Yes, but a single operative that knows what he is going up against is more likely to be able to stay on the trail of this last subject without creating more complications. Besides…" Samantha hesitated.

"Go on."

"Let's face it, the Midnight Teams serve a useful yet limited function for the organization. Sending them after this lone woman is rather like using a flamethrower to light a candle, in my opinion."

Exactly what Jake was thinking in the limo, I'll bet, Kate thought. "Concerned about overkill, are you?"

"More like overspill. On this team's assignment, they shot up a house, chased a car through the streets of London—and I can't remember the last time that happened—which ended with the target vehicle blowing up in Kennington Park."

"All hazards, unlikely as they may seem, of the business," Kate replied.

"Nevertheless, for an agency that relies on staying behind the scenes to be effective, even when bringing in the bigger guns, as you say across the pond, our team certainly wasn't able to deliver, not on completing the entire mission, nor maintaining a low profile. I simply don't think this team is the best choice to send after this person."

"On the contrary, I believe that after this, they will be even more inclined to complete the next phase swiftly and well, to expunge the mistakes that were made previously. If a person knows that the confidence previously placed in them has decreased, they are more apt to try that much harder to regain that trust," Kate said.

"Which may lead them to take higher risks than normal. In an already high-risk situation, the results could be disastrous," Samantha said.

She's tenacious—I'll give her that, Kate thought. "If we pull them now, the psychological damage could be severe enough to hamper their performance for weeks, even months. Although I do appreciate your concerns, I still think that they are the right team for continuing this mission."

Samantha folded her arms. "It seems that we are bound to disagree on this matter. Of course, I will defer to you regarding this decision. However, I will have to note our discussion in my report."

"I wouldn't expect anything else, Samantha." Kate's e-mail monitor chirped. "Hold on a moment, will you?"

She opened the message. "Well, it looks like the team is already on the job." She put the attached pictures from the e-mail up on the large screen. "Broadcast to all operatives on task. This is the subject we are looking for. Last seen in the vicinity of Wyvil Road, London, and is most likely attempting to leave the country. First Team, give me an identity report on her immediately. All other operatives, track her current location ASAP."

Kate switched off her channel and turned back to the other director. "I think this team may surprise you."

"Perhaps. I just pray the surprise isn't more of what they did last night. Let's hope we can pick up her trail before that other team does. I'll keep you informed of any progress on my end."

"Thank you, as will I," Kate said.

Samantha's avatar winked out, leaving Kate to pause for a moment and watch the renewed activity around her, now reenergized with the new evidence they had to work with. For all her defense of the Midnight Team, Kate knew she was taking a chance sticking with them. Just don't let me down, boys and girls—in this game, you're lucky to get a second chance, and there are no third chances.

9

The insistent clamor of her computer's alarm clock jolted Marlene's eyes open, and she yawned and stretched under the thin blanket in her small but acceptable hotel room, luxuriating in the threadbare cotton sheets for a moment before reality crashed down upon her, sweeping away her grogginess in a rush of stark memories. Ray falling down the staircase, blood blooming on the front of his shirt…the black-clad assassin standing over him, firing twice more…the terrifying journey down the clothes chute…the flight through the disgusting sewer darkness, her shoulder blades itching, expecting to feel a bullet punch through them at any moment…staring at the white-sheeted forms being carried out on the emergency carts…

It was anything but a dream. After seeing the deadly proof of the slaughter with her own eyes, Marlene had spent the rest of the night skulking through the London streets. While she had done her best to remain incon-spicuous, it was almost impossible when every slammed door made her flinch, every raised voice jerked her head around to make sure the speaker wasn't coming after her. When she was absolutely sure that no one was following her, she had found a tiny hotel a few blocks away from her ultimate destination, her way out of London, and crashed after picking up a few more necessities in a twenty-four-hour supermarket.

Ray is dead…he's really dead, she thought. There wasn't any coming back this time, not like the blown hack in Philadelphia, when their hotel room had been raided and she squeezed through the tiny bathroom window and ran, dead certain the FBI had nabbed him, only to awaken and see him sitting in that ridiculous hardbacked chair at their safe hotel fifty miles away, covered in mud from the cattle truck he'd hitched a ride on. She couldn't remember the last time she had laughed so hard. She'd gotten up and tackled him to the floor in a bear hug.

I'll never wake up to see his face smiling down at me again. Drawing her legs up to her chest, Marlene wrapped her arms around them and sat very still, head bowed, tears streaming down her face.

After a few minutes, she wiped her eyes and made her way to the bathroom, sniffling with each step. She had paid extra for the privilege of a bathroom so small she was barely able to fit inside it along with a rust-streaked sink, toilet and minuscule shower, all crammed practically on top of one another. But she had things to do before she could go out in public again, and grimly, she set to them.

Forty-five minutes later, showered and dressed, her dark tresses and eyebrows had been transformed to platinum blond, and she had cut her hair even shorter, in case she had to hide it under a wig or scarf. Her clothes she couldn't do as much with, as she had to save her cash for the rest of her trip.

She paced the length of the tiny room. Two strides brought her right up to the musty, fading wallpaper, the pattern of linked roses long since faded to pale shadows of their former color. Marlene's gaze strayed to her laptop in the corner. She knew she needed to clear a path, to get out of the country and meet up with friends, but even with her skills, she knew who might be watching in cyberspace and how they might track her down. Still, it was the best way to go. She'd just have to be careful; that was all. As careful as Ray? her inner voice chided. Shaking her head, she grabbed the case and got moving, heading down the steps and out the back way to Midland Road, right next to the train station.

A couple of blocks away, on the main thoroughfare of Euston Road, she spotted a small café with the wireless symbol she was looking for. Slipping inside, she ordered a large black coffee and a sweet roll that she choked down, hardly tasting it but knowing she should eat. Sitting in a back corner, she unzipped her laptop case and got out her mobile home, office and just about everything in between, a customized laptop that could run rings around anything off the shelf, and even give some other hackers' platforms a run for their money.

Between gulps of steaming, weak coffee, she logged on and navigated to a very secure, very private chat room for folks who dabbled in her kind of work, some still for kicks, some for very serious five- and six-figure business. She pulled down a guest avatar, a plain-John-looking man to hide behind, and strolled around the main room, an endless, bare-bones hall with scattered groups conversing or people winking in and out in a flash.

Marlene kept panning back and forth, watching the conversation bubbles above people's heads. He's got to be here, he's always here. Two things about Aragorn—the man never leaves, and he never shuts up, she told herself.

She finally found the person she was looking for, surrounded by neophyte hackers, all enthralled by a story he was telling that she had heard at least three times. Out of respect, she waited until he had finished—she needed his help, and antagonizing him by interrupting wouldn't help anything.

"—so I wait until the right moment, then send the program. Every telephone in the Pentagon rang at once, and when they picked up, they heard that old McDonald's jingle. They were talking about it for months afterward, and investigating the phone company, and any other phreakers they could get their hands on. Me, I was long gone by then. Course, this was all waaaay back in the day, when geeks like me broke into phone companies with my trusty Commodore 64 and a 1200-baud modem. Times change, boys and girls, times do change."

The sycophants muttered excitedly among themselves. Marlene took the opportunity to send a private message to the tall blond man dressed in a fantasy ranger's outfit, complete with two swords and a long leather coat, holding court at the center of the group.

"Gorn, it's me, Katt."

The avatar's eyes lit up at seeing the guest avatar, but his expression quickly turned suspicious. "You sure you got the right guy, newbie?"

"If I got the guy who went to juvie for eighteen

months because of that Pentagon prank, then yeah, I got the right guy."

The handsome blond head snorted. "Lots of people know that story. How do I know it's really you?"

Marlene tamped down on her anger, knowing that the situation was making her edgy. In his place, she'd do the exact same thing. "Because when we both got drunk one night, you showed my your tattoo, and made me promise never to tell about Betty B—"

"All right, all right, I believe you—no need to be spreading those vicious lies. That really you, Katt? What are you doing running a clone?"

"I'm incognito at the moment. I need your help. Can we continue this somewhere else?"

"Well, that's certainly intriguing. Your wish is my command." Marlene tried not to roll her eyes at his inane chivalry, but simply followed him through what looked like a blank stone wall. Remember, like him all you want, but don't trust him, she told herself. For all his lofty airs and patronizing demeanor toward the newbies, she knew Aragorn trusted one thing above just about anything else—cold, hard cash. Now that Ray was gone, he was the only one Marlene could turn to.

The encrypted entrance led into a lush sitting room decorated in some kind of strange mishmash of Victorian and baroque style, with cut-glass lamps and heavy, ornate, overstuffed, claw-footed furniture everywhere.

Aragorn shrugged out of his coat and slung himself onto a crimson-and-mahogany chaise longue, his appearance totally at odds with the room. He noticed her stare. "Oh, this. Just a moment—" His avatar flickered for a second, and just like that he was dressed in an elegant suit, complete with a dove-gray, cutaway coat with tails and matching trousers, a top hat on the seat beside him, and a raven-headed silver cane in his silk-gloved hand. "Is that better?"

Marlene shrugged. "It'll do. Are you sure we can't be seen or heard in here?"

Aragorn raised his hand and dragged it across the wall in answer. Where his fingers touched, the plush draperies and maple wainscoting faded away, replaced with an endless string of numbers and computer commands. She could read the code that swirled and ran in endless lines along the walls.

"Neat, huh? It's a shifting 128-bit encryption code, with a few tweaks inserted by yours truly, of course." His pixelated expression turned grave, as if he had actually noticed her demeanor, even in here. "Hey, Katt, what's up?"

"Ray's dead." She hadn't meant to blurt it out like that—indeed, her hands resisted typing out the words, fingers unwilling to press the keys, as if by not telling it to someone else, she could somehow will him back to life. But that's not an option—keeping myself alive now is.

"OMG! Really? What happened?"

She gave him an overview of the deal gone wrong and the carnage that had followed. "After I escaped, I holed up, then got in touch with you. I need somewhere safe to hide for a while, until I can figure out my plan."

"What's in it for me?"

"Since I still have what they hired us to get, I still want to complete the deal—the original payment in exchange for the program."

"That doesn't sound like the brightest idea you've ever had."

"Maybe not, but the money to be gained will set me

up for a while, and I need it. Ten percent is yours if you help me out."

"Thirty-five."

"Fifteen."

"Thirty."

"Twenty."

He paused, and she knew she had him.

"Twenty-five, not one percent less."

Marlene knew she could have dickered him down a percent or two, but decided not to bother. She'd still call the shots, and once she was safe, there were plenty of ways to give him the slip, too. He was nothing compared to the people on her trail. "Deal," she offered.

"So, who'd you cross?" he asked.

"I'd rather not say at the moment."

Aragorn didn't like that. "Not a good way to begin our business arrangement, dear."

"Just bear with me for now. I have a pretty good idea who's behind this, but I'm not one hundred percent sure at the moment. I can tell you it's no one you've ever messed with—they deal with security in a more direct fashion."

"Kiss, kiss, bang, bang, eh? Hmm, all right, fair enough. You're near the station for the Chunnel—what a nasty name, sounds like some kind of venereal disease—so all aboard, my dear, and head to the City of Lights."

"All right, what happens there?" Marlene asked.

"It's best if you don't know. That way they can't get it out of you," Aragon replied.

"Oh, please. You don't have anything lined up yet, do you?"

"Give me a break! I don't have rescuers standing by

at a moment's notice, ready to spring into action. Once you're out of the country, I'll contact you with more details, but until then, you're on your own. Suffice it to say that I will have a safe place for you prepared by the time you arrive. Now get going."

"I'm there. Thank you, Aragorn."

The avatar seemed to swell a bit at the mention of his name. "You're welcome—anything for Ray's sister. Now get going."

Marlene logged off, packed up her computer and hit the street. The city was waking up around her, and soon the sidewalk would be packed with people heading into or out of the train station. She strode toward it, as well, trying her best to be just another ordinary commuter in London.

10

Anthony sat in the passenger's seat of the dark gray SUV, dividing his attention between the morning London traffic and the open case in his lap. Every few seconds the LCD screen sent out its quiet, steady beep as it searched for the one signal that would lead them to their quarry.

As Liam wove through the narrow streets, maneuvering up and down car-and-truck-choked lanes, Anthony resisted the urge to glance back at their two replacement men. Headquarters had informed him that he would have to make do with the pair, as there were no other available personnel at the moment. The voice in his ear had silkily informed him that when additional personnel were available, they would do their best to send some along. Anthony read between the lines well enough. You fucked up, so make do with what you've got.

Fortunately, the replacements looked to be more than adequate. Right behind him, his knees pressing into the back of Anthony's seat and the top of his head brushing the SUV's ceiling was a giant of a man. He wasn't overly muscled, but solid from feet to his broad shoulders, with every economical movement combining the best of both agility and strength. His face was narrow, framed by black hair cut high and tight, a jutting beak of a nose and expressionless gray eyes. He was also the quietest team member Anthony had ever worked with, limiting his replies to nods and shakes of his head. The two original team members had thought the menacing man was mute, until he had given his name in an accented deep voice—Gregor Petrov.

The other one was a lanky American named Carl Teppen, with a New Jersey accent that Anthony hadn't heard in several years. Shorter than the Russian, he was leaner, too, almost rawboned. Despite his lanky, almost country-boy appearance, he knew the business. His light blue eyes roved the streets constantly, always checking to their left and behind them for possible trouble. Next to him, the hard-edged Petrov did the same on the right. Both men's hands were always near their waists, ready to draw whatever was necessary to accomplish their job.

Anthony had received and reviewed both their files, and was generally pleased with what he'd seen. Petrov was a former senior sergeant in the Russian army, and Teppen had made lieutenant in the United States Marines before receiving an under-other-than-honorable-conditions discharge for assaulting a civilian while on duty. Anthony wasn't too worried about that; working in the private security sector gave employees a lot more leeway in that regard. Besides, the other guy might have been asking for it, he thought. God knows I run into plenty of assholes every day of my life. As long as these two could take orders and do whatever they had to do to get that girl, then everyone would get along just fine.

He kept a wary eye on Liam, who often took pride in hazing the new team members. But either he understood the importance of not screwing around at the moment, or else the big Russian had intimidated him enough not to try anything. So far, so good, he thought.

They'd been driving around town since 3:00 a.m., making a circuit between Heathrow Airport, the train station and various bus terminals, hoping to pick up the signal from the homing device the company buyer had planted on her a few days ago. Starting at the Wyvil Road location, they had driven carefully past the scattered police cars at the scene, then spent a good hour doing a spiral search pattern with the house as the center, but had come up empty so far. Now, after four hours of fruitless searching, Anthony was finding it hard to contain his impatience. "Goddamn it, did she just vanish off the face of the fucking earth?"

"It still ain't that hard to disappear, if you know what you're doing," Liam opined from the driver's seat.

"Just keep your eyes open. The last thing we need is any more interference." Right as he finished speaking, he heard a faint chirp from the tracker. "Turn left," he said.

"Where?"

"Turn left now!"

Liam cranked the wheel over, garnering a chorus of angry honks from oncoming traffic, which he replied to in time-honored fashion by flipping them the bird. They found themselves on a narrow avenue that wound through a working-class neighborhood, with houses crowding in on both sides of them. Except for an occasional glance ahead, Anthony's gaze remained glued to the screen, with occasional directions given to his driver as the signal grew stronger.

"We should be getting close now." They rounded a curve and came out in front of a train station with yet another odd English name—St. Pancras.

"Clever girl. She's heading for the Chunnel rail link, I'll bet. Find us a place to park—we might be going on a train ride."

11

Kate pushed the remains of her surprisingly good sole *meunière* around on her plate, then speared another asparagus stalk and crunched into it, relishing the springy texture and hint of lemon it had been steamed with. Not quite as good as Mindy's cooking, but it'll do.

The thought of her live-in housekeeper made her smile. Mindy Todd was a college student and crime-TV junkie who served as her girl Friday when necessary, which was pretty much all of the time. Kate had wanted to take her to London, as the bubbly, dark-blond-haired girl had never been to the city. But the board had already put up such a squawk about Kate coming over in the first place, and Mindy's next school term had been about to start, so they had both reluctantly shelved the plans.

She was just coming up for air and a bite or two after a frenetic eight hours of logged-in work, overseeing the sifting of evidence and intelligence and also keeping up on the various other investigations that Room 59 had ongoing around the world. When Kate traveled, the agency traveled with her, and today was no exception. In between keeping an eye on the business at Wyvil Road, she had reviewed after-action reports, interviewed two operatives about a completed mission in South America for potential follow-up and written several dozen memos, addendas, order forms, and signed her name—electronically only, but it still felt like a lot—to more documents than she could count. In the end, while we may all pass on to whatever lies beyond this world, the bureaucracy will continue, implacable, unstoppable. Kate was trying to figure out whether she had just made that up or read it somewhere when her computer chimed.

"Call from—J. Burges. What does she want?" Kate muttered to herself before she hit the button that activated her computer's telecom program. She saw a severe-looking woman with every hair in place, dressed in an almost schoolteacher-plain black business suit, with half-moon glasses perched on the end of her aristocratic nose. "Judy, what a pleasant surprise."

Judy Burges was Kate's liaison to the men and women of Room 59. In theory, she was supposed to handle much of the day-to-day operations, leaving Kate free to handle the IIA Board when necessary, and to keep an eye on the other directors and the big picture. In reality, since Kate loved to get her hands dirty as much as the board would allow, she often stepped in to handle certain ops personally, which irked Judy to no end. Although Judy was an excellent liaison—which was one of the reasons that Kate was able to go on this trip in the first place—she had a tendency to overreach, and Kate was still working on keeping her in line.

Much like I'm probably about to do right now, Kate thought upon seeing the other woman's stern expression. Although she steeled herself for the confrontation she knew was coming, Kate let no trace of it into her face or voice. "How can I help you?"

"Kate, this AA report just crossed my desk—are you really meaning to keep this Midnight Team on duty for the duration of this op?" Judy's upper-crust tone spoke volumes about what she thought of this decision.

Kate bit back the response that sprang to mind—which would have involved a physical impossibility—and tamped down her anger at being second-guessed. "Good, I'm glad that arrived so quickly. Yes, as I outlined in the report, there are several excellent reasons to keep them on the job, not the least of which is the fact that they are familiar with the situation, and are already on-site."

Judy shook her head. "Surely we have other Midnight Teams that could take over. If possible, I'd suggest plenty of downtime, evaluation and perhaps even some retraining. This Southerland operative—it sounds like he's got a definite problem with authority—not what a team leader needs in this kind of situation."

Kate resisted the urge to duck out of sight for a moment to massage her temples. "Judy, you know I like to have team captains police their units unless more drastic action is necessary. After all, they did stop the terrorist plot, recovered the bioweapons and took out two of the hostiles, as well. All in all, a good day's work in my book. And since M-One didn't request any kind of replacement, I am accepting his willingness to go forward as an indicator that his team is operating at full readiness."

"Be that as it may, it's how they did it that is of some concern, on-site or not—"

Kate decided to cut to the chase. "Judy, we have an unknown force running, who is willing to kill anyone in its path to get what it wants. I've made the executive decision to place a team in the vicinity and try to recover this missing person first to see what they're after. Rather than risk an operative, I'm using a Midnight Team because they stand the best chance of taking these people on again and coming out alive. I'm using *this* Midnight Team because they've faced these hostiles before and won, and they will most likely do it again. End of discussion."

Judy's lips pursed for the briefest moment, and Kate knew she had won. "I see. Rather like using a chainsaw to cut up a birthday cake, but I expect they'll manage without causing too much collateral damage. I'd hate to see more news reports like what the tabloids reported this morning."

"Yes, I saw it, too. Typical Fleet Street nonsense." Kate glanced at the front page of a prominent British rag, its headline screaming Joint U.S.-U.K. Anti-Terrorist Squad Loose On London Streets. If they only knew the real story, they'd crap all over their keyboards, Kate thought. "Just reporters grasping at straws to sell more copies. Besides, that's probably Samantha doing a bit of counterpropaganda. Hard to confirm anything when all of your sources refuse to be identified."

Judy barely nodded. "I suppose so. There are several other matters that require your input—if you're not too busy."

"Not at all." She should already know the words "I'm too busy" aren't in my vocabulary, Kate thought, but she merely smiled. They spent the next twenty minutes going over other matters, keeping their interaction at its usual, barely cordial simmer. Kate wanted to draw the call to a close as soon as she could, planning to get up and take a walk around, even if it was just up and down the hotel hallway. But to do that, she had to extract herself from middle-management hell.

"All right, Judy, launch the Vanuatu operation— should be interesting, given its location. Our operatives may be interviewing the local fauna for details about what's going on there. Also, please handle the debrief for the operative who just returned from the Yucatán— if that illegal-immigrant-smuggling pipeline is still there, I want to know the reason why. Thanks, but I've got to run, Judy, I have an important conference that's going to be starting here soon."

The British woman's face wrinkled in a frown of seeming concern. "What? I have your schedule up here, and I don't see anything posted for the next—"

"It just came up, and I'll send you the details afterward. Postop on the law-enforcement conference." Over Judy's surprised protests, Kate terminated the connection and leaned back in her chair with a sigh.

"It's a good thing I don't bother you that much." The low voice in the doorway made her spin around to see Jake leaning against the frame, both hands held up in reassurance. "Whoa, boss, calm down, it's just me."

Kate sighed. "I should be mad, but I guess sneaking up on me means you're doing your job well. How'd the training go?" Seeing as how she was going to be stuck in her hotel room, she had let Jake go for the assignment Samantha had discussed the night before. He had left without a word, leaving her to wonder when he slept.

"These guys are on the ball. Didn't have to show them too much. They were already well versed in most of the fine arts. We swapped a few tricks on covert surveillance and shadowing, and then spent a good hour on tactical driving." A grin split his serious visage for a second before vanishing as quickly as it had appeared. "That was fun. On the way back, I checked with the lab about that pistol—no luck there. The serial numbers have been removed. It did have a fairly rare threaded barrel to accept a silencer, but they removed the numbers on it, as well. Looks like another dead end. How you doing here?"

Kate pulled off her headset and tossed it on the desk. "I'm about ready to climb these very nice hotel walls. What say you to a couple of hours of sightseeing?"

Jake bowed slightly from the waist and motioned toward the door with his hand. "I'm yours to command."

"Well, yeah, that is the idea. Just let me change and—" The insistent trill of the computer brought Kate back to reality, freezing her in midstep.

"Is our chariot turning back into a pumpkin?" Jake's face showed no trace of a smile.

Against her will, Kate sank back down into her chair. "Just a minute—maybe it's something that can be dealt with quickly." She slipped on her headset and connected. "This is Primary."

A twenty-something kid with green hair and several piercings dotting an eyebrow, ear and lip appeared on the screen. "Primary? This is Autom8. I got a line on your dead merc."

Turning the rest of her body toward the screen, which had her full attention now, Kate waved Jake off with one hand.

"Subject is—or was, rather—one Jordan Tancreo,

formerly of Rio de Janeiro, Brazil." The man's picture appeared in a split screen next to the hacker's metal-decorated profile. "Former army military sergeant, then a police officer below the equator, but he apparently decided neighborhood bribery and shakedowns weren't enough for him, so he went for the big time and joined Mercury Security, Inc."

Kate leaned in. "You're sure about that?"

"Employed with the company for two years before his untimely demise."

Kate drummed her fingers on the desk. What does this mean? Was it pure coincidence that Terrence Weatherby, who had spoken to her at the conference yesterday, had no idea who she really was? Or did he? After a moment, she dismissed the thought. Paranoia is a way of life in this business. These two events had to be connected only by the merest of coincidences. However, she couldn't have been handed a better way to investigate them....

Kate moved the microphone away from her mouth. "Rain check, Jake—I've got something here I have to follow up on."

With a silent nod, he ghosted out of the room while Kate turned back to the monitor. "Good work, Autom8." She didn't pause at his online handle—Kate had been dealing with various hackers for far too long to be amused or concerned at their unusual idiosyncrasies. "Get me all current data on the company."

"It's uploading now for you, both public and private data. They seem to be having some cash-flow problems lately."

"That would explain their trolling for business at the convention. Great, this is great. Keep digging, but be sure to stay out of sight."

The hacker recoiled as if she had slapped him. "Naturally."

"Right, no offense." Kate winced—sometimes her intensity about the job could be taken for brusqueness.

"None taken. Autom8 out."

Kate disconnected and leaned back for a moment, weighing possibilities. Making her choice, she hit a key on her computer's speed-dial directory, listening to the phone ring.

"Hello?"

"Samantha, this is Kate." There was an odd kind of echo on their connection that Kate couldn't figure out. "Where are you?"

"I'm standing in the entryway of your suite."

Kate pushed back from her improvised office to see Samantha, her face pale, standing right next to Jake, who was holding her long cashmere coat. He shrugged and disappeared into the adjoining bedroom.

"Well, I guess we don't need these anymore." Kate took off the headset and waved her in. "What's going on?"

Samantha slid the recessed door closed behind her. Taking a small device from her pocket, she quickly swept the room for bugs, even going over Kate and her computer. She then attached it to the window and pressed a button, making the device emit a faint, high-pitched whine that vibrated the window ever so slightly. "Okay, we're clean. What I have to tell you cannot—*cannot*—go beyond this room. Do you understand?"

Kate slowly closed her laptop. "Samantha, you know I can't give you that assurance. If this is really that sensitive a matter, then perhaps I'm not the one you should be speaking to."

Samantha walked in and sat on the sofa. "That's the

issue at hand, since this does involve the current mission. It's just—there's a particular aspect of it that is of vital importance to the security of Great Britain—and America, as well."

Kate mulled it over for a second. "All right. Tell me what's happening, and let's see what we can do about it. Would you like something to drink?"

"No, my digestion is already in knots as it is." Samantha brushed back her hair and continued. "Here's what I can tell you. It is imperative that we recover that woman who escaped the Wyvil house, and any data storage devices she has on her."

"Okay, we're working on that. May I inquire as to the sudden paramount leap in her importance to your government?"

Samantha actually glanced at the door before speaking. "Yesterday, the headquarters at MI-6 was infiltrated on-site, and our computer system was broken into from the inside."

Kate had been prepared for anything but that. "My God, I thought the new headquarters building was impregnable."

"So did the architects and builders. The hackers found an old, abandoned sewer pipe that ran exactly where they needed it—from Wyvil Road. They broke through and were able to access the mainframe undetected. It seems they used a backdoor—even though we were sure we had eliminated all of them. We're still getting an idea of the damage, but it appears that they might have our entire playbook—classified information, agents in place, everything. If word of this got out, you can imagine the black eye it would give the department. I can see the headlines now—MI-6 Can't Even Protect Its Own Headquarters."

Kate's mind whirled as she absorbed the magnitude of the news. "Not to mention the damage caused in the intel community if any of the data is leaked to the public. I can think of dozens of organizations that would pay handsomely for even a fraction of what those files contain."

Samantha nodded. "Exactly. Long-term operations scuttled, deep-cover agents blown, informants exposed. It might set law enforcement back a decade or more worldwide. There are terrorist and crime rings around the world who would love to know just what we know about them. No matter what, that woman—and every bit of stolen data—must be recovered."

"We're doing everything we can at the moment. I assume that MI-6 has scrambled everyone they have to work on this?"

"Every available officer is scouring the city for her. That's another thing—there may be cross fire if the Midnight Team runs into anyone from MI-6. They're under orders to consider anyone attempting to approach or assist her as an immediate threat, and to capture or neutralize them using whatever methods are available. Even she is expendable, as long as the data is recovered."

"Understandable. I'll let our boys know. If MI-6 gets to her first, we'll break off our pursuit. If we get her first, we'll arrange a handover as soon as possible," Kate said.

Samantha took a deep breath. "Kate, with what I've just told you, does that change your mind in any way about using the Midnight Team?"

"I have the utmost faith that they will be able to get the job done, even with this new wrinkle. Our teams have not failed in executing an assignment yet, and despite what others have been saying, I'm counting the Wyvil Road operation as a win. I expect this one will be no different."

"I hope you're right." Samantha rose. "I've got to head back—they've pulled me in to consult on this. I'll do what I can to keep you informed."

"Check in whenever you can. If anything breaks on our end, you'll be the first to know after me." Kate got up with her and walked Samantha to the door. "Don't worry, with all of us on the job, she won't get away."

"Yes, but more operators in an area also means a higher chance of something going wrong," Samantha said.

"Then we'll just have to do our best to make sure that doesn't happen. Stay in touch, and good luck."

"You, too."

Like a silent butler, Jake appeared to help her on with her coat. Samantha flashed a wistful smile at both of them, then let herself out.

"I take it that wasn't a social call," Jake said.

"Not in the slightest." Kate's computer chimed yet again. "Damn, when things happen, they really happen fast." She crossed the room to the computer and stabbed a key. "Yes?"

"Primary, this is NiteMaster. I have a fix on your target with a seventy-eight percent chance of accuracy."

Kate sank into her chair again. "Where?"

"You're not gonna believe this, but—" a photograph popped up of the outside of the house on Wyvil Road, and of the crowd surrounding the police vehicles "—she actually went back to the scene of the crime." The picture zoomed in on a woman in a baseball cap, denim miniskirt and leggings, with a laptop case over her shoulder.

Although she was watching the police work with the rest of the crowd, she also did her best to keep her head down and face away from the news cameras. "When she left, she forgot to keep herself covered, and a watch camera on the next block got a good front-on shot."

He showed the ball-cap-clad girl next to the grainy shot of the woman they had obtained from their specialist on the Midnight Team. She had cut her hair, and her clothes were completely different, but the face was the same, albeit happy in the first picture, and haunted in the second.

"That's her, all right. How are you doing following her trail?" Kate asked.

"She's good, I'll give her that. She crossed into several areas that weren't covered by surveillance programs, so there are gaps in our coverage. However, using the general timeline, as well as the average walking speed of a five-foot-eight female—"

Kate cut him off. "NiteMaster, I don't need to know how, I need to know where she is *now*."

The hacker blinked as if being brought back to reality from his virtual version. "Oh, right. Anyway, using a spiral search correlated with the time-stamp data, I found her outside a hotel near the St. Pancras railway station this morning. She's a blonde now, by the way, and I last spotted her coming out of a coffee shop near the train station."

"Fantastic." Kate was already dialing. "See if you can locate a more recent sighting, and also watch for tickets being bought within twenty minutes of that time to Paris, and the name of each purchaser—we might be able to get a name out of this. Great work."

"Thanks, I'll let you know if I find anything more. NiteMaster out."

Kate's call was answered on the first ring. "Go for M-One."

"This is Primary, we have a lead. St. Pancras Station. Must warn you that locals are involved."

"MPS?"

"Government."

"Mmm. Just have to watch our steps even more, then. Will report in when we are on-site. M-One out."

"Primary out." Kate disconnected and sat back, rotating her shoulders to relieve some of the tension that had tightened them into knots. She kept a careful watch of the time, waiting to tick off the seconds. When five minutes had elapsed, she dialed a familiar number.

"Hello, Samantha. Yes, we just got something. Our target has been sighted near St. Pancras Station…"

12

Marlene quickened her pace as she approached the St. Pancras Station, barely glancing up at the refurbished building's Italian gothic facade with its new, ornate clock tower that was currently tolling eight o'clock. She hurried past the bustling rows of brand-new retail shops, cafés, bookstores and bakeries that catered to the commuting and tourist crowd in the packed station. Thousands of travelers flowed to and from the neighboring King's Cross Station, as well as catching or getting off trains heading to Scotland, the East Midlands, Sheffield, Yorkshire and elsewhere.

And of course, there was also the Chunnel rail link, which allowed a passenger to step onto a single high-speed train in London and step off in Paris. If all went well, that was exactly what Marlene planned to do.

She got in line and nervously counted her money— a little over two hundred pounds at the moment. Once she got a ticket, she'd still have to cool her heels at the station for fifteen minutes until the train was ready for boarding. First things first, she thought, concealing her nervous impatience as the line inched forward. At last, she got to the ticket window, and even though it cost more than she would have liked, she secured her seat— the last one in her traveling class—on the eight-thirty train departing for Paris. If she'd had more cash, she would have bought several tickets to different destinations, hoping to confuse anyone monitoring the system. But getting out of the country was the most important goal at the moment, so she had to take the direct route and hope she was still ahead of her pursuers.

Now all she had to do was sit and wait inconspicuously until the train was ready for boarding. Marlene found a bench under the Barlow train shed, which she had read about in the *Times* having suffered from cost overruns during its restoration. All looked fine now, with new steel framework supporting clear Plexiglas panels that let in the wan English sun. Marlene tried to at least appear as if she was enjoying the morning, but she couldn't help glancing around her, trying to see everywhere at once. Stop it, you only look more suspicious, she thought as she leaned against the back of the bench, trying to blend with the commuting crowd once again.

The announcement to board the London-to-Paris train echoed from the loudspeakers, jolting Marlene into alertness. She pushed off the bench, making sure her laptop case was secure, and walked down the platform, keeping a wary eye on anyone who looked to be taking any sort of interest in her. She saw the doors only a few yards away. Just a few more steps, and she'd be safe—

Marlene felt a hand grip her arm at the same moment something needle-sharp pricked into her back.

"Just keep walking right on past those doors," a tony British voice said in her ear. "We're going to keep going for a few more steps, then you'll stop as if you forgot something, and we'll retrace your steps and walk right out of the terminal. Any attempt to resist me will be met with a painful deterrent." The point of the knife jabbed her rib cage to emphasize the instructions.

Marlene tensed, then forced herself to relax and keep moving with him. "Are you from Mercury?"

"Let's just say my employers are very interested in talking to you about an item of ours that you have in your possession. All right, we're going to stop in the next few steps."

While he spoke, Marlene had been looking around for what she needed. Up ahead, she saw him—a uniformed Metropolitan Police officer patrolling the platform a dozen yards away. She whirled around, pushing the laptop case between herself and her captor to not only break his hold, but also to keep the case between his blade and her body. Before he could grab her again, she picked up the laptop case by its handle and shoved it into his face, knocking him off balance, while screaming.

"Help, police, he's trying to kidnap me! Help, police!"

The effect was immediate. The uniformed officer turned and began trotting toward the scuffle. At the same time an unremarkable man who had been waiting for a nearby train dashed up and tackled the man, sending his blade skittering across the floor.

"Knife, he's got a knife!" Blowing a whistle, the uniformed cop piled onto the melee, and the three men fought and cursed as they wrestled each other. Marlene looked around, fearful that the scuffle had attracted too much attention, but other than a few passersby stopping to stare while giving the struggling, swearing men a wide berth, the platform was still fairly clear. She edged toward the platform, willing the doors to open as if she could pry them apart by her desire to escape alone. For some reason the train still wasn't ready, and she glanced at the main entrance one more time, and that's when she saw them.

Two men, one a lean, blond-haired man with an alert, wary gaze and a slightly hunched posture, as if he was hiding something in his Windbreaker that Marlene certainly didn't want to know about. The other man was pure predator, scanning the crowd with measured sweeps of his gray eyes, his dark brown hair cut short to his skull, his stance alert, ready.

Their gazes met, just for an instant.

Although Marlene had never seen either man before, she knew they were there for her.

13

"Damn it, of all the times to catch the morning traffic! There's got to be a faster way over there than this!"

Although David usually wished Robert would just shut the hell up, this time he couldn't help agreeing with the wiry Welshman. Even with the congestion-charge plan introduced in central London a few years ago, the morning traffic was still as thick as the city's legendary fog, with the bumper-to-bumper crawl trapping them on Gray's Inn Road, still a half mile away from their destination.

"Isn't there a quicker way than this?" David asked.

"Yup." Cody swiveled in his seat. "Kanelo, you're with David as Team One. Tara and Robert, Team Two. Get out and get up there. I'll stay in touch via cell. If all goes well, by the time I get up there, one of the teams will have spotted her and made contact. Try not to cause a scene—just get her out of the station quietly. I'll meet you by the front entrance. If anything strange goes down, report it immediately."

"What if the other shooters are there?" David asked.

"If any fireworks start, defend yourselves or the target only—do not intervene if other civilians get in the line of fire. Also, we know that MI-6 is on the hunt, as well—so be careful and do not engage them if at all possible. Team One, get out at the next intersection, cut up one, then move over to the station. Team Two, you'll go at the next light, head down one block, then come up the back way. Stay alert and watch for trouble. Team One, you're up."

Robert's eyebrows waggled up and down. "Looks like it's you and me, girlie. Hey, Kan, bet you a tenner we get to her first."

David caught Tara's eyeroll in the side mirror. The tall black man loosened his sport coat and put his hand on the door, ready to move.

The SUV lurched forward, then just as quickly came to a halt. "Team One, move out."

David pushed his door open and stepped out into the street, barely closing the door and flattening himself against the SUV as a cyclist whizzed past, tossing an incensed "Stupid yob!" over his shoulder as he wove through traffic, the only wheeled vehicle moving for blocks. With Kanelo beside him, David stepped quickly through the packed traffic and onto the far curb as the cars crawled forward again.

"Let's go," David said.

As they ran, David slipped on a pair of sunglasses that also connected him with Primary, Room 59 headquarters. "Map to St. Pancras Station," he said under his breath. The combination earpiece and mike picked up his words and projected a small map in the lower right-hand corner of his left eyepiece, giving him distance,

estimated time of arrival, a map and turn-by-turn instructions to the front entrance. "Argyle Street doglegs
north across Euston to Pancras Road to the entrance on
the left." David repeated the instructions, committing
them to memory as he and Kanelo trotted down the
street, the SUV disappearing from view.

The two men settled into a comfortable pace, neither
one saying anything. For his part, David was glad for the
silence, which allowed him to concentrate on the job
ahead. Their long legs ate up the distance quickly, and
soon the large brick facade of the rail station came into
view. Traffic on Euston Road was moving fast, and the two
men had to wait until the striped pedestrian pole signaled
that it was safe to cross, slipping through the increasingly
thick crowd as the pair got closer to the building.

At the door, David radioed it. "M-One, Team Two,
this is Team One. We are in position."

"Team Two in position," Robert replied.

"M-One affirmative. Sweep the building for your
target, and keep your eyes open for anyone else looking."

"Affirmative." David caught Kanelo's eye, and the
two men headed into the station, caught up among
hundreds of other people coming and going. David kept
his hand near the waist of his trousers and the HK pistol
snugged into a clamshell holster at the small of his
back. He kept a wary eye out for security—he figured
the measures taken near the Chunnel train would be
strict, and didn't wish to bring down any attention on
himself or his partner.

Threading their way through the crowd, David and
Kanelo scanned the dozens of faces around them,
dividing up the huge room by unspoken agreement.
They appeared casual, sweeping forward from the main

doors and moving toward the various platforms, intent on checking every face they saw. David's gaze alighted on different faces just long enough to realize it wasn't the person he was looking for, then moving on.

Over the clamor of the train shed, David heard the piercing, high-pitched blast of a whistle. He locked eyes with Kanelo. "Police whistle."

"Team Two, this is Team One. Whistle and commotion near the Chunnel train—we're moving to investigate."

Kanelo nodded, and they both headed toward the noise, skirting the outside mass of commuters heading into London from the outskirts of the city. David had to use all of his dexterity to move against the throng, bobbing and weaving as he tried to get closer to the commotion on the platform near the HS1—the high-speed Chunnel train.

A crowd had gathered, and as David forced his way to the front, he was elbowed aside by another man who was very intent on where he was going.

"Sorry," the man grunted as he disappeared into the crowd. David immediately checked his wallet and his gun, aware that the man could have been either a pickpocket or the accomplice who distracted a mark while another thief lifted the goods. Both were still in place, however.

"M-Two, I have possible target sighting," Kanelo said as he nudged David and surreptitiously pointed, not at the high-speed train, but at another one on the other side of the platform.

David stood on his tiptoes in time to see a flash of short, blond hair and deep blue eyes, the exact shade that had held his gaze in the grainy video frame. She disappeared into a train car, followed by the dark-haired man who had bumped into him a moment ago.

"Shit, that's her, and she's already got a tail. Come on!" David pushed his way through the crowd toward the train, part of his mind catching that the high-speed train was making its final boarding call. What's she up to? he wondered.

14

Anthony nudged Carl with his elbow and walked a little faster. "Don't lose her." Even though he'd be more comfortable with Liam at his side, the first thing Anthony always did was evaluate new men assigned to his team, and the best way to do that was to see how they did in the field.

"Don't worry, I got her. Looks like the drapes don't match the carpet anymore." Carl's head didn't move, but his eyes scanned to his right and left. "Sure is crowded around here."

The team leader knew the newbie wasn't talking about the general crush of passengers. They had spotted the woman right away, and had been moving in to apprehend her when she had been accosted by another man. Anthony had held them up, hoping the guy might get away with it—it would be much easier to move on him later in a less conspicuous place—but she had gotten away with her distraction, running for the other train and leaving the furious man behind to be hauled away by two Metro police officers. Anthony was pretty sure there were more agents around the station, although whether they were from MI-6 or that mystery shooter team, he had no idea. We'll just nick her first, and fuck over anyone who gets in our way this time.

The two men trotted through the crowd toward where they had seen Marlene board the train. More clever than I thought, Anthony mused. Now she had options, stay on board or exit from either side.

"Stay outside and follow the cars down—she'll come out either here or there. I'm going in," Anthony directed.

Carl nodded and slipped through the crowd, paralleling the train cars, always watching the windows for a glimpse of their target. Anthony stepped inside and, after a glance behind him to make sure she hadn't pulled the old "sit down and blend in with the crowd" trick, walked unhurriedly down the center aisle, past old people struggling to put away their bags, young people slouching in their seats, bored and disinterested, already staring out the windows or falling asleep, and professionals in their suits and ties, clicking away on their laptops or talking too loudly on their cell phones. He gave all of them no more than a cursory glance, his eyes roving for the one face that would mean his job was done.

When his earpiece vibrated slightly in his ear, he tapped it. "Go."

"I've spotted her, in the next car ahead of you. She's stuck in behind a bunch of students. You should be coming up on her in the next twenty yards," Carl reported.

"Watch for other interested parties."

"Will do. You just get up there and get her out."

"Just watch your own ass, and let me worry about

hers." Anthony strode to the door between the cars and into the next compartment, but before he could take another step, he felt a hand clamp down on his shoulder.

"Terry, is that you? I thought I recognized you back there!"

Anthony spun around to see a man he didn't recognize—no, that wasn't quite true. He had seen him before, in the crowd near the altercation, had even bumped into him on the way over to this train. The guy was a pretty good actor, with a huge smile plastered across his face as he waited for some spark of recognition. The only giveaway was his too-intent gaze, boring directly into Anthony's.

"I'm afraid you have the wrong person, sir. Now please excuse me—" Without waiting for a reply, Anthony turned to head deeper into the car, only to be stopped again by the other man's hand.

"Naw, I'm sure it's you, Terry Westing from Eton College, class of '93, right?"

This time Anthony didn't say anything, but whirled around so fast that he broke the other man's hold on his shoulder and pinned the offending hand between his right arm and his side, trapping him. Curling his fingers so that the second knuckles protruded in what was known as a ram's-head fist, he pistoned his left arm out, aiming for his opponent's solar plexus and a quick end to this delay. To any bystanders, it would have seemed that he had just tapped the other man, but would leave him winded and gasping on the floor.

Instead, the man moved with Anthony's attack, turning sideways to let the intended blow sail past his chest while he grabbed the outthrust hand with his own. "Now, that just isn't very nice." The man's voice had dropped in volume and tone, and matched Anthony's own cold intensity.

The merc's eyes widened in surprise. Shit, he's another pro! Anthony realized. Before he could move, a loud voice from behind them piped up. "Hey, get moving, other people would like to get on board here!"

Anthony released the man's hand and twisted out of his grip, shoving him backward into the crowd of people jamming the entryway. Turning around, he scrambled past the knot of people ahead of him, shoving through and climbing over when necessary. "Where'd she go?"

"She's getting off at the next door. I'm moving in—What the hell do you—?" The connection was suddenly cut.

"Carl, what's going on out—damn it!" Anthony vaulted over a row of chairs, narrowly missing kicking a backpacker in the head. Clambering over another row, he heard another disturbance and raised voices behind him, and knew his adversary was after him again. Reaching the door, he raced outside just in time to see Marlene duck into the Chunnel train as the doors swung shut.

"Son of a bitch! Carl, where in the hell are you?" Hearing a shout, Anthony looked up the platform to see Carl trading vicious blows with a tall, well-built black man in a torn sport coat. "Priority members, abort, repeat, abort." Taking a running start, Anthony leaped into the air just as the black man's back turned to him, his high side kick slamming into the guy's ribs and pushing him to the ground.

"Let's go!" Anthony saw more uniformed men approaching from down the platform, and pulled Carl away. "Move out, now!"

The two men ran down the platform and out into the yard, disappearing into the maze of trains, tracks and cars that covered the rail yard.

15

Her heart hammering in her chest, Marlene squeezed through the doors of the high-speed train just as they closed. Grabbing a pole near the entryway, she leaned against it for support as she glanced backward to see the brown-haired man burst from the other train. He spotted two other men fighting, and went to help one of them, leaping into the air to kick the other one, then the pair ran off, pursued by police officers.

Marlene closed her eyes and swallowed hard, concentrating on not vomiting. Her stomach lurched, and not just from the slow movement of the train as it began its long acceleration out of the station. I could have been killed out there, she realized. Stepping onto the other train had been an act of desperation, and she had been surprised it had worked so well. But I also had help, of a sort, she thought, puzzling over the different groups of men who had fought each other on the platform. She knew none of those men would be caught;

they knew all kinds of ways to evade the law, and they would keep coming after her, all of them, until one side or another caught her. MI-6 wanted the data—that, and to throw her into prison and toss the key, most likely. The other side, her erstwhile employer, wanted the data, too, and her dead.

"Miss?" The voice right next to Marlene brought her out of her reverie with a startled squeak. Straightening up, she opened her eyes to see a man dressed in a smart uniform holding a small device. "If I could see your ticket, please?"

"Oh—of course." She extracted the vital slip of paper from a pocket on her laptop case and handed it over. He inserted it into a slot on the machine, which whirred and made a buzzing noise, then spit the ticket back out into his hand.

"Just made it," he said.

"Yes—yes, lucky me."

"Good thing you weren't caught up in that fray outside, eh?" He held the punched ticket out. "Thank you, and have a pleasant trip to Paris."

"Thank you." Taking the slip of paper, she walked down the center aisle on unsteady legs to her compartment in the middle-class accommodations. Finding an empty foursome, she sank into the nearest window seat, leaning against the cool glass and watching the graffiti-covered walls of South London fly by faster and faster as the train picked up speed.

"Excuse me, is this seat taken?" Marlene looked up to see an impeccably dressed, dark-haired man with a kind smile. He was pointing at the seat across from her, and although she didn't really want to be sitting next to anyone at the moment, she didn't feel as if she could refuse him.

"No, it's open."

"Thank you." His speech was colored with an accent she couldn't quite place—Italian? Greek?—and despite herself, Marlene couldn't help watching him as he sat across from her, setting a folded newspaper on the seat beside him. "Some fortune, eh? The ticket booth said every seat in here was sold, but here we are, with no one nearby."

"Mmm." Marlene returned to staring out the window.

If the man caught her unspoken cue to leave her alone, he gave no sign of it. "I just had to get out of the city one last time before winter, and I thought Paris would be nice to see this time of year. Just playing hooky, I suppose. And you, are you playing hooky, as well?"

A ghost of a smile tugged the corners Marlene's mouth up for a moment, before she shook her head. If only, she thought. "No, I'm traveling to Paris on—personal business." One might even say a matter of life or death.

He nodded, his liquid brown eyes never leaving her face. "That does not surprise me, although I had hoped you would be going to the City of Lights for a vacation. It is so beautiful, and there is so much to see there."

"Well, it's likely I won't be staying long. I'll be meeting friends there, and we'll be driving through Europe for a few weeks."

The man's expression grew rueful, almost as if he had caught her in the lie, even though there was no way he could have known anything about her. "Are you sure I cannot tempt you with a few days in Paris on the arm of a handsome tour guide?"

Marlene covered her mouth with her hand to hide the foolish smile on her face. *I nearly got kidnapped on the* platform a few minutes ago, and now this guy is hitting on me? "You are very confident, *monsieur.*"

"Well, in my line of work, I have to be. I have to know what I want, and move to take it quickly, before someone else does." He smiled, transforming his face from utter seriousness to the lighthearted expression of a carefree man ten years younger.

"Oh? And what is it you do?"

As quickly as it appeared, the smile flitted from his face as he leaned forward. "I work for Mercury Security, Incorporated, and my current assignment is to locate you, Maggie Britaine."

16

"Son of a bitch!" David resisted the urge to kick the side of the departing train in his anger, and instead ran to help Kanelo, who, trying to hold his head and his back at the same time, was failing at both.

"Stay still, you might have a concussion. This might hurt a bit." David took his head in both hands and turned his face up to the light, checking his pupils.

"I can't tell what hurts more, the muscles where that bastard booted me or your fingers on my aching skull."

"I think you'll be okay, but we'd better get out of here—we've attracted enough attention as it is." Indeed, David realized, if it wasn't for those other two guys taking off down the platform toward the tracks, they'd probably be surrounded by police right now. "Come on, let's get you up and moving."

He bent down and slung Kanelo's arm around his shoulders, then pulled him to his feet. The taller man swayed a bit, and David steadied him with one hand while hitting his earpiece with the other. "M-One, this is M-Two, we are pulling out. Be advised, we did not recover the target, but ran into other interested parties. Have one injured, we're moving toward the exit now."

"Is target still in sight?"

David glanced over at the train pulling out of the station. "Negative, target is out of reach at the moment."

"Copy that. All teams, withdraw. Repeat, all teams withdraw."

David heard muttered cursing from Robert. "Not again! What happened, Two, she get a look at your face and run off screamin'?"

Cody's authoritative voice cut through the chatter. "That's enough. We'll debrief when we've regrouped. Do you know where she's headed?"

David and Kanelo had been on the move during the brief conversation, and were almost at the main doors. "Yeah, she's on the HS1 to Paris," David replied.

They were about to push through the exit when a voice called out behind him. "You there, at the door!"

Both men froze just inches away from the door. "Keep going?" David asked.

Kanelo sucked in a breath and winced before answering. "No—too suspicious. Let's see what they want. Let me stand."

David took his arm away and turned around to see a man who looked as if he worked for the railroad approaching them. "Gentlemen, there were reports of a man attacking you in front of witnesses. I'm afraid that I have to keep you here until the police can take your statement, and I'm sure you'll want to press charges—"

Kanelo interrupted him with a loud groan, and slumped against David, who ran with the improvisation.

"I appreciate that, but as you can hear, my friend isn't feeling too well, and I'd like to get him to a hospital to get checked out."

"Sir, I'm sure an ambulance can be called for him, but you must remain—"

"Oh, God, my head—splitting open—everything going dark—" Kanelo clutched his temples and practically fell over on David, who held him up with both hands.

"Thanks for your offer, sir, but we really must get to a hospital right now!" David shoved his teammate at the door, wincing as the unprepared Kanelo's head smacked into the glass. Reaching around him, David pushed the door open and helped him through over the protests of the administrator.

"Good acting there, Kan." David ushered him down the steps toward the idling SUV.

"Ugh, it wasn't all acting—my head is pounding, and for a moment there I thought I was blacking out. Ribs hurt like hell. Is he still back there?"

"Don't know, and don't care." David yanked the front passenger's door open and hustled Kanelo inside, then jumped in the back, barely getting aboard before the vehicle was moving.

"We're picking up Team Two around back, so before they get here, why don't you fill me in on what happened?" Cody said.

"I think the same team we ran into last night was at the station." David related what had happened inside, leaving nothing out. "The plan had been to stop the man pursuing our target and flush her out for Kanelo to take into custody. I got a good look at one of them. However, he got a good look at me, too, I'm afraid."

"Unfortunately, their backup spotted me, as well,

and intercepted." Kanelo rubbed the back of his neck. "He was pretty good, too, for a white boy."

"So while the four of you were beating on each other, she scooted between you all and got on her original train? Where was your second team?"

"Well, here they are, so you can ask them directly." David leaned back in his seat, and looked around for any nearby police presence.

Robert and Tara piled into the SUV, and moments later they were moving north on Pancras Road, away from the commotion. The two-tone wail of European sirens could be heard in the distance. David tuned back in to hear Team Two's report, and learned that they had been barred from coming onto the platform once all of the commotion had started.

"Then we got the call to leave, so we did." Tara slumped back in her seat. "At least tell me we know where she's going?"

"Yeah." Cory navigated while calling another number on his phone. "Primary, this is M-One. We sighted target at the station, but the other team was there, as well, and she escaped in the confusion…. Yes, we do know where—Paris, on the Chunnel train…. A helicopter would be best, but it'll be close…. Very well, we'll meet you there…. M-One out."

He turned and scrutinized everyone in the passenger compartment. "David and Kanelo, get online and go through Facemaker at Primary for your two hostiles. Maybe they can come up with a jacket on these guys. We're going to France."

17

Who is this woman?

For Kate, it was the million-dollar question. And how is she able to waltz out from under trained professionals not once, but twice in the past twenty-four hours?

She patched into the virtual HQ, ignoring the slight headache that came with spending too much time in virtual reality. "Do we have anything yet on our target?" she asked.

"Still searching, ma'am."

Kate tried not to clench her fists in frustration. She thought that she had long ago gotten used to the interminable waits while their personnel and massive computer systems searched for that piece of useful intel in a vast, ever-changing ocean of information. And so she was always annoyed when her temper got the better of her, and she felt like going to the nearest computer and wringing whatever she needed out of it. Even though they knew where their fleeing target was—

indeed, one of the virtual screens had mapped out the Chunnel route, as well as the speed of the train that was a few minutes from entering the thirty-one-mile-long underwater passage, with an estimated time of arrival at its station in Paris—every second meant that she was getting farther away.

Normally this wouldn't be a problem, since Kate had already scrambled agents from the French Room 59 Directorate to meet their target at the station. However, given her unusual ability to elude danger, Kate wouldn't have put it past her to manage to get by them, as well. And if she does, everyone goes back to shadowing and target-interception training.

A ping from her computer signaled incoming messages from the Midnight Team. Kate opened up two of them to reveal two faces, and a similar message on each one:

Primary:
Here's a picture of one of the men encountered in the St. Pancras Station. Hope it helps get a line on who we're up against. Good luck.
M-One

Kate studied both pictures as she uploaded them to their networked criminal-profiling program, which could draw on law-enforcement databases around the world for suspects, and got their man or woman more often than not. The full-frontal picture had been created with Room 59's imaging program called Facemaker, an advanced version of the computer programs used by police around the world to create pictures of suspected criminals. A witness selected the remembered features—eyes, nose, hair, distinguishing characteristics—

and assembled a picture of their suspect. Facemaker then took the process a step further, and extrapolated a three-dimensional picture, with near photo quality, of the suspect's face. The result was a more recognizable picture, at least for computers, which made it easier for them to better match the points of recognition on a human face and get higher hit results on a jacket search.

Kate looked at one glowering face, for even though the program presented its subjects in a neutral expression, the heavy eyebrows and hooded eyes, combined with the strong nose and jaw, gave the man a decidedly unpleasant aspect. She hoped the computer would come up with something soon. *God, I hate waiting.*

Even as she did that, a part of her already had a pretty good idea of what they were going to find. With that in mind, she dialed a number.

"This is Samantha."

"Samantha, this is Kate. How goes it?"

"As well as can be expected. I understand there was a bit of commotion at St. Pancras Station this morning."

"Mmm, I'd heard that, as well." Kate didn't squirm in her chair often, but Samantha's matter-of-fact tone told her that the other woman had a pretty good idea of who had caused the disturbance. *However, if she's not going to come out and say it, there's no need to elaborate.* "I'd also heard that the suspect got away, unfortunately."

"Yes, it seems she's due more credit than we've been giving her."

"Funny, I was just thinking that. But the real reason I've called is that I have a line on the people who may be behind this—or at least one of the parties that's after her—probably to get back what they hired her to steal."

"She's a contract employee?"

"Surely MI-6 has had the same thought. No hackers go to this much trouble—take this much risk to go on-site and get access the only way they could—unless they're being paid incredibly well by somebody."

"You may have something there. So, who do you think it is?"

"Mercury Security," Kate said.

There was a pause. "Terrence's organization?"

"The same."

"I thought their cash flow showed they were nearly broke."

"Perhaps broke enough to go all-or-nothing on a data strike they could auction off bit by bit to the highest bidder, or get a blanket bid for the whole enchilada. It's not like we don't know people, or governments willing to spend that kind of cash to get what they want."

"True, too true. What do you intend to do about it?"

"Well, I was hoping that you'd be interested in serving both of your loyalties at the same time by agreeing to do a bit of fieldwork."

"Oh, God, you can't mean you want me to be a swallow."

Kate smiled wryly at the term. In tradecraft parlance, a swallow was an agent with the sole purpose of subverting a target using whatever means necessary, including sex. "Hopefully it wouldn't come to that."

"You're damn right it wouldn't—I can barely stand the man as it is, but to think of doing that…I'd better have the fastest acting sedative you've got available with me."

"And you will, along with plenty of backup. In fact, I'll assign Jake to the case—it would be good for him to get out in the field, keep his reflexes sharp. So what do you say—shall we set it up?"

There was silence on the other end as Samantha thought it over. "I'd do just about anything for my country, but I didn't know I'd have to endure a sacrifice like this."

"What, dining in a five-star restaurant with a handsome man who's at least charming on the surface? Every woman should have your problems," Kate said.

"No, they shouldn't—you've only had a small dose of him. Let me run this past my superiors here—they may insist on a joint op."

"That's fine. I like to think we play well in other people's sandboxes when we have to. Call me with particulars once you have the op in play. And Samantha—thank you. You're doing the right thing."

"I know, I know. It's just—I'm going to feel so unclean afterward. Ah well, for queen and country, as we say."

"That's the spirit. And if you need anything that MI-6 can't provide—although I can't imagine what that might be—let me know."

"I will, Kate. Thanks for passing this along. I'll be in touch."

Kate disconnected and leaned back in her chair, massaging her temples. She had been up for the past twenty hours without a break, and it was starting to catch up with her. Just enough time to catch a nap before the team touches down in Paris. No, I'd better update Louis of what's coming his way—I'm sure he's not going to be happy. With a sigh, she dialed again, with only a brief, longing look at the bed a few feet away.

18

Maggie Britaine had seen plenty of movies where the heroine or hero, when faced with an enemy who had incontrovertible proof of his or her real identity, just shrugged it off with a smile and a careless remark that deflected the intended verbal thrust while preserving the air of mystery.

Real life, however, was much different, and her hand flew to her mouth as her eyes widened when she heard the man's astonishing revelation. She knew there was no point trying to pretend her name was Marlene anymore.

He sat back, smug and comfortable. "Yes, I'm afraid that while you evaded my partner quite effectively, I won the coin toss to pursue you onto the train if necessary. He was so sure that he'd be able to handle you himself…a mistake he won't make next time, I'm sure. Unfortunately, our employer will not be happy that he landed himself in jail, either."

Maggie only half listened to her new captor as he

prattled on. The rest of her mind was already preoccupied with trying to figure out some way to escape. No weapons—not that I could shoot or stab him—and I'm sure he could overpower me without thinking twice. No, I'll have to come up with something else. She had never really been comfortable with violence—hence her career in computer crime, white-collar and oh-so-bloodless. But now she might have to get up close and personal with this guy to get away.

She tuned back in to his conversation, hoping to find something she could use against him. "…since there is literally no place to go for the next two hours, you might as well relax and enjoy the ride."

Maggie's eyes flicked to her laptop case on the seat next to her. "What if I was able to give you what your employer wanted right now? Would you let me go?"

The mercenary smiled. "I'm afraid it is too late for that now, my dear. My employers would be very disappointed if I didn't bring you back with me. Although perhaps I should hold on to your computer case for the time being."

"Why? As you rightly pointed out, I'm not going anywhere, and carrying this case would ruin the lines of that excellent suit."

The man appraised her, his eyes sliding up and down her lithe body. "At least you appreciate good fashion, even if you, ah, do not seem inclined to wear it."

"Oh, this?" Maggie let her fingers trail up the side of her leg, noticing his eyes dip down, drawn by the movement as she readjusted her skirt. "Well, I was trying to disguise myself after your goon squad came after me. Trust me, this isn't my usual attire." Crossing her legs, she let her hand float to his wool-clad knee, caressing it ever so gently. "Isn't there any other way I

might persuade you to overlook this chance meeting?"
While she spoke, she also slipped the small flash drive
out of her pocket and wedged it into the crack between
the two seats, pushing it down until it was completely
hidden.

He laughed at the suggestion, right to her face. "Oh,
you are delightful. However, I would save that gambit
for any other men who might be interested later on. As
for me, my tastes run in other directions. Your charms
don't interest me."

"That certainly explains your excellent wardrobe
taste." Unbelievable—just my luck to get caught by a
gay mercenary, Maggie thought as she slumped back in
her chair. "I could scream, you know. Get a conductor
over here to investigate why a young, attractive woman
is making such a racket."

The man removed a folded sheet of paper from his
pocket. "Then I'd have to show him this, which says that
you are my cousin, and that you suffer from paranoid
schizophrenia, you have escaped a mental health facility
in England and you're in my care while we seek treatment in Paris. And, if it comes to that, I would have no
choice but to sedate you." He rattled a small bottle of
pills at her. "But I'd much rather enjoy your company
until we arrive. The choice, of course, is yours."

"Give me that!" Maggie grabbed for the paper, which
rose out of reach as the man held it above his head. She
sighed. "It would seem you have me neatly trapped."

"Well, you did elude us for almost an entire day—
that is not something that many people can claim."

"You'll excuse me if I don't consider that to be a
point of pride."

He shrugged. "You may take it as you wish. However, I can assure you that you would have been caught sooner or later—it was only a matter of time."

"Says you. I hope you don't expect me to be very sociable for the remainder of the trip," Maggie said.

Her comment provoked another eloquent roll of his shoulders. "The journey can be as pleasant—or as unpleasant—as you wish."

"It's very unpleasant already, thanks to the company."

"Alas, that I cannot change for you. Perhaps you might feel better if you were to eat something? You must be famished after all that running around last night."

Although Maggie wanted to say that she was just fine, her stomach rumbled loudly at the mention of food. "Sure, why not? Maybe I'll just get drunk instead."

"I would hope you might refrain. It would demean us both." He stood and offered her his hand. "If I may?"

She glared at him and pushed herself out the chair, grabbing her laptop case and slinging it over her shoulder. "And you can save the gallant act—you're nothing but a hired thug."

Although he let her walk ahead of him, he slipped a hand on her elbow, squeezing hard enough to let her know that any resistance would be punished. "My dear, it is you who are the criminal here. After all, you were the one who did not deliver what we had hired you to acquire."

"There wouldn't have been any problem if your company had not suddenly gotten cold feet about its reimbursement clause for expenses, which were higher than we had initially expected. But when we invoked the percentage-overage clause, suddenly you folks stopped returning our calls and sent out hired guns to kill us and anyone else who got in the way, conveniently avoiding paying us the second half of our fee, as well," Maggie said.

"I have no knowledge of how my superiors intended to recover what was ours. As for the terms of your employment contract, that is something you would have to take up with our contract attorneys. But you did sign our agreement, so I can only assume that you read it first."

"Yes, all seventy-seven pages of legal jargon. One wonders how clients in other nations fare when you hold them over a barrel."

"Unlike you and your brother, they usually have excellent lawyers on retainer to handle contracts like these. Once you are finished in our employ, I suggest that you avail yourself of a similar firm next time."

"Yeah, that's exactly what someone in my line of work can do—just walk into an old-money law firm and demand representation."

He shook his head in mock disapproval. "You of all people should know money can buy anything."

As they walked, Maggie looked at the various passengers they passed, hoping to find someone who might be able to help her. Well-dressed couples chatted and gazed out at the English countryside as it blurred past. A smartly dressed conductor passed by, and for a moment Maggie thought about accosting him, but a painful squeeze on her arm nixed that idea, almost as if her warden knew what she was thinking.

She huffed in exasperation. "At the very least, you could tell me your name, so I don't think of you as Mr. Asshole all the time."

"Fair enough. You may call me Carlos."

"Spanish? I thought you were from Greece."

"I have traveled all over the world, as I expect you have, as well."

"Here and there," Maggie said.

They walked into the dining car, where a large crowd of travelers clustered around a buffet table laden with steaming trays of food. The smell made Maggie's mouth water, and she suddenly realized just how hungry she was, in spite of her circumstances. No choice, so I might as well eat while I can—who knows when I'll get the chance again.

She got in line and picked up a tray, plate and silverware, resisting the urge to whirl around and bash her captor in the head with it. The buffet ran to salad, pasta and what looked like chicken and beef dishes, so Maggie loaded up on the carbs while waiting for the elderly couple ahead of her to progress. All the while her mind created and discarded escape plans. Stab him in the eye with a salad fork and run for it? Hope he's allergic to the antipasto salad? Fake an epileptic fit myself? That last idea she held on to—it wouldn't be pretty, but would be an effective distraction at least. What she'd do after that, however, she had no idea. She didn't know if there were any medical personnel on board, and while she could hope for a doctor, if there wasn't one, she'd have to shake and tremble all the way to Paris.

Her thoughts were interrupted by the gentleman ahead of her. "Lucille, don't forget your purse—we don't want to lose your medications at the start of the trip."

"Thank you, Joseph, why don't you just hand it to me—whoops!"

As soon as she had heard the word "medications,"

Maggie had waited for the right moment, then lurched forward, her plate smacking into the overstuffed purse to send it and its contents flying. "Oh. I'm so sorry! Here, let me help you with those." She bustled around on her hands and knees, picking up containers and shoving them back into the woman's trembling hands, which caused her to drop them all over again, delaying everyone even more. Maggie knelt to pick them up again, using the confusion to slip a bottle into the waistband of her skirt. She picked up the rest of the woman's belongings, and loaded them into the voluminous bag, apologizing loudly all the while. The couple thanked her, then shuffled off to their table, while a server came out to clean up Maggie's overturned plate of food on the carpet.

Her mission done, Maggie turned to get another plate and go back to her seat, but was stopped by Carlos, who held out his hand. "Give it to me."

"What are you talking about?"

"The pill bottle you took off the old woman. I want it right now."

Maggie jabbed him in the breastbone with her finger. "All I did was help an old lady pick up her medicines—"

Carlos's hand shot out like a cobra to latch on to her wrist, firmly moving her to one side of the car, out of the buffet line. "Don't lie to me. I saw you slip the bottle under your shirt. Now either hand it over, or else I take you into the restroom and search you myself."

"You even try, and I'll scream my head off."

"You forget, I have my own sedatives. You'd be out in seconds, just another hysterical female traveler in the tunnel." Still gripping her wrist with his left hand, he held out his right. "Hand it over."

Her lips pursed in anger, Maggie's shoulders slumped. "All right." She reached down to her waist and plucked the small bottle from her waistband, thrusting it at him. "Here."

He took it out of her hand and examined the label. "Valium. And what, I wonder, were you planning to do with this?"

"Since shoving them up your ass isn't an option, I think you have a pretty good idea where they would have gone," Maggie said.

"Of course." Carlos flagged down a server and gave him the bottle, explaining that they should be returned to the old couple eating at the far end of the car.

Maggie crossed her arms to keep from trembling with fear and anger. "Your kindness knows no bounds."

He ignored her jibe. "I wish you hadn't tried such a desperate ploy. Now I may have to restrain you. Come on, let's eat before everything is gone."

She simply nodded, and they got back in line again. Once they had full plates and found two empty seats, Maggie stood up again. "I'd like to get some Parmesan cheese from the table, and I promise I won't do anything foolish."

He eyed her speculatively for a moment, then nodded. "Yes, the primavera is rather bland. I'll be watching, however, and would appreciate it if you didn't bother trying anything."

"I'll be right back." She got up and turned to walk to the buffet table, slipping out the pack of individually sealed, foil-wrapped capsules that she had also taken from the old woman, and punching them all out into her hand, holding them in her fist as she approached the table. Don't look back, she admonished herself, knowing he'd interpret it as a sign that she was up to something, which, of course, she was.

A server was clearing things at the now nearly deserted table, and she was able to pick up the small container of shredded cheese, which was almost empty.

"Could you please bring some more out?" she asked, sending the waiter scurrying into the next car. While she waited, she picked up a napkin and emptied the capsules into it, her eyes flicking left and right to make sure no one was taking too much interest in what she was doing.

When the waiter returned, she took the small covered container from him. "Thank you."

He turned to finish his work, and she immediately dumped the powdered drug into the dish, careful to keep it all on one side of the container. As she'd hoped, the white granules were indistinguishable from the finely shredded cheese. She only hoped it didn't have an odd taste.

As she brought the dish back to their section, she stirred a bit of the Parmesan over the powder to conceal it. She set it down, and sat, helping herself to some on the untainted side of the small bowl. She offered the spoon to Carlos. "Here you go—it does improve the flavor somewhat."

He sniffed as he reached for it. "Yes, I had expected better from Eurotrain. Ah, well, you forced me to sit in the second-class compartment, after all. Perhaps we'll take first class on the way back."

Maggie tried not to look too eager as he scooped out two heaping spoonfuls of the cheese and sprinkled it on his pasta, then mixed it into the meal. She sipped the sparkling water that a server had brought around, grimacing at its metallic taste. She concentrated on her meal, but couldn't help sneaking a glance at Carlos from time to time, wondering if he had ingested enough of whatever medicine she had stolen to affect him, and how long it would be before it took effect.

God, I hope I didn't just give him some kind of vitamin supplement, she prayed. She knew he'd be suspicious of her clumsiness with the old woman's medications, which was why she had given up the Valium so easily. Whatever these other pills were, she hoped they would make him sick, or affect his normal bodily functions adversely enough to incapacitate him. The biggest problem now was that she didn't know what was going to happen.

They finished their meals, and Maggie saw with disappointment that he had eaten only about half of his pasta. They left the dishes to be cleared, and headed back to their seats.

As she walked, Maggie felt strangely light-headed, and the floor in front of her blurred as she walked forward. She felt Carlos's guiding hand on her arm again. "You don't look so good, my dear. We're almost to our seats. Perhaps a nap will clear your head."

Oh, shit! He drugged me! She had been so preoccupied with enacting her plan that she had forgotten the first rule of being a prisoner—trust nothing supplied by her captors. "You…son of a bitch… That's…why the water…tasted funny."

"I'm afraid so. You have a penchant for wriggling out of these kinds of situations, and I simply cannot return to my company without you in tow. Here we are. Just sit down."

Everything around her seemed to be floating away, receding down a long, gray tunnel, and Maggie was absurdly grateful for the hand that guided her to her soft, comfortable seat. She fought to stay awake, knowing it was very important that she do so, but suddenly unable to remember why. All she wanted to do was lay her head back on the seat cushion and sleep. Her eyes drooped closed and the last thing she heard was Carlos's voice again.

"You rest your head and get some sleep, and I just might entertain myself with seeing what goodies you have on your computer."

Ha..ha…the joke's on you, she thought wearily. You don't have the password for that file. Even I don't have the password for that file right now…. It was her last conscious thought before blackness overwhelmed her.

19

Anthony drove like a man possessed, weaving in and out of the afternoon traffic as he headed for the English coast.

Once he and Carl had gotten out of the train yard, they had scaled the tall fence and vanished into the crowd on the other side. After calling Liam to pick them up, Anthony slid behind the wheel and took the route out of the city. Now they were on a direct course to Dover, where they would hire, hijack or buy a boat to get them across the Channel to Calais, where he hoped to pick up her trail again.

Liam muttered into his cell phone, confirming the schedules of the daily ferry, and Anthony had assigned Carl to pose as an American tourist and see what private vessels might be available for a quick jaunt. When the lanky American had asked why they didn't use company vehicles, Anthony had snapped, "Because by the time we got to the airport and got cleared, up and back down, she'd be a hundred kilometers from the train, that's fucking why." In truth, he hadn't wanted to bring in any more Mercury personnel than necessary—it was already embarrassing enough that she had gotten away not once, but twice now, and he was going to make sure she didn't succeed a third time.

The opening bars of "Werewolves of London" sounded in his ear, and Anthony hit the receiver. "Go for Team One."

"Where are you right now?"

It was his handler. Like you don't know, he thought. Every company vehicle was equipped with a GPS tracker that personnel followed back at headquarters. "I'm heading to Dover." No need to give him any more information than necessary.

"Really? Last I'd heard, our quarry was at the St. Pancras train station, so I cannot imagine what awaits you at the seaside."

"Last I'd heard, our quarry got through the net at the station, and was on the Chunnel train to Calais."

"Ah, yes, I had heard that, as well. Curiously, I didn't find this out from you. One can only suppose that there was cellular interference that rendered you unable to call."

"Yeah, those sunspots can get pretty bad this time of year," Anthony said.

Anthony heard a noise that might have been an amused snicker from the man on the other end, or he might have been clearing his throat. "I have confirmation that our target is on the train, but I got it from Aleix, who is also on that very same train."

Anthony's jaw tightened at the news, but he didn't let up on the accelerator. "He's there? He's got her?" He was aware of every head in the SUV turning toward him, but he kept his eyes on the road.

"He sent me a picture from his cell phone of her out cold in front of him, sleeping as pretty as you please. The poor dear must be simply exhausted." There was no trace of warmth in his tone. "Once they arrive, he'll have her on the first return trip back, and she'll be here in about six hours, tops. So you might as well pack it in and return home. Your part in this is done."

Anthony's mind raced for alternatives. "Maybe we should continue on and rendezvous with him in Calais as an escort—after all, she's escaped before." He hated saying the words, knowing they told of his failure to keep her contained, and his handler's reply confirmed it as such.

"Yes, she's eluded you, what is it, twice now? And yet you expect us to let you oversee her return? I don't think so. After all, I'm pretty sure Aleix can handle an unconscious fifty-kilo woman. At least, he seems to have captured her quite easily."

Gritting his teeth, Anthony fought for control before he replied, the SUV swaying as he navigated a turn a bit too sharply, sending the vehicle swerving close to the shoulder of the road. "Let's not forget she had a bit of help on the first one."

It was the wrong retort.

"And yet she escaped your formidable dragnet with ease at the train station. The only mitigating circumstance was that she also pulled the wool over Desmond's eyes, as well, so at least you had some company on that one. But now you can forget all about it. You and your team are done. I want you to report back to headquarters tomorrow morning at 0800 sharp for debriefing. Maybe you can use the rest of today to figure out how you're going to explain this failure to the board."

Anthony grimaced. The board was the three-person case-review panel that evaluated personnel and the overall success or failure of a mission when warranted. Anthony knew that it would be more than warranted in this case. He was looking at an official reprimand, or if things got any more cocked-up, demotion from team leader. That simply wasn't an option.

"Yes, sir." He broke the connection and glared at the rest of his team. "What the hell are you all staring at?"

Liam broke the silence, the only man in the vehicle who could do so under the circumstances. "What's goin' on, boss?"

"Officially, we've been pulled off the assignment. HQ wants us back by tomorrow morning for review."

Carl leaned forward, sticking his head between the front seats. "What's that mean?"

"For you, nothing—you just got stuck with a job that had gone to shit before you got here." He left the second part unsaid, that he and Liam might face disciplinary action from the company. "However, Liam and I are going to continue with the plan as originally stated. You two are free to come with us, or you can take the SUV back when we reach Calais—the choice is yours. I'll tell you one thing, though—I don't plan on coming back unless I have that bitch in tow."

Carl leaned back in his seat and thumped the roof with a bony fist. "Shit, man, I'm in it to win it. Don't want the stink of failure hanging on me my first time out. Let's go all the way."

"How about you, Gregor? You in or you out?" Anthony asked.

The tall Russian's gray eyes pinned him in the

rearview mirror, and it was several seconds before the man spoke. "I'm in."

"Excellent. Then, Liam and Carl, back on the phones, and get us a boat." Anthony settled back in his seat and smiled to himself. The new men were going to work out just fine.

And that bitch is going to get everything that's coming to her and then some for making us look bad, he thought. The instructions just say bring her in alive—not uninjured. The thought comforted him as the coast-line of England came into view, and just beyond the horizon to the southeast, the coast of France, where his salvation awaited.

20

Concentrating on looking out the window, David tried not to let the others see his fingers tightly clutching the armrests of his chair. The headphones over his ears muted the roar of the Agusta A-119 Koala helicopter's turbine engine that was ferrying them across the southeastern peninsula of England, and soon over the azure-emerald waters of the English Channel at nearly 200 miles per hour.

They had driven to Heathrow Airport, where they had bypassed the main terminal, customs and any other sort of organization that might have delayed them. At a small hangar on the outskirts of the sprawling airport, they pulled up to a sleek helicopter, its main rotor already carving through the air in a blur. Ducking down, they had taken their cases of equipment, run to the spacious passenger compartment and climbed inside. Cody had patted the pilot's shoulder, and they had lifted off.

It wasn't that David disliked flying—he loved to

travel. But there was something about the ungainliness of helicopters that always set him on edge, even though he had traveled in them extensively in Afghanistan. Maybe it was the idea of the entire aircraft being supported by a thin blade of composite materials or aluminum or steel, beating at the air to keep the whole contraption aloft. Maybe it was just that passengers seemed closer to the elements in a helicopter, seemingly not as protected as in an airplane, although both were equally as safe. Maybe, on some fundamental level, he just didn't trust the damn things, having known too many men who had died in chopper accidents, either from enemy fire or mechanical problems. It wasn't a phobia, and it certainly didn't impede his job performance, but he was very careful not to express his concerns to the other members of his team. As in most spec-ops units, any sign of perceived weakness was always exploited and teased mercilessly.

Even now, Kanelo and Tara were engaged in a deep conversation that had started back in the SUV, something about treatment of trauma in a combat situation. For a change, Robert was silent, just staring outside at the countryside they were passing over. David had been researching the city of Paris, trying to get a handle on their target location, but had put away his cell phone and was about to join his sullen team member in silent reverie when he felt a light tap on his knee. Glancing up, he saw Cody pointing to his headset with one hand and holding up four fingers on his other one.

Casting about, he saw the channel control where his headset was plugged in, and switched over. "What's up?" he asked.

"How would you handle this extraction?"

David blinked while he processed the direct question. Cody was known for doing this—tossing the ball to one of the other team members on the fly to see what they'd come up with. Now David was up to bat. "Well, assuming that we can keep the chopper as our primary vehicle, I'd have us dropped off next to the train station, head down to the platform, find and acquire our target and withdraw the same way."

"So you'd just have us slip into the heart of Paris and touch down just like that, huh?"

"Yes, sir, that would be the plan." David brought up his Paris map, which currently showed the area around the Gare du Nord, the train's final destination in France. "See the big building right next to the train station? That's a hospital. It has a helipad. I'll bet a quick call to HQ can insert us into their schedule just like that."

"Okay, what's our cover?"

"A visiting team of specialists from London—something regarding a fellowship, so it's a long-term study and there's no chance they would want us to kibitz with the rest of the staff. We're in, at the station, and out in under an hour, target safely acquired."

"You seem pretty confident," Cody said.

"Well, if the train is running on time, and we were about thirty-five minutes behind once we took off, it's gonna be close. But if I were in charge, it's how I'd go in."

Cody nodded. "All right, I'll set it up. Good work." He made to adjust his channel, but was stopped by David.

"Hey, I'm not doing your work for you, am I?" The question wasn't rhetorical—David thought he already knew the answer, but he wanted to hear it from his team leader.

"Nope—it's exactly the same game plan I'd come up

with. I was just seeing how you handled your premission intel and planning. From what I've seen, it's first-rate—another sign that you aren't a cowboy."

"Thanks, M-One."

"It's my job, M-Two. Now get to work figuring out how the five of us are going to find her among several thousand Parisians and tourists." Flashing him a grin, Cody plugged his phone into the headset and began clearing their way into Paris.

David got on his phone to check with Primary to see if they had gotten any updated pictures of their target from the St. Pancras cameras. He was aware of the other three team members looking at him, but remained engrossed in what he was doing, not even pausing to look out the window at the beautiful countryside blurring by beneath them.

21

Maggie felt as if she were being shaken apart. Every limb—except her left hand—was flopping about, and she felt a pressure on her shoulder that moved it back and forth, back and forth. Her head throbbed, and her eyes, ears, nose and mouth felt as if she had been dining on cotton balls instead of pasta primavera with a glass of tranquilizer water.

"Hey, are you okay?" someone asked.

She pried her bleary eyes open to see a young blond-haired boy, dressed in a stained T-shirt and shorts, standing on the seat next to her, pushing on her shoulder like he was trying to shove her into the wall of the train compartment.

"All right—all right, I'm awake!" She wrenched her shoulder out from his grubby hands and tried to fend him off with her other hand, but it refused to move from the armrest of the seat. She looked over to see that she was secured to it with a flexible lock-tie, like the kind SWAT teams and police used to subdue their suspects.

Seeing it brought back what had happened to her with more chilling clarity. "Where—where's the man who was sitting across from me?"

"He had to go to the bathroom." The boy wrinkled his nose. "He smelled bad."

"Smelled bad, huh?" Maggie smiled, in spite of how she felt. "Like poo?"

The boy grinned at the forbidden word and nodded, his head bouncing up and down.

"Jeremy!" A woman, obviously the boy's mother, swooped in like a mother hawk on one of her errant young, grabbing his hand and almost pulling him off the seat in her mingled relief and dismay. "Miss, I'm terribly sorry if he was bothering you. You are in so much trouble, young man!"

Bothering me? More like saving my life, Maggie thought as her head cleared. "Actually, your son and I were having a delightful conversation, weren't we?"

He nodded hesitantly, going along with the story now that she wasn't going to turn him in.

The mother, a harried-looking woman with dark circles under her eyes and two other small children in tow, smiled tightly. "Well, come along, children, back to our seats."

"Ma'am—there is one thing you could do for me, if you can." Maggie's voice stopped the woman in her tracks as she was about to herd her brood into the next car.

"Yes?"

"Would you happen to have a nail clipper I might borrow for a moment?"

Puzzlement creased her pinched features, but she rummaged in her purse. "Um, here." She held out a pair of child's safety scissors. "Will these do?"

"I think so." Maggie bent over and, hiding her actions

from view, placed the scissor edge against the armrest and pressed down with all of her strength on the tough plastic tie. For a moment, nothing happened, then the metal blade sunk into the plastic and the restraint began to give. With one final push, she snapped through it. Straightening, she gave the scissors back to the mother while flexing the suddenly tingling fingers on her numb left hand. "Thank you very much." The mother raised an eyebrow, but didn't say anything, just hurried her children through the door.

Maggie winked at Jeremy as he was hustled out of the compartment, then shook her head, trying to clear it. The stuffed-cotton sensation was receding, but she still felt off, as if she were a half second out of step with the rest of the world. She flagged down a passing conductor. "Sir, how far are we from Paris?"

"We shall be arriving at the station in approximately twenty-five minutes, miss."

"Thank you." After he left, she dug the flash drive out from between the two seat cushions, then looked around for her laptop.

Of course he's got it. I wouldn't leave it out in the open, either, she realized. Just to be sure, she checked the top luggage rack, but came up empty. Her carefully crafted plan of hacking into the train's control systems and stopping it in Calais to throw off her pursuers was shot to hell, and now she also had to figure out how to get her laptop back. Although Carlos couldn't get into it, there was every chance that the people back at his headquarters could, and that simply couldn't happen.

Pushing out of the chair, she rose to her feet, nearly falling over as the rush of blood to her head made her world go white for a moment. Leaning against the wall until the feeling passed, she walked unsteadily into the aisle bisecting the rows of seats. Ignoring the odd looks from other passengers, she made her way to the bathroom, which was occupied, with several people waiting impatiently for it. Maggie couldn't decide on whether to wear an innocent or pained expression, so she settled for the pained one as she approached. "Taking a long time?"

"Bloody git's been in there for more than ten minutes, so yeah, you could say that!" The first man in line, a ruddy-faced Englishman in shorts and a short-sleeved, flower-print shirt, looked as if he was about to kick the door in.

"Oh dear, that's my fiancé in there, and I think the meal may not have agreed with him," she said. "Perhaps we should get some help—he might have passed out."

"Hey, here comes someone." The group, united behind Maggie, stopped a conductor and explained the situation to him. The short, balding and bespectacled man, immaculate in his neat uniform, looked as if they might have asked him to carry a dead squirrel around for the rest of the day when they suggested he open the door. He agreed to knock first and check on the occupant before doing anything else. Stepping up to the door, he rapped on it with his knuckles while glancing up and down the cars as if afraid he would be overheard. "Sir? Excuse me, sir? Is everything all right?"

After a few seconds, they all heard a strained and weak voice. "I'm fine...thank you. I just...need a moment—oh, God!" The exclamation was followed by a series of distinctly unhealthy sounds that caused everyone near the door to shy away.

Maggie did her best not to laugh. "Oh, sir, I'm so worried about him. Can you please open the door?"

The conductor exchanged a stricken look with the Englishman, who appeared ready to take charge. "Miss, if your fiancé says he is fine, then perhaps we should—"

"Oh, my God!" The cry from inside the restroom snapped everyone to attention.

"Or maybe he needs help before something worse happens." Maggie frowned and leaned into the conductor, lowering her voice. "I'd hate for the train company to be held liable because prompt treatment wasn't given to him."

Those magic words did the trick. "Very well, I'll open the door, but perhaps it would be best if you examined him first, miss."

"My, er, pleasure." She waited for the conductor to produce a small key and unlock the folding door. Not knowing what to expect, Maggie took a deep breath and held it before opening the door. Even so, the smell that wafted out made everyone recoil, stepping back from the offending stench, even though there was no place to hide from it in the vicinity.

Carlos was huddled inside, all his former suavity— along with everything else liquid—drained out of him. His once immaculate wool trousers were now puddled around his ankles, and a fine sheen of sweat gleamed on his brow. He looked up in panic and embarrassment, his eyes widening upon seeing her. "How did you get free? What do you think you are doing?"

Maggie spotted her laptop case on the floor in front of him. "Getting this first." She leaned over and snatched the case off the floor. Carlos tried to lunge for her, but his state of undress, as well as a fresh attack of flatulence, followed by more liquid sounds, forced him to stay on the toilet.

"You did this to me!" he shouted.

"Of course I did. Turnabout is fair play, don't you think?" She slid the door shut saying, "You'd better stay in there until you're finished, love."

Carlos frantically waved at the people outside the bathroom. "Conductor! Conductor! Help me, please! I've been drugged—"

Maggie closed the door and leaned on it. "I'm afraid he's becoming a bit irrational. He's always been afraid of enclosed spaces. I have an idea—let him know that you've sent for medical help. I'll be right back." Without waiting for a reply, she trotted off into the next cars, looking for a familiar, elderly couple.

She found them three cars down, holding hands and gazing out at the scenery. Maggie cleared her throat. "Excuse me—"

"Yes? Oh look, Joseph, it's that nice young woman that helped me in the buffet car. What is it, dear?"

"I'm so sorry to bother you. I'm afraid that my fiancé has become a bit agitated during the trip. While I was collecting your medicine bottles, I happened to notice that you have some Valium. I wouldn't normally ask this of a perfect stranger, but he's growing increasingly restless, and I'm worried about trying to calm him down."

The woman was already rummaging through her cavernous purse. "Of course, my dear, I understand completely…. Now let me see, where did I put that?"

"He's usually so calm, but something about this trip has just brought out the worst in him. It would just be to settle his nerves. I would be very grateful."

The woman dug out the plastic container, and laboriously unscrewed the cap, her wrinkled fingers trembling with the effort. "All right, I think one should do, don't you?"

"Well, he's a big man, so I'm not really sure." Maggie said.

The woman's lips pursed. "Be careful, dearie, too many at once might knock him right out."

Maggie leaned down, her face a mask of weary exasperation. "At this point, that might not be such a bad thing."

The woman discreetly pressed a few pills into her palm. "I understand completely. These should settle him down soon enough, and then you two will have a better trip afterward."

"I'm sure we will." Maggie held the pills loosely in her hand, stopped to get a bottle of water from the buffet car and headed back to the bathroom. Along the way, she checked the pills. They were round and blue, with a line scored through the middle for breaking them in half. Nothing identified the type of medication.

Back at the restroom, she held out her hand to the conductor. "Here, a doctor suggested that we give these to him. It's an antidiarrhea medication. He needs to take all three at once."

The conductor examined the pills briefly, and Maggie's heart almost skipped a beat when she thought he might recognize what they were. She cracked the water bottle open. "Don't worry, he doesn't have any allergies. These should take care of the problem."

"All right—if the doctor suggested it." The conductor cracked the door open again, leaning away from the new stench wave that rolled out. "Sir, we've consulted with a physician, and he has suggested that you take these pills for your—condition."

Although clearly in pain, Carlos was also suspicious. "Does—did she have anything to do with this?"

The conductor glanced at Maggie in surprise, and she twirled a finger near her temple in the universal "crazy" sign, then shook her head.

"It's better if I'm not involved," she whispered.

The conductor leaned in again. "Ah, no, one of our other staff located this person."

"All right…all right."

"I'll pass the bottle of water in to you first, then the pills, okay?"

The conductor passed the water into the restroom, then followed it up with the medication. Maggie held her breath, hoping that in the dim light and because of his condition Carlos wouldn't look at the pills too closely. She tried to detect what might be going on inside, but heard only silence.

"All right, I've taken all of them. When will they begin to work?"

The conductor looked back at Maggie, who whispered, "Twenty minutes."

"They should take effect in about twenty minutes. Perhaps—perhaps you should remain in there until they have taken hold, so to speak."

"That's…probably a good idea…."

Maggie wasn't sure, but his voice sounded less steady, as if the pills were already affecting him. Probably just wishful thinking on my part, she thought.

"Ladies and gentlemen, I'm afraid that I will have to ask you all to return to your seats, as we are going to arrive at the Gare du Nord station in just a few minutes.

Miss, I will have to ask you to return to your seat, as well. I'm sure your fiancé will be fine, and there is a hospital right next to the station, in case you would like to have him examined. You will see the signs as you walk onto the platform."

"Thank you, sir, I think we will do just that. You've been most kind and helpful, and I appreciate everything you've done."

"It was my pleasure, miss, and I hope that your fiancé is feeling better soon."

"I'm sure he'll be just fine. If you don't mind, I'll just sit here near the lavatory, to keep an eye on him."

"Very well, miss." The conductor hurried off and Maggie sank into the nearest seat, across from two scruffy, backpacking students who were fast asleep, their heads resting next to each other, oblivious to the commotion only a few yards away. Envying their carefree freedom, Maggie leaned back in the seat, but dared not close her eyes, waiting for the second those doors opened, and she could get the hell off the train.

22

It was a feat of driving and navigation that Anthony would never be able to duplicate for the rest of his life.

After they had barely caught the high-speed ferry that was minutes from heading out of port—which cost Anthony an extra fifty pounds to ensure they got on— they had docked at Calais fifty-seven minutes later, and he had driven the SUV onto the broad expressway that would take them right into Paris. Even though the posted speed limit was 100 miles per hour, with the updated GPS speed camera detector and radar detector, they were able to drive an average of 125 miles per hour, weaving in and out of the traffic like madmen. They had hit the outskirts of Paris in ninety minutes, rather than the two and a half hours the distance would normally take.

Anthony had been behind the wheel the entire time, deftly guiding the vehicle across the lanes, slowing only when they detected a speed camera or hidden police officer. It was just as well they hadn't been pulled over;

given Anthony's mood, he would have been just as likely to shoot the officer and damn the consequences. However, the heavier traffic as they plunged into Paris proper had slowed them to a crawl, and even now he wasn't sure they were going to make it to the station on time. He stared straight ahead, as if he could make the traffic part by sheer force of will. "Come on, come on!"

The other three men remained silent, all aware that it would be best to let Anthony concentrate. They were crawling south on Barbes Boulevard, waiting for when it turned into the Boulevard de la Magenta, which ran right past the train station. At last, they found themselves outside a large hospital complex, and then they saw the large, neoclassical face of the Gare du Nord train station.

"Time."

Liam checked his watch. "Eleven fifty-three. If the train was running on time, it arrived three minutes ago."

"Well, let's hope they weren't."

"Do you think the tracker might help us here?" Carl asked from the backseat.

"Sure, if you want to carry it so I can read the damn thing while we walk through the station—that won't be conspicuous at all. Besides, there's too much interference in a place like that. It would be too hard to ensure I was receiving the right signal."

Liam rolled his eyes. "According to my street map, there's parking on this side street. Take the next right."

Anthony turned onto the small avenue, and sure enough, there was a small, multilevel parking structure on his left. "Probably packed full of commuters and damn tourists," he muttered. But their luck held. A

Volkswagen hatchback was just pulling out of a space in the lowest level, right near the exit. Anthony claimed the space as soon as it was empty, cutting in front of a sedan loaded with what looked like students who had been waiting for it. They pulled up, looking ready to complain, but one look at the four hard-faced, grim-eyed men who got out and simply stared at them, and the students slunk away to find another space.

Anthony brushed past Carl and headed to the back of the SUV, opening the back door and removing a small square of carpet on the floor of the empty cargo compartment, revealing a recessed keypad. Entering a seven-digit code, a panel rose slightly with a hydraulic hiss, allowing him to pull it up with his fingers. Anthony didn't need to look up to know that Liam, Carl and Gregor had established a perimeter, keeping an eye out for anyone who might be watching.

He distributed pistols, silencers and magazines first. "Carl, you and I know what our target looks like. She should still be in the station, possibly meeting someone here, or else continuing on by herself. In case you need to clear a path quickly or create a distraction, use these, but only if necessary." He handed a pair of small fragmentation minigrenades to each team member, pocketing two himself. "Remember, use them only if necessary. We should be able to acquire the target and remove her without attracting undue attention."

Carl hefted the golf ball–sized grenades for a moment before slipping them into his cargo pants pockets. "What if we see any of those fuckers from that other team?"

"If you spot them, and they've already acquired her,

then follow to a position where you can engage without attracting attention. If you can take them out, do so— especially the black man or his dark-haired partner." Anthony slapped a magazine into his Walther P-99, chambered a round and slipped it into the pancake holster at the small of his back. "Carl, Gregor, you're Team Two, Liam and I are Team One. Keep your earpieces on and active at all times. Let's move."

Anthony led the way to the street outside, setting a ground-eating pace to the train station's main building. Liam caught up with him at the edge of the street. "Hey, boss?"

"Mmm?" Anthony didn't look at him, as he was too busy checking traffic for a time to cross the street.

"If we've been pulled off the case, then doesn't that mean someone else has her already?"

Antony spared him a quick glance before heading across the wide street. "Control said she had been picked up by Aleix, but I'll bet she's already gotten away from that fuckin' poofter."

"Okay, fair enough—but what if she didn't?"

"If she didn't, then you just let me handle him, all right?"

"Fine by me."

The interior of Gare du Nord was very similar to the London train station—shops, announcements over the loudspeaker system, and people going every which way. Anthony scanned the electronic boards for the London arrival, catching the platform number. "Gate *cinq,* number five. Team Two, head down to the far end and work your way up. We'll start from here."

The tall Russian and lean American disappeared into the crowd, heading along the main wall of the building.

Anthony and Liam watched them go for a moment, then turned and began checking faces in the crowd, looking for their target before she spotted them.

23

"Louis, I know—"

"There is a certain way we do things here in Paris, and having a Midnight Team gallivanting through the city is not one of them!"

"Louis, calm down. Look, I understand that you're annoyed by the short notice. Obviously we'd prefer to handle this with local operatives—"

"That's another thing. I wasn't even informed until your team was practically on-site, despite having agents already scrambled to intercept this woman at the station. We had to pull every string I could to get those covers set up in time."

"And I'm sure you did your usual spotless job on them, correct?" Kate asked.

"Of course."

Kate took a deep breath now that she had appealed to the French director's vanity. Louis Planchard, formerly of the French intelligence agency Direction

Générale de la Sécurité Extérieure, or the DGSE, was a staunch believer in the goals of Room 59. However, his was a classic Gallic personality, and like most directors, he tended to be territorial, as well. He rightly believed that his operatives were the best resources to handle certain situations—like recovery of an asset on the run in Paris before another hostile team got to her. And while Kate could understand where he was coming from, at this particular moment, she didn't have time to argue the point. Of course, the fact that she had heard through the Room 59 grapevine that he had wanted her position when it had come open, and had been very disappointed when he hadn't gotten it, might have also had something to do with the conversation they were having.

"Look, if there had been time, we certainly would have run a joint op with you overseeing it. But events are happening very quickly, and this team is the best equipped to handle it at the moment, so they are in charge. Any of your people who are on-site are to defer to the Midnight Team leader, is that clear?" Kate said.

"All right, Kate, you haven't steered me wrong yet, so I trust that you know what you're doing."

"Good, I'm glad you're on board. You said there were operatives free who could get to the train station?"

"I alerted two as soon as I got the message. They should be there by now. You've sent me the photos of our team members, so they know who to expect, as well as a photo of our mystery woman who has escaped us twice before, *n'est-ce pas?*"

Kate sighed. "Yes, she's proven surprisingly adept. However, now that she's on your turf, I trust that she won't be a problem to pick up. We've also sent over two Facemaker pictures of the two members of the Mercury

Security team that may also be trying to apprehend her, so make sure your operatives are briefed."

"Of course. Assuming this Midnight Team doesn't do anything overreactive, I shouldn't think it would be a problem. My people will be in position to observe and assist if necessary."

"Thank you, Louis. I'll be in touch with you as things proceed. Good luck."

"And to your people, as well."

Kate waited until he had broken the connection before shaking her head. Of all the directors, he had been the most resistant to the idea of the Midnight Teams in general, saying that their use was overwhelming blunt force when the delicate touch of a scalpel was needed. Kate had created the concept of the Midnight Teams with Room 59's North American director Denny Talbot. They knew there were some situations where the application of controlled, deadly force was the only solution. And rather than leave it to the special forces units of the country where the mission occurred, she wanted Room 59 to have its own black-ops force. They'd be ready to go anywhere and do whatever was necessary to accomplish their mission. So far, it had worked well—until this last op.

Kate's phone rang again. "Yes."

"Samantha here. I've set up the meeting."

"Do you think he was suspicious at all?"

"Hardly, I just mentioned that you—as Donna—had said his company was looking for more work with government agencies, and that we at MI-6 were interested in seeing what they might be able to provide. He fairly leaped at the opportunity. I could almost hear him panting over the phone. It'll be in a public place, you understand. I suggested the Grill at the Dorchester Hotel—if I cannot enjoy the company, I will at least enjoy my dinner."

"Stop, you're making my mouth water already. When will you be meeting him?" Kate asked.

"Tonight, at seven-thirty. It seems that Mercury has a standing reservation there—again, I thought their financial numbers didn't look good?"

"What we saw indicated that they've been running their operation pretty close to the bone recently. They've been working smaller contracts—training in Third World countries, some executive-protection work, that sort of thing."

"Appearances must be maintained, hmm?" Samantha said.

"I suppose, but it's an expensive proposition. Still, enjoy yourself."

"That will be the last thing on my mind this evening."

"Well, since I'll be overseeing this recovery and stuck in my hotel suite with room service as my only consolation, I'm still going to assign Jake to provide security for you. Nothing against your own people, you understand. I'd like my own man on the scene. I haven't been out in public for so long, I'd probably forget how to act and end up stabbing my date with my shrimp fork."

Samantha chuckled. "Of course you wouldn't. However, I will take you up on that, particularly since his face won't be immediately recognizable. In fact, we might as well provide him with a suitable companion for his own meal, as well. I have just the operative in mind, too. Someone might as well have a pleasant evening out of all this."

"Samantha, remember—it is your duty, after all."

"Yes, yes, you may need to keep reminding me of that tonight."

"I'll send Jake out to recon the hotel and set up a time to meet with you beforehand to run through how things will be set up."

"Thanks, Kate. I'll talk to you soon."

Kate broke the connection and stretched her arms over her head, beginning a set of isometric exercises to maintain her physique during the long hours in the chair, especially since it didn't look as if she was going to be getting out of it anytime soon.

As if on cue, her computer chimed again. It was Autom8. "You'd asked to be patched in when the team touched down in Paris?"

"You got it."

"All right, here comes the feed. They just set down on the roof of the hospital."

"Thanks, I've got it." Patched in to all five of the Midnight Team's specialized sunglasses, each with a miniature camera built-in, Kate settled in for yet another round of high-stakes television watching, where the bullets and blood were all very real. She could only observe as men and women fought and died when she gave the command, like a puppeteer with invisible strings that stretched around the world.

24

The Agusta helicopter touched down lightly on the helipad above the French trauma center. Located on the southwest corner of the facility, it was right next to the train station, so close that they could easily see the large yard where the high-speed engines arrived and left.

As soon as the chopper hit the tarmac, a man ran toward it, reflexively bending over to put a little more distance between himself and the whirling rotor. He opened the door and extended his hand to Cody. "Dr. Wesson, it's a pleasure to meet you."

"Thank you, let's get inside, shall we?"

David and the rest of the team took their small overnight bags with them and trotted to the stairwell. Once inside, the man handed out red-and-white badges with their cover names on them. Tara and David looked at theirs with odd expressions on their faces as they walked behind the others.

"Dr. Ladysmith?" Tara frowned.

David examined his badge and shook his head. "Yeah, and I'm Dr. Browning. Hey, Robert, what'd you get?"

"They made me Dr. Barrett."

Cory frowned them all into silence as they followed their host into the building. "Who says the French don't have a sense of humor? All right, it's showtime—let's keep our eyes on the prize here." He switched over to another channel. "M-Flight, keep those engines hot. We won't be here long."

"Affirmative." The pilot kept the helicopter's rotors moving, although he powered down his engine to what passed for idling, David supposed.

Once inside, the heavy fire door closed, cutting off most of the outside noise. A stairwell stretched down in front of them, and next to it were the doors of a large elevator for transporting crash carts and hospital beds. They all walked into the elevator, which sank into the hospital proper.

Their guide kept talking as they descended. "I must say it's a pleasure to have such a distinguished assembly of doctors to review the progress of our fellowship. While we were a bit surprised to discover that you were coming, our staff has been able to put together a presentation that we think will impress you."

Behind the man's back, David exchanged worried glances with Cody and his other team members.

Cody took the lead. "We're looking forward to seeing their current lines of work. If you don't mind, why don't you give us a little sample?"

"Well, I don't want to give anything away—"

"Don't worry, we won't tell anyone you briefed us ahead of time," Cody assured him.

"Very well. Of course you know that the fellowship

is to explore alternatives to sclerotherapy on prolapsed hemorrhoids."

Tara and Kanelo glanced at each other, and the woman covered her smile with her hand. Robert almost didn't stifle his chuckle in time, but managed to turn it into a strangled cough. Only Cody and David didn't change their expressions. "Ah, I see. You know, on second thought, perhaps we would rather wait until the presentation. I'm sure it will be very enlightening. If we could just have a few minutes to freshen up, we'd appreciate it," Cody said.

"Of course. We'll be ready to begin the presentation at your convenience. We'll take you to a room on the third floor and begin in say, twenty minutes?"

"That would be fine. We're looking forward to it. Thanks very much for setting this up on such short notice."

"Not at all—it's our pleasure." Their guide's pager beeped and he checked it with a glance. "Your room is down this hall, third door on the right. I'll be back up here to collect you in fifteen minutes." With that, he hustled off in the other direction, disappearing around the corner.

As soon as he was gone, Robert guffawed, the sound echoing down the corridor, and causing more than one nurse to frown at them and hold her finger up in the universal "quiet" sign. "Well, what say we world-famous team of ass doctors get to work?" he said.

"I didn't even know there was a fellowship for hemorrhoids." Tara shook her head. "I wonder how long the French have been working on this."

Robert snorted. "Given their general attitude, not long enough."

"All right, can it, all of you." Cody sighed. "At least

he didn't stick around to wait for us." He nodded toward the stairwell door. "Let's go, people, we're running out of time."

25

So far, so good, Anthony thought. This time, they were in control from the start.

He had established a surveillance position with an excellent view of the entire first half of the high-speed train. Sitting on the shoe-shine booth, above the constantly changing heads of the crowd, he had given the shoe shiner fifty Euros and told him to take an early lunch, which the man had quickly agreed to, his protest at losing out on the midmorning rush silenced by the look in Anthony's cold eyes.

He pretended to read that day's newspaper, using the time as he flipped pages to scan the crowd for his target. Liam was farther down on the platform, watching the rear half of the train. Between them they had almost the entire train covered, with Gregor and Carl covering the other side, just in case she exited the train in a more unusual way. Once she appeared, Anthony and Liam would close in until they had her between them, at which time they would escort her off the premises, with Carl and Gregor following as the backup team in case someone else was lying in wait.

After several minutes of watching the steady stream of people flowing out from the train to join the already crowded throng on the platform, Anthony spotted her, doing her best to blend in with the rest of the disembarking passengers. Gotcha—and you're damn sure not getting away this time, he vowed.

"Target exiting the sixth car. Moving to apprehend. Close in behind." Anthony folded his newspaper under his arm, slipped off the shoe-shine booth, and blended in with the masses, just another faceless traveler. He paralleled her, walking a few yards behind and to the left, dodging clusters of reuniting families and groups of friends greeting each other. He was about to move in when his cell phone vibrated. With a silent curse, he checked the caller ID, then answered. "Yes?"

"I was just wondering why your vehicle is sitting outside the Gare du Nord train station?"

Anthony risked being seen by standing on his tiptoes to keep her in sight. She had been stopped by two men, and was producing her passport. He'd bet her life they weren't French customs officials, either. "Just a minute." He switched to his walkie-talkie mode. "Liam, get up here immediately. Carl, Gregor, assume trailing position at head of train. Wait until you see us to move." He switched back to his caller. "You said the rest of the afternoon was mine, so I decided to take a drive through the French countryside. Why, has something come up?"

"You always were a smart one. We're having— trouble contacting Aleix." The pause was slight, but definitely audible.

Anthony grinned. "Do tell. As it so happens, I'm standing in the train station right now, about three meters from our missing lassie, and Aleix is nowhere in sight. Why don't you let me handle this—as you should have done in the first place—and I'll be in touch once I've got her." He cut his connection just as Liam came up on his right side, not looking at Anthony as he spoke into his wireless earpiece.

"I'm in position. Target is with two hostiles, confirm?"

"Confirmed. Incapacitate only. On my mark." Anthony walked through the crowd, approaching the trio, getting close enough to hear the woman's rising voice.

"I don't know what your problem is, I've just gotten here, and already I'm being hassled—"

She does have guts, to try and brazen this out like that, Anthony thought. He heard one man reply as he edged even closer. "*Mademoiselle,* I'm sure if you will come with us, we can clear all of this up. If you would be so kind—"

Anthony caught Liam's eye and nodded.

He and Liam stepped up, one on either side of the woman, and each brought up small aerosol sprayers, which they aimed at each man's face. A small cloud of concentrated, atomized sedative puffed out into the men's faces. Coughing and spitting, they reached under their suit coats, but the fast-acting mist was already taking hold, and both men slumped to the floor, out cold. The strange event engendered a few puzzled looks from passersby, but Anthony and Liam were already moving, each taking one of their target's arms and firmly propelling her away from the scene. She made a token attempt to twist away, and Anthony took great pleasure in jabbing the pistol in his left hand, hidden under the newspaper, into her ribs hard enough to make her groan.

"Ms. Britaine, I would appreciate it if you would just keep walking and not make any kind of disturbance or attempt to draw attention to us. It's been a long day already, and I am most certainly not in the mood."

She looked over at him, and nearly sagged off her feet in fear, held upright only by his strong grip on her. "You're the man from London—you're with Mercury, aren't you?"

"Correct, and if you do exactly as I say from now on, you're going to be just fine." Of course, Anthony was lying through his even teeth—he planned to extract a vengeance from this bitch that would brand his face in her memory for all time, assuming she survived it in the first place. But first he had to complete his mission, and that meant getting her back to HQ in one relatively un-damaged piece. When they were through with her, then it would be his turn.

"Carl, Gregor, we are heading to the main entrance. Follow at distance."

Although a crowd had gathered around the two fallen men, Anthony, Maggie and Liam had almost made it to the main doors when they hissed open, and five people walked in that Anthony hadn't expected to see. They were led by that grinning bastard who had stopped him from getting her back in London.

26

David's reaction, along with the rest of his team, was immediate. His right hand darted into his open bag to grab the butt of his pistol and casually aim it at the two men. Around him, Robert, Tara and Kanelo also reached into their bags, the four of them looking like a group of salesmen interrupted in the middle of their sales pitch. David heard Robert muttering into his earpiece, and knew he had alerted Cody, who had taken his customary position high above everything, and was observing events through his rifle scope.

David only had eyes for the brown-haired man, who had immediately moved behind the woman, one hand on her shoulder, and his other one obviously holding some sort of weapon hidden behind her back. The other man stood a few feet away from his partner, hands at his side, his gaze boring a hole in the Midnight Team members. For a moment, all eight of them stood in the entryway, oblivious to the stream of people flowing around them, many throwing dirty looks their way as they passed.

"Hold up, gentlemen." David raised his bag slightly, making sure both men saw it. "I'm afraid we can't let you take her out of here. Let her go, however, and you can walk away, no questions asked."

The brown-haired man had the temerity to grin in reply. "That is just as impossible, since we have just met. We are leaving, and since we have her, you will not be stopping us, unless you want to be taking just her body back."

David shook his head. "Ah, that's where you're wrong, since we don't need her alive—but apparently you do. So I already know you're bluffing. And since we outnumber you, that really takes the decision out of your hands."

"You're a confident little arse, aren't you?"

"Runs in my family. This is your last chance. Release her and walk away, or we're going to take her from you," David said.

The man gripped her shoulder even tighter, making the woman gasp in pain. "Looks like you're caught between two big fucking rocks, lass. And since things have a way of changing ever so quickly—"

His head darted behind the woman's for a moment, while David tried to figure out what he meant. Dropping his left hand behind his back, he signaled Tara and Kanelo to watch for flankers.

As he did that, Robert's head snapped to one side, and a spray of pink-and-gray matter splattered over David. It was followed by the cough of a silenced pistol, and the wiry Welshman fell to the floor, his normally nonstop mouth still hanging open in surprise.

"Cover!" David still kept his eyes on the two men

even as his team scattered for whatever concealment they could find. He heard more coughs, followed by the impacts of subsonic bullets. A pained grunt came from nearby, then a scream as a civilian was hit and collapsed in the entryway.

The obviously dead man had a galvanizing effect on the nearby people, who screamed and scattered, the fear radiating outward as they turned in a blind, panicked mob, seeking cover or flight away from the danger.

"M-Two, report," David heard in his ear.

"M-Four is down. Repeat, M-Four is down! Watch for hostiles coming out the main doors. We have engaged at least three of them inside. Have not recovered the target yet." More bullets thudded into the bank of pay phones David had taken cover behind, smashing open one of the machines and scattering coins across the floor.

"Do you have the target in sight?" M-One asked.

"Negative, I can't see her—shit!" A bullet careened off the floor near David's foot coming from behind and to the left of him. Scooting over to his right, he looked up to see a tall man standing on a green-railed balcony with a perfect sight line over the entire lower level. David raised his pistol and triggered three shots, aiming below the railing at the man's crouched form. He saw the man convulse, and knew he'd hit him at least once, but a fusillade of return fire made him duck back behind the phones.

Next to him, David saw Tara behind one of the tall green columns that supported the roof high above them, which was now scored from bullets ricocheting off its surface. "You got anyone?" he asked.

"I think he took her behind the ticket counter, but

we're going to be hip deep in National Police in thirty seconds! We need to get her and get out!" she replied.

"All right, cover me from the shooter at eight o'clock!"

Tara turned and quickly sent four shots at the balcony, making the gunman duck for cover behind some kind of sculpture. David used the distraction to crawl over to the ticket booth, which was already pocked with bullet holes. A row of advertisements mounted on Plexiglas panels meant to funnel people out of the station extended in a line back from the large booth, but David thought there was just enough room to squeeze between the first one and the cubicle wall. He peeked underneath to make sure no one was on the other side, then sucked in his breath and forced his way through the narrow gap. Behind him, he heard more shots, followed by the loud report of unsilenced pistols, which meant the French police had arrived.

David slid to the far corner of the booth and listened hard, trying to hear who was around the corner. He heard the rustle of movement, then a man's voice speaking. "Liam, evade and head out the back way. Carl, Gregor, cover us until we're out the main door, then follow. I'm moving out right now."

Without hesitation, David half stepped out from behind the corner, aiming his pistol at the voice. Scarcely a yard away, the woman crouched, the man behind her, his arm around her waist and his other hand holding a pistol pointed up. His head snapped around at her indrawn breath. "What the—?"

David had him in his sights, about to squeeze the trigger, when the woman moved, blocking his shot. Throwing an elbow into her captor's chest that shoved him backward, she scrambled toward David, who wrenched his own firearm up so as not to shoot her. The man recovered fast, bringing his pistol down to aim at both of them even as he fell to the floor. David grabbed her and pulled her around the corner just as the other man shot.

The hiss of the passing bullet was overwhelmed by a sharp explosion in the middle of the train station that sent shrapnel whizzing by. David covered the woman with his body and ran a quick check on her with one arm while keeping his pistol trained on the corner, ready for their assailant to come at them again. "Are you all right?" he asked.

"I—I think so," she said.

"M-Team, M-Team, this is M-Two. I have the target. Repeat, I have the target. All members withdraw. Repeat, withdraw to extraction point." David heard the singsong wail of the French police cars in the distance, and got up on the balls of his feet. "I need you to get ready to run as fast as you can, following the line of ads to the main doors. Once outside, turn right and head for the hospital next door. Can you do that?" he said.

The woman nodded. "Who are you?"

"Don't worry, we're on your side. Okay, ready— go!" David propelled her toward the main doors, doing his best to keep himself between her and any gunmen who might be pursuing. They were almost there when a shot from above them and to the left scored across the top of David's shoulder, making him gasp in pain and stagger to the doors.

She skidded to a stop and looked back. Raising his right arm across his body, David shot several times at the figure. "Keep moving!" He almost shoved her into the door, and together they staggered out into the Paris street.

"Jesus, Louis, what the hell was that?" Kate watched in helpless horror as the Gare du Nord train station erupted in gunfire and what looked like small explosions. "Where are your operatives?"

Louis sounded agitated, which, along with the public gunfight playing out in front of her, was Kate's confirmation that things had really gone to hell. "We're trying to raise them—they made contact with the target, then something happened and we lost contact."

"Well, keep trying, damn it! Okay, it looks like one of our team has the target, and has exited the station, so at least she's in our hands now. The National Police will be swarming all over that place, so you'd better make sure your people are going to be all right."

"I'm sure they will be fine. I'm more concerned about the Midnight Team doing something rash as they leave the area," Louis replied.

Kate scowled at the insinuation. "Like recover the

target, exactly as they were supposed to? Knock it off, Louis, they're professionals. They came in to do a job and get out, that's all."

Kate checked the log hanging in virtual reality in front of her. It told her the location of each member of the Midnight Team at that exact moment. When they joined the agency, every Room 59 operative had a small transmitter implanted in his or her body. It was used to monitor their location at all times. Instead of five small green dots, there were four, which meant they had lost a member during the op. Kate pushed the unpleasant thought from her mind and concentrated on the here and now, watching through the M-Two's camera as he hustled the woman through the hospital. He may be a cowboy, but he sure got her out of there in one piece, she thought.

"All right, the target and her escort have reached the roof. I see two others entering the hospital, but we have no line of sight on the hostiles." That was the one drawback with their system—she knew exactly where her people were, but the bad guys had never gotten the memo to wear radio transmitters, so she never knew exactly where they were.

Kate dialed in. "M-One, this is Primary. What's your sitrep?"

"Upon entry, the team ran into a pair of hostiles on the way out with the target. The standoff distracted them long enough so that a backup pair was able to ambush, terminating M-Four. We have recovered the target, and she is on her way up now with M-Two. M-Three and M-Five are also withdrawing, and I expect them to arrive shortly."

Kate checked the feeds for M-Three and M-Five, watching them walk to the hospital doors, one of them limping, from the herky-jerky picture she saw. "Okay, listen up." This was the part she hated. "When the target is aboard, you give your people ninety seconds to arrive, and if they're not there, you withdraw."

"Say again, Primary?"

"The rest of your team has ninety seconds from when the target arrives to get to the evacuation vehicle. If they don't make it, you leave them behind. Acknowledge." Kate couldn't risk giving the other team another chance to acquire the woman—they had gotten too close to her twice already.

There was silence, then the team leader replied. "Affirmative."

"If they are left behind, we'll arrange for the French division to pick them up. The target is the important thing right now."

"Understood, Primary. M-One out."

"Louis, you got that?" Kate asked.

"I heard the whole thing, Kate. Don't you worry, if anyone is left behind, we'll be sure to get them to ground safely."

"Thank you." That was the other problem with Room 59's standard operating procedure. Although the agency had the approval of practically every other intelligence agency in the world, they were expected to execute their operations as quietly as possible. If they were caught, they were often treated like any other criminal, or, in these times, a suspected terrorist. Of course, Kate thought, shaking her head, any civilized country would look askance on people waving a gun around in a public place. The National Police would have little mercy on whomever they caught, friend or foe.

Kate wanted to pull off the eyewear and go take a

long, hot bath, but that was an impossibility now. Instead, she leaned forward in her chair, silently rooting for the rest of the Midnight Team members to make it to the roof in one piece and get out of there.

28

I'm gonna kill that fucking bastard!

It was Anthony's overriding thought, almost swamping his years of military training and iron discipline that kept the beast inside at bay. Ironically, it was the loud cracks of the French policemen's pistols that distracted him from the almost overpowering red rage to burst around the corner—and most likely take a bullet to the face for his trouble—in the vain hope of putting a round right between that smarmy git's eyes.

"Anthony, we've got locals on our ass," he heard.

"Follow the plan, but take cover first—fire in the hole." Anthony plucked a grenade from his pocket and sent it skittering into the main area of the building, now completely deserted, as the crowds bustling through the station had either taken cover or fled into another tunnel. The grenade detonated with an echoing bang, making the approaching officers duck for cover. Anthony used that time to bolt for the door, hitting it with both arms outstretched after holstering his pistol under his jacket.

A National Police car screeched to a halt nearby. Anthony twisted his features into a mask of fear and staggered over to them. He pointed to the station, talking wildly. *"L'intérieur!"*

The officers pulled him down behind the car and told him to stay there. They then approached the main doors of the station. As soon as their backs were to him, Anthony got up and walked off, past two more police cars that screeched to a halt in front of the station. He kept up his cowering-civilian persona until he reached the corner of the building, and once around it, he looked in all directions for the woman and her rescuer. They were nowhere to be found. He skirted the side of the building, past a taxi stand, peering into the windows of idling vehicles.

An angry horn blare made him look up at the hospital across the street, just as a blond-haired woman and brown-haired man entered the doors. His gaze instinctually went up to the roof, in time to catch the briefest glare of sunlight off glass. Like a sniper scope.

No sooner had the thought gone through his brain than Anthony acted, picking the narrowest slot and running into traffic, heedless of the blaring horns and curses flying in his direction. He expected to feel a heavy rifle slug punch through his neck, or maybe even his skull and be done with it, fading him to black before he could even register he had been hit. However, no sudden death rained down on him from above, and in another second he was at the entrance to the trauma center, or what passed for it in Paris. "Liam. Status?"

The reply that came back was between pants for breath, as if he had been running. "I'm at the…far end…of the train shed…" His voice was washed out by the roar of an incoming train. "West side of the building."

"Excellent, you should almost be able to see me. They're heading to the roof of the trauma center, right next to the station. Must be going to a helicopter. Get over here and follow me up."

"Affirmative."

Anthony was already heading inside the trauma center, pushing through the white-jacketed crowd, ignoring their questions as he scanned for the entry to the staircase. "Gregor, where are you?"

"Outside, on the east side of the station," came the reply.

"Are you hurt?" Anthony asked.

"Bullet glanced off my vest, but I'm fine."

"Good. Get back to the car. The code for the back is three-three-one-six-six. There's a rifle inside. Take it and get to a vantage point where you can see the hospital roof to the right of the museum. Once there, take out anyone you see that isn't one of us or the woman."

"Affirmative."

"Carl, status report."

Carl's reply was drowned out by a flurry of gunshots. "Didn't make it out. I'm pinned in a corner, low on ammo, and I just used my last frag. No cavalry coming to the rescue, huh?"

"I'm afraid not," Anthony said.

"What are your orders?"

The question made Anthony hesitate for a second, not just because Carl was still enough of a professional to ask it, but because of the answer it required. While he didn't like leaving a man behind, he knew there was no hope of saving him at the moment. If taken alive, he might talk, but there were ways around that. Unfortunately, nowadays a dead body also told tales, but less so than the living, and there were ways around that, as well. "Hold them off as long as you can. Surrendering is your call," Anthony said.

Now at the doors of the stairway, Anthony peered into the reinforced safety-glass window to see if anyone was lurking on the other side. He couldn't tell, so he put his shoulder to the door while drawing his pistol with his other hand, ready to shoot. The heavy door swung open, and he burst inside, eyes scanning everywhere for potential enemies. Finding no one, he eased the door closed.

He heard several more gunshots through his earpiece, then he heard a bitter laugh. "Surrender to the French? I'd never find decent work again!" Carl said.

"That's the spirit. Good luck, and be sure to destroy your phone before they take you."

"Affirmative. It was a pleasure working with you, sir."

"You, too." Anthony disconnected before he heard anything else. He could well imagine what the young man was about to go through. He didn't need to hear it confirmed. With luck, Carl would distract the police long enough so that they could recover the woman and get out before they threw up roadblocks around the city.

He was about to begin his sprint up the stairs when he heard voices from the hallway.

"Take the stairs?" a deep male voice asked.

A female answered. "Not with this leg, we won't."

"I could carry you—"

"Leaving us both defenseless if the hostiles are still around. Hold up—damn it, that hurts. "M-One, this is

M-Three and M-Five. I took a hit to the leg, but we got out…we're coming up now…hold the chopper…yes, sir, that's great news. Thanks for letting us know… M-Three out. Come on, we've got ninety seconds to get to the roof, or the chopper's leaving without us. Orders from Primary," she said.

Anthony crept up the first flight of stairs, then ran as fast as he could up the remaining five flights, the plan sprouting in his mind as he went. His powerful legs ate up the distance as he reloaded his pistol, yanking back the slide with a vengeance, then threading a compact silencer onto the barrel.

Reaching the top, he saw a small landing with the elevator doors on one side, and the double doors leading to the roof on the other. In the dim light, he caught a dark splotch on the ground, and bent over to wipe it up with his fingers. Sniffing it brought the coppery scent of blood. They were here.

The chime of the elevator straightened him up, and he quickly scrambled over the railing to press against the wall of the elevator shaft, above the empty stairwell, one hand grasping the railing, the other holding his pistol. He balanced on the edge of the landing on just his tiptoes, the rest of his feet hanging out in space.

The doors slid open, and a pistol extended out, covering the landing and the stairwell. Anthony held his breath and tried to blend in with the shadows. If the soldier looked his way, he'd take him out, but lose the element of surprise.

"It's clear." The quiet male voice still echoed in the stairwell. "Come on."

Leading with the pistol, the two came out of the elevator, the woman leaning on the taller man, who

Anthony recognized as the man he'd kicked into next week at St. Pancras. They stepped out fast, even though each movement was hurting the woman, as evidenced by the little gasps she let out as they moved forward.

Anthony visualized his movements in his mind, waited for them to take one more step, then it was his turn. Leaning out, he lined up his Walther's sights on the back of the man's head, exhaled and squeezed the trigger once. The subsonic bullet tore through the soft muscle at the back of his target's neck where the skull met the spine, killing him instantly. He turned from support to deadweight in a second, collapsing on top of the woman, who grunted in surprise.

In that second, Anthony moved, vaulting over the railing and stepping over the woman, his pistol pointed at her head. For a second, his vision blurred, and her brown hair became blond, her features sharpened from round to more angular, with defined cheekbones. She looked very much like the woman who had gotten away from him.

Anthony blinked before he could squeeze the trigger, and suddenly his target was gone, and the wounded soldier—or whatever she was—was in front of him. He put a finger to his lips, stilling her to silence, then waved his pistol to make her raise her arms higher in the air.

"I'm going to lift you to your feet, and you won't try a thing, or I'll cripple you permanently. Nod if you understand."

She hesitated, then nodded, her eyes dark and venomous. Anthony didn't mind; he'd seen that look many times before. Keeping his pistol trained on her face, he grabbed her arm and hoisted her up, ignoring her grunt of pain as he did so.

"All right, we're heading out now, you leaning on me like so—"

The squeak of a boot sole on linoleum below caught his ear, and he turned enough to listen for more noise while still keeping an eye on her. He dragged her to the other side of the corridor, so he could watch the stairs to his left. "Do not move or make a sound," he whispered.

They stood there, face-to-face, with Anthony listening for the next noise from below. A soft tone in his earpiece signaled an incoming call, and he answered. "Go."

"I'm a floor below you, and thought I'd call ahead to avoid getting shot."

"Come on up—the party's about to begin." He took his gaze away from her for a split second, partly to confirm that it really was Liam down there, and partly to see if she would try anything. Her eyes narrowed, and he turned his hip just in time to block what would have been a vicious low punch to his testicles. She tried to follow up with a rake across his eyes, but he snapped his head forward, his forehead slamming into the bridge of her nose, the cartilage of her nose crunching under the blow. The back of her head bounced off the wall and she sagged limply, with only Anthony's arm holding her up. Moving his free hand to her mouth, he aimed at her right shoulder and squeezed the trigger, the 9 mm bullet burrowing through her flesh like a voracious, punishing insect. The shock brought her around again, and she screamed into his hand, just as Liam crept up the last flight of stairs.

"Found yourself a playmate, I see."

"You recognize her," Anthony said.

"Sure, she's one of them."

"Simple exchange, one bitch for another."

"I doubt they'll go for that."

Anthony shook his head. "Yeah, me, too. So we'll just have to kill them all instead. How're you fixed for ammo?"

"Got a full mag in, and a half on me. You?"

"Two full, one three-quarters up. I wanted to give Gregor more time to get into position, but we need to go now. Follow behind me and cover the right. I've got the left." He hoisted the semiconscious woman up like a rag doll, wrapping her left arm over his neck and hiding his pistol below her other arm. "Let's move."

29

The roar from the helicopter's blades made it difficult for David to hear anything. He stood in front of the open door of the chopper, his short hair ruffling in the powerful wind kicked up by the blades. When they had arrived, Cody had insisted on checking his injury, and slapped a pressure bandage on it, but David had insisted he was all right and could cover the rest of the team as they came up. They had placed the woman, still clutching her laptop case, in the far seat of the helicopter, and made sure she was belted in before taking their positions to cover the rest of the team. Cody stood a few feet off to David's right, covering the door, and David stood where he was to protect the helicopter and its cargo.

He had been half-right. The wound on the top of his left shoulder burned like a mother, making it nearly impossible to lift his arm for the time being. His HK pistol was in his right hand, but he couldn't pull off a Weaver's grip to save his or anyone else's life, so he'd have to shoot one-handed, which increased the chances of a bullet going astray—

Don't think about that right now—just concentrate on helping to get your team out of here alive, he told himself. David didn't dwell on what had happened to Robert—those were the hazards of the job. He just hoped that when it was his time, he went out like that— totally oblivious to it if at all possible.

The stairway door creaked open, and David's grip on his pistol tightened as two figures walked out, one supported by the other. David caught his breath as he recognized the one being helped along. Tara was a complete mess, her face, right shoulder and left arm all bloody, as if she had gone ten rounds with a heavyweight boxer.

The man helping her kept his head down, as if concentrating on his steps. David knew immediately it wasn't Kanelo. He brought his pistol up, aiming at the man, who suddenly stepped behind Tara and pointed a gun at her head. Another man popped out from behind him and aimed at Cody.

The brown-haired man had to bellow to be heard over the whirling main rotor. "All right! Everyone just relax, and nobody else will have to die today."

David took a step closer, his pistol aimed at the visible part of the man's face. "Drop your weapon right now and step away from her!"

"M-Two, hold your position!" Cody shouted, his own pistol aimed at the second man, who had him in a standoff, his gun aimed at David's leader.

"Simple exchange. You give me her—" the man nodded at the helicopter behind David "—and I give her back to you." He lifted Tara's head up so David could see her battered face, now crusted with drying blood, her eyes rolling back in her head.

"Not gonna happen! I said put your weapon down now!" David took another step forward, making the brown-haired man grab Tara by the hair and shove the silenced muzzle of his pistol under her chin.

"Don't—take—another—step!"

David kept his gun trained on the man's head, torn between taking the shot and concern that he might hit Tara. For a moment, no one moved, David swallowing his rage for the moment. Then he saw it.

Tara's eyes cleared, and she looked straight into his own.

Her left arm was free.

Her direct stare spoke volumes. Give me an opportunity—any opportunity.

David gave her the tiniest of nods.

Cody shouted back. "You know we can't do that!"

"You don't have a choice!" The brown-haired man turned to regard Cody for a moment, and Tara struck.

Her arm whipped up and levered the pistol away from her chin, catching the man by surprise, the gun firing as he reflexively squeezed the trigger. At the same time, she threw her head back, slamming her skull into her captor's cheek.

"Take them!" she screamed while trying to twist away, struggling to hold the pistol away from herself.

But while her attack had put the man off balance, he was still behind her, bringing the pistol back down toward her face. David tried to line up his shot, but they were both ducking and weaving so much he couldn't shoot without taking the chance of hitting Tara.

Even above the howl of the blade, David heard the

loud crack of a rifle, and looked over to see Cody fall to his knees, pistol clattering to the rooftop as bright blood jetted from his neck, which looked oddly misshapen now, as if something had taken a big bite out of him. Clasping both hands to the wound did nothing to stop the spurting crimson, and before David could go to him, or even say anything, he fell face-first on the gravel, legs twitching as the arterial blood colored the gravel around him.

"David!"

He looked back to see Tara still struggling with the brown-haired man, who was slowly, inexorably bringing his pistol down to bear on her. Tara was giving it everything she had to keep the gun away, but her good arm and leg were both trembling, and the gun muzzle was getting closer and closer to her face.

In the split second that David saw that, he also registered the other man bringing his pistol around, as well—about to shoot him if he didn't fire first.

David's reflexes, instincts and training all combined to spur his body into blurred motion as he made his move.

Sighting on the second man, he fired three times as his target's gun spit flame and lead at him. David's bullets hit him high in the chest, while the other man's hurried shots whistled by, punching through the helicopter's canopy. The man tried to keep his weapon on David, but he staggered backward and sat down, then fell backward, his face already turning a flushed pink as he struggled to breathe through a punctured airway.

Immediately David sighted back on Tara and her opponent—just in time to see him fire. The bullet punched through her jaw, into her brain and out the side of her head, sending a chunk of skull and gray-pink matter flying into the air.

David squeezed off several shots, but the guy held up Tara's body, using her as a shield as he retreated to the iron door, shooting wildly the entire way. Once behind more solid cover, he let her shredded, lifeless form drop.

Popping open the helicopter door, David threw himself backward on the floor. "Go! Go! Go! Watch out for a sniper at five o'clock!" he shouted.

The pilot engaged the throttle and the engine roared as they prepared to take off. David smashed away the rest of the broken side window with the butt of his pistol for a clear field of fire, expecting the last man to rush at them at any moment. Tara's body lay near the door, a few yards from Cody's. David wanted to look away from the bodies, but he knew he couldn't—he had to remain on guard, in case the remaining attacker did something stupid.

The helicopter left the ground, rising away from the slaughter on the rooftop. David scrambled into one of the backseats and buckled himself in, trying to divide his attention between the door and his lone passenger. "You all right?" he yelled at her. A mute nod was her only response. "We'll get you back to England. You'll be safe there—"

She stared at him, her eyes wide with fear, and David trailed off, aware of how hollow his words sounded in his own ears.

His stomach dipped as the helicopter lurched, and at the same time David heard a strange noise, as if someone had thrown a watermelon at the windshield. The inside of the canopy was speckled with red mist, and the pilot's head lolled to one side, his hand loose on the collective.

The sniper got the pilot!

David wrenched his seat belt free and lunged into the cockpit as the helicopter's formerly steady engine stuttered, and the aircraft sideslipped through the air, losing altitude and almost crashing on the roof. Grabbing the collective from the pilot's motionless hand, he pushed it down, decreasing the rotor's attack angle and dropping the helicopter like a rock onto the next building.

The chopper skittered across the roof of the building next to the trauma center, and a vision of his life ending in a fiery collision flashed before David's eyes. He tried to remember how to power the engine down, and realized he was holding the throttle control—it was built into the collective. David twisted it with all his might, but the engine revved up even more, making the helicopter bounce faster along the roof. Looking out of the one section of canopy that wasn't covered in blood, David saw the end of the roof, then some kind of open-air courtyard. He twisted the handle the other way, and the helicopter skidded toward the very edge before grinding to a halt, the blade still slicing furiously through the air above his head. David searched for the power switch on the main instrument panel just as one of the skids slipped off the roof, making the entire helicopter lean precariously to one side.

Finding the main power switch, David flipped it, killing the engine, but the still-whirling blade shook the aircraft, threatening its already unstable position. David leaned back from where he stood and slowly—placing his hands and feet with care—crawled toward the door that led to the roof.

He turned back to the woman, who sat frozen in her

seat, clutching a black laptop case. "We have to get out of here. I'm going to open the door, and then I want you to unbuckle your seat belt and come to me," he said.

"I can't—if I move, we'll go over," she said.

"If you don't move, we're gonna go over!" The helicopter shuddered and tilted even farther, the screech of tortured metal grating through David's skull. "Come on, you have to move. I'm going to open the door." He reached for the side door and pushed on the latch, shoving the door open. Grabbing the lip of the floor with his good hand, he reached out to her with his wounded arm, steeling himself for the pain that was about to come. "Unbuckle your belt and take my hand."

She sat frozen for a long moment and, just when David thought he'd have to go back for her, slowly moved her hands to her waist and unfastened the buckle. Setting it down carefully to one side, she slung her computer case over her shoulder and reached out to him, taking a cautious step across the slanted floor, then another, until their hands were almost touching.

The helicopter settled a bit more, and David knew it would go over at any second. He grabbed her hand and pulled as hard as he could, ignoring the fiery pain searing through his injured shoulder. "Come on!"

He scrambled to the edge of the helicopter's floor and jumped onto the landing skid that now hovered in midair beneath him, feeling the machine shift again at the sudden shift in ballast. With a last, agonized tug, he pulled her out just as the aircraft teetered, then hung on the lip of the roof for a moment.

"Jump!" Holding her hand, David leaped off the skid, pulling her with him. Unbalanced now, the chopper slipped over the side of the building to land with a deafening crash in the courtyard below. David heard shouts and screams from below at the helicopter's impact.

David collapsed on the roof, sucking in a breath and clutching his injured arm. Beside him, the woman panted from a combination of terror and shock.

"I can't believe we're still alive—" She put her hand on the roof to steady herself before she fell over.

"Hey, hey!" David took her chin and turned her face to his. "Take a deep breath. Now take another. You gotta stay with me—we're not out of the woods yet. Are you hurt?"

The woman sat up and examined herself. "I don't think so, other than skinned knees and hands. You're bleeding, however."

"Yeah, I know." David glanced at his shoulder.

"Not just there." She pointed at his left side.

David followed her hand and saw a large red patch where his shirt had adhered to his skin. The wound in his side flared with the movement, and he knew he'd have to treat it as soon as possible before it got infected. "Crap, the son of a bitch must have tagged me. Thank God for adrenaline, I guess. Come on, we gotta get down from here."

"Wait a minute, why should I go anywhere with you?" the woman asked.

David tested his legs and found them slightly wobbly, but otherwise stable. "Well, your choices are to either come with me, or I can leave you for those goons we met in the train station."

She shuddered at the idea, then shot to her feet. "Those other two on the roof—they were your fellow agents, or something like that, right?"

"Something like that." There really hadn't been time to explain. David had just rushed her to the roof and into the helicopter before all hell broke loose. He scanned around them, spotting what looked like a door on a roof to the north. "Wait for my signal, then follow my trail exactly," he said.

"Why?"

"Because that sniper might still have a vector on us. And when you do move, try to stay low." He loped off across the roof, away from the trauma center, keeping a wary eye on their surroundings. Reaching the thin cover of an air conditioner unit, he crouched down, ignoring the steady burn in his side, and watched the area past the trauma center roof, looking for any sign that the sniper might still be searching for them. A thick gray column of smoke rose into the air as something on the helicopter caught fire. That's as good a cover as we're going to get, he thought, waving her toward him. The wail of emergency vehicles reverberated in the distance, echoing off the tall buildings around them. As she walked—following his path exactly, he noted—David studied her during the short journey. She seemed to have shaken off her earlier hysteria, but he could just be watching her slip into the early stages of shock. Have to keep an eye on her for the next few hours. Other than that, she moved well, low and fast. Of course, the idea of a high-velocity bullet aimed at one's back makes just about anyone move fast.

Once she got to his position, David had already plotted the rest of their route to the door. "We need to get street-side, find transportation and get out of the area immediately. We can go to a safehouse to hole up in until I can arrange to get us safely out of the country."

"Um, okay." The woman hurried to match his stride. "Hey, what's your name?"

David had any one of several cover identities in place for just such a question, including the doctor one that had been prepared for their incursion into the hospital, but at the moment, he had been through too much to give them any thought. "David," he said.

"I'm—Maggie."

The pause had been slight, but David caught it all the same. He glanced at her and smiled. "Don't worry, you're with the good guys now."

"That's good *guy*, remember? I'd really feel better if the rest of your friends were here."

David's expression tightened, but he quickly smoothed his features over, not wanting to alarm her. "Fair enough, but I'll be calling in reinforcements like nobody's business. Now, Maggie, let's get the hell off this roof."

They came to another metal door, this one locked with pass-key access. "Finally, something going our way," David said.

Maggie's eyebrows rose. "What, the locked door?"

"Yup." David drew his cell phone and extended two small metal prongs from the top. Inserting them into the slot where the card would normally go, he slid them down through the narrow opening once, then again. After the second time, the mechanism clicked, and when he pulled on the handle, the door swung open to reveal another staircase, this one much more utilitarian that the last one. Retracting the prongs on the phone, he sheathed it again, then started down the stairs. "I never get locked out at home."

"I'll bet. We should probably find something to cover

your wounds—otherwise you're going to attract all sorts of attention."

David was pleased that she had thought of that, and annoyed that he hadn't. "Good point. I'm sure we'll find something along the way." He paused in the middle of the flight, leaning against the railing as a wave of dizziness swept over him.

"Are you all right?" she asked.

David shook it off, inhaling deeply. "For someone who's been shot twice today, I'm just ducky. Let's keep moving."

They continued down to the second floor, where David's rudimentary French told him there were patients on this floor, but he couldn't tell what department of the hospital they were in. "Let's take a quick look around here—see if we can find a lab coat or something."

"All right. Let me go out first," Maggie said.

"Sure, but I'll be watching you, so no funny business."

"Don't worry, I'll stay in sight the whole time."

"Okay, go." David leaned against the wall next to the door, sucking in a breath that made his side ache with the effort. When he took his hand away from the wound, bright red blood oozed out. That's not good, he thought. Remembering to watch his charge, he looked through the window to see the now empty hallway.

Oh, shit! David peered one way, then the other, trying to see as far down as he could without opening the door. There was no sign of her in either direction. Damn it! He was just about to open the door and go after her when it swung toward him, almost hitting his face.

"Where the hell were you?" he asked.

Her arms were full of medical supplies, along with

a white jacket. "Hey, relax, I found a storeroom and took advantage of it. I got bandages, gauze, tape, alcohol, everything we need. Now hold still." She knelt down and lifted his shirt, wincing as she peeled it away from his wound. "Ow, that's nasty."

"Just get something on it and let's get out of here," he said.

"Hold still, and I will. This wing seems pretty quiet. No one's running around or anything—it's almost like they haven't even heard of the crash yet."

"Good for usss!" David's breath hissed between his teeth as he tried not to cry out when she swabbed alcohol on his wounds.

"Sorry, I know this isn't the nicest treatment, but it'll have to do until you can get treated by a professional."

"That's irony for you—surrounded by doctors, and we can't ask a single one for help," he said.

The comment brought a smile to Maggie's lips as she worked. "You always crack jokes when you've been shot?"

"Takes my mind off the pain."

"Well, I'm sure any doctor here would say try not to include so much lead in your diet, then call the police next. Sorry, but you're stuck with me for the time being." She folded a bandage into a double-thick pad and securely taped it over the side wound, then did the same with the shoulder injury, re-covering the entry and exit wound. "That'll do for now. Here, clean up your hands, and wipe down your face while you're at it." She held out a handful of self-sealed antiseptic wipes for him.

"You thought of everything," he said.

"Well, you did save my life back there—twice—so

I figured I should probably start pulling my weight somehow."

"So far, so good."

"All right, Doctor." Maggie held out the lab coat. "We should be able to get outside with this and to the street. I hope your little gizmo can open car doors, as well. It'd be embarrassing to see a doctor standing next to his car with a bent coat hanger." Her words were light, but David still detected the undercurrent of fear in them. Which is probably just how I sound when I talk right now, he thought.

They took the last flight of stairs down to the ground floor, and once again Maggie poked her head out to make sure the coast was clear before David emerged. Although this level was crowded with people, no one gave them a second glance, as they were all intent on their own business. As they walked, David heard snatches of conversation about something that had happened on the premises.

"…hélicoptère…"

"…accident…"

"…quatre personnes mortes…"

David stiffened at that last bit, but Maggie kept him moving toward the double doors that led outside. They came out into a broad thoroughfare that led to other areas of the hospital grounds. "All right, wheels."

A sleek silver hatchback pulled in from the street to the north and parked near an entrance about ten yards down from them. A harried-looking man dressed in a suit and tie got out and rushed into the hospital, barely slamming his door closed behind him.

"That'll work. Come on." David headed over, glancing casually around to make sure no one was watching. He extruded the prongs on his phone again and pressed a button. After a few seconds, the locks popped open on the car. "Get in."

"Hey, it might be best if I drive, given your condition," Maggie said.

David regarded her for a moment, then nodded. He went to the passenger's side and sank into the leather seat with a grimace. "Ow."

Maggie got in the driver's seat. "Okay, start 'er up."

"Right." David extended the second prong, making it longer this time. "Put that into the keyhole and press seven three times."

Maggie did so, and the ignition turned over without her hand moving, the engine purring quietly. "Wow."

"Yeah, now let's hit the road before the suit comes back to find us boosting his ride."

Maggie adjusted the seat, belted up, shifted into gear and pulled out, aiming for the same entrance the man had come through. She slammed on the brakes as a large cargo truck lurched into the entryway, blaring its air horn as it screeched to a halt. The driver threw up both of his hands in the universal gesture of exasperation, shaking his head and mouthing what were no doubt aspersions on Maggie's dexterity, ancestry and anything else he could think of. Smiling sweetly, she squeezed the car through the narrow opening, turning right on the street and accelerating away.

David had just managed to get his seat belt fastened before slamming into it, the restraint locking up across his chest and lap, and making his injuries flare with so much pain he nearly blacked out. His vision was dimming, turning gray around the edges, and he couldn't move, couldn't talk, couldn't think. His last conscious memory was seeing her turn to him and ask, "Where to, David—David?"

30

"Damn it, David, don't you fucking die on me now!"

Maggie tried to divide her attention between staying on the road and checking the agent, or whatever he was, to make sure he was still breathing. She placed a hand on his chest and was relieved to find he was still alive. "Oh, thank God." Alarmed horns alerted her to her drifting car, and Maggie quickly straightened up before she sideswiped somebody.

With that minicrisis over, she concentrated on where they were, and more importantly, where they were going. She found a broad avenue and turned left onto it.

A chirping noise filled the car, and Maggie nearly strained her neck, whipping her head around to see where it was coming from. After a startled few seconds, she realized David's cell phone was trilling.

"Crap, what now?" She pulled over and, holding her breath, she removed the phone from the ignition, amazed to find that the car still kept running. She stabbed the green connect button, holding the phone to her ear gingerly, as if it might attack her at any second, as she pulled back onto the road.

"Hello?" said a clear, calm, female voice on the other end.

"Hello." Maggie's response was automatic, but she didn't say anything more.

"May I ask who this is?"

"No, you may not. In fact, I'd rather you told me who the hell you are first."

"I'm a friend of the man in the car next to you. You might say I'm his boss," the voice said.

Maggie grimaced. Wonderful, more double-talk bullshit. Without realizing it, her speed began creeping up as she tried to escape the city faster. "Great, but that doesn't really answer my question. Who are you affiliated with?"

"I'm afraid I don't quite follow you."

Maggie jerked the phone away from her ear and rubbed the mouthpiece on the seat belt. "Hmm, the connection's breaking up here. Now, stop jerking me around. Who do you work for?"

"We're an independent organization, if that's what you're wondering."

Son of a bitch! Is this guy with another mercenary group? she wondered, alarmed. "And if I said the name Mercury Security, your response would be?"

"We are not a private security organization, if that is your concern."

"That's just one of my concerns at the moment."

"I'm sure it is. May I speak to the owner of this phone, please?"

Interesting how she never says his name, Maggie

thought, shooting her unconscious passenger a sidelong glance. "I'm afraid he can't come to the phone right now—in fact, I gotta go, too."

"Miss, wait, is he hurt? Please, don't hang up, we can help you—" was all she heard before Maggie clicked off the phone. She held the sleek unit in her palm for a moment as she wondered what to do. *What else does this thing do, I wonder? Can it track us? If she hadn't had both hands occupied, she would have smacked her forehead. Shit, of course they can triangulate on our position. Hell, if this guy's with the government—no matter what she said—I gotta ditch this thing.*

At the next intersection, Maggie pulled up to a truck with an open-topped flatbed filled with broken concrete. She held the phone for another moment, then lowered the window and tossed the chirping device up into the back of the truck, which was turning left onto another boulevard.

Okay, what to do, what to do? At the next light, she wrestled her laptop out of its case and inserted her mobile satellite Internet card. Her encrypted connection would pop up on the Web for a few minutes, but since she was moving, she felt it was worth the risk. Besides, *I need help right fucking now.*

Logging on, she placed a scrambled VOIP call to a number known only by a handful of people in the world, inserting her wireless earpiece into her ear while she waited. Next to her, David moaned and stirred restlessly in his seat. A fine sheen of sweat gleamed on his forehead. *And this is just what I need, as well, to haul around a wounded secret agent.* As soon as the thought popped into her head, Maggie felt a bit guilty. After all, the guy had been standing between her and that other gunman when he'd gotten shot.

Come on, come on… At last, someone picked up.

"Hello?"

"G?"

"Is this who I think it is?"

"Yeah."

"Girl, what the hell happened? My guy was ready to meet you, and the next thing he knows, crazy fools are capping each other and setting off noisemakers all over the place." Even on his secure line, Aragorn was careful not to refer to guns or explosives or any actual locations. "They've pretty much shut down the trains coming or going out of there, you know."

"Good thing I'm in a car, then," Maggie said.

"Do I want to know how you acquired it?"

"Through my new friend," she said.

"The kind of friends you got, I'd hate to see your enemies."

"Yeah, ask your buddy—he probably saw them up close and personal before the fireworks started."

"He did mention something about that."

"Well, look, since I was unavoidably diverted from making my connection, I still need the hookup."

Maggie heard a long, drawn-out hiss of breath in her ear. "Should I assume that what happened today involved you?"

Maggie thought about lying for a second, but discarded the idea. She needed Aragorn more than ever, and if he found out she'd lied to him, he'd disappear like smoke in the wind—or worse, hang her out to dry. Besides, he probably had a voice-stress analyzer monitoring the call anyway. "Yes," she said.

Aragorn murmured in disapproval. "Heat like that I do not need, you know."

"I know, I know. I wouldn't ask if I didn't need the help—you also know that."

"Maybe so, but I think you need to level with me, so I know what the hell I might be getting myself into."

"The shit I got myself into involves men who would do the kind of stuff that went down today. They're the kind of men who would wax my brother without even thinking twice. That's the kind of shit I'm in, and I need help—your help—to get out of it, all right?" Maggie's eyes gleamed with tears as she spoke about her brother, but her voice was as cold and clear as ever. *I'll be damned if I give him the satisfaction of hearing me cry—or beg for that matter.*

There was a long pause again, and Maggie was sure Aragorn was just playing with her. He'd always liked to pull juvenile shit like that.

"All right, but I'm gonna need another ten percent. No negotiating this time. I've already laid out expenses on this, and now I gotta set up another net for you on short notice. Where are you right now?" he finally said.

In her haste to get out of the city, Maggie hadn't paid any attention to where she was going, and now looked up in surprise as a jumbo jet airliner roared over the avenue she was on, crossing her vision from west to east. She waited for the ringing in her ears to die down. "I'm near an airport, if you hadn't guessed."

"Do you know what direction you're heading?" he asked.

Maggie scanned the dashboard for any help, and found a digital compass to her right. "Yeah, north-northeast."

"Good, I can work with this. Keep going on this road

until you're out of town, then follow the directions I'm sending you. Call me once you get to the outskirts, and we'll go from there. Drive safe, and for God's sake don't get pulled over."

"No shit. Hey—thanks."

"Thank me only once we get you safely tucked away. Now hang up and concentrate—you've got a ways to go."

"I'll see you soon."

"Not if I see you first." Aragorn clicked off, and Maggie disconnected her call just as a chime from her computer announced an e-mail had arrived. Opening it revealed a map and the quickest route to Brussels, Belgium. Settling into the seat, she glanced over at David, still breathing shallowly, and focused all of her concentration on quietly getting them out of France without any more bullets whizzing by, explosions going off or cold-eyed, brown-haired men coming after them—apart from the one in the seat next to her.

31

During her two years as head of Room 59, Kate couldn't remember an op going so bad so fast.

There was always a chance, of course. Agents got themselves into trouble, getting arrested or injured in other countries, sometimes getting killed while trying to execute their missions, but they had never had what should have been a simple extraction blow up in their face like this. Four Midnight Team members were dead, at least two members of Mercury Security were dead, as well, plus two French police officers dead and three wounded. Besides that, there were reports of at least four civilians injured, two severely. That was something that Kate couldn't stand. It was the one ironclad rule that she had made sure was instilled in every agent. An innocent—a true innocent, not someone who just didn't know what Room 59 was about—should not be harmed unless the operative simply had no choice in the matter. And while she was sure that none of her people would have been responsible, she knew how it was going to look to her superiors.

As if sensing the worst possible time to interrupt her train of thought, Kate's computer chimed. She answered it wearily. "Yes?"

Judy's grim face appeared on the monitor. "We've heard what just happened at the Gare du Nord. The board has convened a special session to decide what, if anything, needs to be done."

Kate barely kept her mouth from dropping open. The board of the International Intelligence Agency was made up of nine people, each from a different country around the world, who provided oversight of Room 59. They selected the missions the agency sent its agents on, and could veto or otherwise modify a mission to their liking but they didn't interfere once a mission was underway. Kate had never heard of an impromptu meeting like this being called, and she immediately smelled a rat.

"I'm sorry to contact you on such short notice, but this was the best time they could meet. I'm taking you in now."

Before Kate could protest, the picture dissolved into the standard virtual reality conference boardroom where they discussed all Room 59 business with their superiors. Usually the boardroom was plush and inviting, with leather swivel chairs and a rich mahogany table that stretched almost the length of the rectangular room. Now, however, it looked dark and forbidding, matching the appearance of the nine silhouettes that materialized to sit in the chairs on both sides of the table. A small national flag floated above each dark form, representing the United States, the United Kingdom, France, Germany, Italy, Saudi Arabia,

Russia, Australia and China. Although the U.S., the U.K., China and Russia had permanent seats on the IIA board, the other five positions were held on a rotating schedule. And even though Kate had no idea who was behind the faceless human figures in each seat, she had ascertained enough to get a general feel for how the old guard would react to this breach. It was the new members—Saudi Arabia, Italy and Australia—that she hadn't gotten a handle on yet. At the moment, however, all of the silhouettes appeared more menacing than they ever had before, vague shadows that could destroy everything she had been working for, if they felt she wasn't working in the agency's best interests. That realization brought with it a cold feeling in the pit of her stomach that Kate rarely, if ever, felt—fear.

Steeling her gaze, she remembered what Denny Talbot, the North American Room 59 director, had told her the very first time she had gone before the board when a mission had gone wrong. "Never let 'em see you sweat. Our people are going to make mistakes, but our job is to fix what went wrong as quickly as possible, and get back on track. The examination, recriminations and punishment, if any, will come later." She had gotten through the inquiry that time, and she would get through this one, too.

No time like the present, she thought, reaching for her virtual glasses. She slipped them on, putting her on an equal footing with everyone else. To her left, she saw Judy sitting quietly two seats away, her expression inscrutable.

The black figures hid any trace of gender, but Kate always made sure to address both, just in case. "Ladies and gentlemen, no doubt you have all heard of the incident that occurred in the Gare du Nord train station in Paris at approximately 1035 hours local time. Rather than rehash the details, I will fill you in on what we know. The target has been acquired, and is under guard by one of our operatives at the moment. We are making arrangements to bring both of them in as soon as possible, using every available resource."

As she had figured, the announcement brought a wave of mutters from the board members. Out of the corner of her eye, she saw Judy stiffen in her seat, her eyebrows narrowing at the news. Didn't think I'd pull that one out, did you? Kate thought grimly.

The flag above the United States representative glowed in the dim room as the figure below it spoke. "In the interests of security, only the four permanent seats on the board have been made aware of the exact nature of the target's value to certain parties. I apologize for this necessity, but wish to reassure the other members that it was vital that this level of security be maintained. However, given what we know at this time, do you, Director, believe that the sort of force sent to recover this target was necessary, when perhaps a standard operative would have been more successful?" Although Kate didn't know who the U.S. rep was, she knew he was someone new and not familiar with her work.

"As I stated in my mission action reports, all of which should be before you—" the dig was a jab at Judy, who didn't react this time, but remained stoic and unmoving "—you will note that our team encountered unexpected resistance at the primary mission site. Once the target was mobile, I authorized the Midnight Team to continue their pursuit, in the event that this other hostile team was also still trying to reacquire her. As they seem to have disabled the two French operatives who had been at the train station and made contact with the target, it seems obvious to me that a team trained to handle this sort of response was necessary." Sorry, Louis, she thought.

The red-and-gold Chinese flag lit up. "That operational lapse will be dealt with separately. While it is true that the target was recovered, there is some concern from the board, and from your liaison, as well, about your insistence that this Midnight Team continue with the mission when this sort of operation is not what they had been designed for, to our understanding." Several other heads nodded in agreement.

Kate darted another glance at Judy, who might have been carved from marble for all the reaction she displayed. But the Chinese member's words were enough to confirm Kate's suspicions that Judy had gone over her head.

She returned her attention to the members in front of her. "Ladies and gentlemen, every operative in our employ is a clandestine agent first, dedicated to accomplishing their mission at all costs. The members of the Midnight Teams have been trained in urban infiltration as extensively, if not more so, than standard agents. I have every confidence that they can be relied on to do the job we ask of them every single time. Unfortunately, at times their missions may take them into public venues, and incidents like this may occur, despite our best efforts. Regardless, I can tell you that if those men and women hadn't been there, the body count could have been much higher."

"Or a single operative might have found a way to extract the target without leaving such a public—and messy—situation." This observation came from the

Saudi Arabia representative. "I mean, it is one thing if a civilian is caught in the cross fire, but we have a full firefight occurring in a very public place with dozens of witnesses, followed by a shoot-out on a hospital roof, and the crash and total destruction of a helicopter. All of this will be investigated by the local authorities, and will require extensive cleanup and media handling. The aftermath may place our entire operation at risk. Our invisibility is what lets us accomplish so much, but not if our activities are splashed across every front page and on every network—as is currently happening."

Despite her mind racing to stay a step ahead of the Saudi speaker, Kate was impressed with his eloquence, particularly as a new member. Might have to keep an eye on him in the future—or try to cultivate him as an ally, she thought.

"Strong points all. However, I'm sure that the director and all those in her employ are aware of what they need to do, and the best way to do it." This unexpected support came from the U.S. member. Kate seized the opportunity.

"That is true. Ladies and gentleman of the board, we play for the highest of stakes every day, with the world as our game board. If that sounds facile or simple, let me assure you that it is not. The men and women who perform these missions always know what is at stake— they have to be aware of it to do their jobs. Although we can glean a fairly complete picture of what happened earlier today, I am sure that the men and women of this Midnight Team acted completely appropriately under the circumstances. However, I also prefer not to dwell on what might have happened. What we know, based on the information we have, is that the target is in our hands and is on the way to us, and that is the most important point. The mission was accomplished."

And as long as David was still alive and with the target, that was her story, and she was going to stick to it. His implanted chip was still reading as live, so she had independent confirmation other than the woman's word. Kate had scrambled all available resources to track down the location of the cell phone, and sent a team to find and follow the car David was registered as being in, since the last intel they had gleaned had shown that it and the phone were now heading in separate directions.

"I'm coordinating our resources in Europe to ensure that her journey back to us will be safe and uneventful," Kate said.

The Russian flag glowed. "All prudent decisions. Still, I think we should move to suspend all new Midnight Team operations until further review. Any teams currently in the field will have the chance to complete their missions if absolutely necessary, and if not, they will be recalled immediately and placed on indefinite hiatus until a formal recommendation has been made."

Kate resisted the urge to bolt up from her chair, but couldn't let this proposal to sideline one of Room 59's assets pass without a response. "If that is the board's decision at this time, I will of course abide by it. However, I would request that each member carefully review the operating reports of the various Midnight Team missions. Overall, their success ratio exceeds our regular operatives. They have succeeded in completing missions that would have been beyond the abilities or resources of our regular operatives, and have proven their dedication to the goals of this agency many times over."

"Of course we will review all pertinent information before making a final decision," the U. S. rep said. "If there are no other questions, I move to call the vote on the suspension of all Midnight Teams until a formal review can be made."

Small lights appeared above each board member, green for approval, red for disapproval. The vote was six to three for the motion, with Australia, Germany and the U.K. opposing.

"The vote is six for, three against, and is carried. Director, we'll leave you to work out the details of placing the teams on inactive standby as soon as possible. Only vital operations that are already under way should be continued," the U.S. representative said.

"I understand. Thank you, everyone." The board members began to fade away, and Kate sent a private message.

"Judy, a word before we get started." It wasn't a request.

Kate shunted her liaison into a private room on the agency network. As soon as Judy appeared, she looked as if she was going to say something, but Kate cut her off.

"Save whatever excuse you've cooked up. You went above my head to the board, and that is inexcusable."

The unflappable British woman didn't back down an inch. "I did what I did to preserve the agency. It is my job," Judy said simply.

"Fine," Kate replied. "From this moment on, everything you do will be run by me first. Every order, every request, *everything*. If I find out a single document has gone out without my approval, I will do everything in my power to remove you from your position."

Judy frowned. "But—you can't possibly mean that.

The paperwork alone will double your load. I'm only trying to assist you!"

"Assistance like what you just provided in front of the board I do not need. You should have come to me instead of going over my head. I expect to see updates on all current operations in the next hour. Get to it." Kate turned on her heel and stalked to the door, but stopped there. "And one more thing—you're off all Midnight Team operations—I'll be overseeing them from this point on personally."

Her avatar left the room, and Kate pulled off the glasses as she closed the VR door behind her and leaned back in her chair, her heart pounding. She knew Judy really was just following procedure but in such a high-stakes mission, procedure could get people killed.

I sure hope David has the situation under control. Otherwise Judy might get another shot at me sooner than I'd like, she thought. As much as she wanted to take a break, there was still more work to be done—there was always work to be done. She leaned forward and dialed a number, slipping on her headset again. "Hello, Jonas. There is quite a situation developing at the moment and I was thinking your skills would be quite useful. I expect you might be taking a little road trip immediately…."

32

David's eyes fluttered open to see the sunlight filtering in through the windshield, bathing his face in its warm glow. It was almost worth being blinded as he woke.

"Hey, you're up. Good, I was starting to worry." Maggie regarded him with cautious glances, dividing her attention between him and the two-lane highway they were speeding down.

"Why?" he asked as he tried to remember what had happened.

"You were moving around in your seat. I thought you might be having a seizure or something. I'm just glad you're not."

"That makes two of us." Rubbing a hand over his face, David looked at the countryside. "Where are we?"

"About two hundred kilometers north of Paris. Where we're going, that's for me to know at the moment."

"Fine, play coy if you want. I've got to check in." David searched the car's interior, patting his pockets as he did so. "Where's my phone?"

"I, uh, I got rid of it."

David's head snapped around, heedless of the pain it caused in his shoulder. "You what?"

"I couldn't take the chance of them tracking us, so I ditched it. I have no idea where it is right now."

"That's great. Well, we need to find a public phone, then, don't we?" He wasn't concerned about the phone's loss. When Room 59 figured out it wasn't with him anymore, their techs would lock it down and broadcast a message to anyone who found it to mail it to a drop box for a handsome reward. The problem was that he had one less link to headquarters and backup now. He was sure they were still tracking him—the subcutaneous chip in his body was good for decades, probably long after he was gone, in fact. He quickly assessed his situation. He didn't have a weapon—he'd lost his pistol in the helicopter crash, he recalled. He was wounded, and at the moment he was at the mercy, more or less, of this woman, unless he wanted to try to wrest control of the car from her. That was an unattractive prospect at best.

"They're going to keep coming after you, you know," he said.

"Who, your people or the other people?"

"Both, I expect."

"Yeah, well, that's why I'm going underground with people I know."

"Okay. If that's true, why am I still here?"

Maggie shot him a sidelong glance out of narrowed eyes. "I may be a thief, but I'm no killer. Besides, I couldn't have gotten out of there without you, so I certainly wasn't going to repay the favor by leaving you in an unconscious heap by the side of the road."

"I appreciate the thought." David's words came out without a hint of irony or sarcasm.

"You're welcome."

"Of course, you know I still need to continue my mission—bringing you in," he said.

The car swerved toward the shoulder. "Well, then, that hospitality could be rescinded at any time. You may be some kind of hot-shit government agent, but I doubt you'd be able to put up that much of a struggle," she said.

That's closer to the truth than you know, David thought. His side wound had clotted, but still ached, sending pain all through his chest. His shoulder was worse, however, stiffening a lot and rendering his entire arm pretty much useless. He was sure he could take her if necessary—hell, he could probably still overpower her if he was in a body cast—but there was no need to rock the car right now. He was sure Room 59 was tracking him, so she'd be brought into the fold regardless—she just didn't know it yet. Best just to let her think she's got the upper hand at the moment.

"So what makes you think these people you're meeting can help you more than I can?" he asked.

"Let's just say I have an aversion to organized anything, whether it's government or crime."

"The ultimate freelancer, eh?"

"Yup."

"The question still stands, particularly in light of what happened earlier."

"My friends prefer evasion to shooting people or trying to blow them up. Once I'm with them, we'll disappear, and go off where no one will be able to find me, electronically or otherwise," Maggie said.

"Good idea, if you can pull it off. So you're a thief, eh?"

"Yeah, what of it?"

"Hey, I'm just making conversation. So what'd you steal that's got everyone so hot and bothered over you?"

She frowned at him for a moment. "Are you serious?"

He nodded.

"What are you, like, some kind of killer mushroom?"

Now it was David's turn to frown. "I don't follow."

"Do your superiors keep you in the dark all the time and feed you lots of shit?"

He chuckled at the analogy. "No, not all the time. But you say you're a thief, yet you're hanging out with ecoterrorists. They don't have a lot to steal—unless you like diseases, I suppose."

"No, I'm a data thief. System hacker, that sort of thing. The greenies were just a cover, they were conveniently located next to where my bro—where I did a job."

David thought about the Wyvil Road house for a moment and he had difficulty wrapping his mind around it. "But the nearest target with any data worth having is—MI-6."

"I can neither confirm nor deny that statement." Maggie actually smiled for a fleeting second. "Isn't that what you government types say when you want to tell the world something but can't?"

"I've never had the opportunity to use it myself. So the guys chasing you—they're not MI-6 security. They wouldn't have cleansed the house—they would have arrested everyone there. They know you have what you have because—" he blinked again at the realization "—they hired you to do it?"

"Maybe you should have been a detective instead of a hired gun. You seem to have the knack for it."

"So, what happened? Is the adage true—no honor among thieves?"

Maggie looked over, and the ferocity on her face startled him. "You're lucky I'm driving. Otherwise I'd slap that look off your face. I've already lost more on this job than any amount of money can replace." She took a deep breath and collected herself, bringing the now racing car back down to the speed limit. "Even with my experience, the job was much more difficult and time-consuming than expected, leading us to invoke the additional-expenses clause in our contract. Our employer chose to disagree, and tried to enforce their decision with those assholes at the house and train stations."

David noticed the change to plural, but continued the conversation. "They almost succeeded, too. What makes you think they aren't still after you?"

"I've been keeping an eye out for tails, and haven't seen anything behind us. Besides, we gave those guys the slip at the hospital. I can't possibly see how they'd find us again."

"If I had my phone, I could make sure of that. I could scan for bugs, tracking devices, that sort of thing. That guy might have planted something on you in the station."

"Not likely. He was too busy trying to get me outside," she said.

"Do you mind if I take a look at your computer bag anyway?" David asked.

"I don't see any reason," she said.

"Humor me. Besides, it will keep me occupied during the trip."

She sighed. "Very well, but don't open it."

Turning awkwardly in the bucket seat, David

managed to retrieve the case from the backseat of the car with a minimum of jostling to his wounded shoulder. It was a simple padded nylon case, with plenty of pockets on the exterior to hold just about anything a computer geek—or hacker—would need. David examined the pockets first, carefully emptying them and running his free hand along every inch of the interior. He next turned his attention to the case's exterior, and after a long examination, found what he was looking for, embedded in the nylon near one of the plastic feet the case rested on when it was set down.

"You mean he couldn't have planted something like this?" he said.

The item he held up was no bigger than a grain of rice, and matte black, to blend into the case's surface. It had a little claw that would hook into just about anything. David found it was surprisingly difficult to remove.

Maggie peered at the black speck in his palm. "Is that what I think it is?"

"If you think it's a tracking device, you're right." David rolled down the window and opened his hand, pitching the tiny bug outside. "When you have a chance, I'd suggest getting rid of all your clothes and that case and scanning your computer, in case they were able to plant a program in it, as well."

"That I know they didn't do—my firewall is impossible to crack. Nobody gets inside but me."

"Maybe so, but doing the rest of it wouldn't hurt—preferably, before we arrive wherever it is we're going."

"Why are you so helpful all of a sudden?" Maggie asked.

Because I already know who's going to win this

round, and it isn't going to be you, or those other guys, he thought. "Because I want to show you that I can help you—out of this situation, maybe even out of this life you're in. If you want me to."

"Here, we can stop here and change." Maggie pulled off the highway at a small town. "But no phone calls. In fact, I think you'll stay here in the car altogether."

"If you insist. I suggest leaving the engine running—it would be much harder for me to hotwire it with a bum arm."

"At least I know you won't take off on me," she said.

"I could leave you stranded here, you know," he replied.

Her level gaze met his. "You could, but I don't think you will."

The corner of David's mouth quirked up a passable half smile. "We'll never know. Here." He held out a folded sheaf of Euros. "Find me something loose and comfortable. A hooded, zip-up sweatshirt would be fine. And a belt to sling my arm."

Maggie looked from the money to his eyes, her brows narrowing with suspicion.

"Go on, it's fine. If you're really running off the grid, you can't have much, and you need to change out of that outfit."

"Are you saying you don't like it?"

"Somehow I see you wearing something more tasteful in your everyday life."

With a final squint at him, as if trying to see if he was putting her on, she snatched the banknotes from his hand and also took the laptop case from him. "Thanks."

David leaned back in the seat, content to just keep an eye on her. He knew Room 59 agents would have been dispatched to all major cities in the area. Given their direction, he was pretty sure he knew where she was going, and he fully expected that there would be a welcoming party there—just not the one she was expecting.

33

Anthony sat in the helicopter seat as he and Gregor flew
north, toward Belgium. His face was set, betraying no hint
of emotion as he stared straight ahead, trying to come to
grips with what had just happened over the past hour. Not
only had he lost the woman again—but that cocky,
smiling bastard had killed Liam right in front of him.

He had worked with Liam for three years—an
eternity in the PMC trade. They had functioned like perfectly matched bookends, with the laconic Brit seeming
to read his mind at times, always backing his play, yet
knowing when he might be pushing the odds a bit too
far. They had crossed the globe a dozen times over,
fought and schemed in backwater villages on rivers that
had barely been named a few decades earlier, and run
operations in the largest metropolitan cities in the world.
And now he was gone. To Anthony, it felt much as if
one of his limbs had been cut off, leaving him crippled.
Not that he would show it, but he felt it inside—a hollow
space that might not ever go away.

At least Gregor took out their leader. And I got two more, which leaves only him. After the helicopter went down, Anthony had almost chased the two survivors when he saw them climb out of the aircraft before it went over the side of the building. But the jump to the lower level of the other building was too much to risk. And besides, he had cleanup to do.

He had carried Liam's body back inside and taken the elevator down one floor, where he found a wheeled cart and a sheet to cover his partner with, along with a white lab coat for himself. In the confusion over the crash, he had managed to locate a janitor's closet, where he had wrapped Liam's body in heavy-duty garbage bags and borrowed a uniform and a janitor's cart. From there it had been a simple matter to walk out a side entrance and make his way back to the SUV, where he had ditched the cart and packed Liam inside, ignoring Gregor's questioning glance. Anthony had instead offered him a cigarette, which the tall Russian had accepted. "Covers up the smell," Anthony said, lighting up himself. He hated smoking, but didn't want to take a chance on an alert cop smelling the distinct odor of burned gunpowder.

They had slipped out of the parking structure and headed the opposite way from the sirens and cordons and roadblocks. There had been one close incident, when two police cars had blocked the street in preparation for setting up a roadblock. A car coming the other way had screeched to a halt, narrowly missing the squad car, and setting off a furious argument between the driver and the two cops. It had ended with the driver in the back of the squad car, and Anthony and Gregor being waved through with just a cursory examination of their papers, which were in perfect order.

Anthony had plotted a route out of the city, but had to admit defeat, pulling out his cell phone and hitting the speed dial, then setting the phone on the dashboard.

"You certainly know how to attract attention to yourself," the voice on the other end said.

"Sod off. My team just got cut to shit by these fuckin' assholes."

"I'm aware. By the media furor, one would think the Germans were marching down the Champs-Elysées again. And…?"

"And the bitch got away again, goddamn it. In fact, she's with the last survivor of the fucking team that tried to rescue her. Do you have anything pertinent to the situation, or are you just going to keep shitting on me?" Anthony didn't care anymore what his handler thought of him.

"Since the girl is approximately thirty kilometers away from you and traveling farther every second, I'd suggest you shut your fucking gob and listen very carefully."

Anthony looked at the phone in amazement; his handler never came close to losing his temper. "Go on," he said quietly.

"We've just concluded a deal that will deliver this woman right into our hands. All we need to do is send someone to collect her at an address in Brussels."

"Where?"

His handler supplied an address on the outskirts of the city. "You know that since she's with the other side, they will no doubt be moving reinforcements to keep what they think is theirs."

"That will not happen," Anthony said.

"Your declaration doesn't fill me with too much confidence, for while you certainly are adept at killing everyone around her, the woman keeps slipping through your fingers. Go to this airfield on the north side of town." He rattled off another address. "Transportation will be waiting for you to get to Brussels ahead of them. Once there, you will take charge of the woman and bring her back to us. You'll have everything you need to get the job done. And you'd better keep her this time—otherwise don't bother coming back."

"She'll be on your doorstep this evening. Oh, one more thing—I recovered one of ours."

"There in the vehicle with you?"

"Yes—it's Liam."

There was silence on the other end for a few seconds. "That is a pity. Let the desk person know—they'll handle it."

"Thank you."

"I'm not doing it for you. I'm doing it for him. Liam was one of our best. I'd planned to give him his own team after this one, instead of him constantly cleaning up after your messes."

"After this one, you won't have to worry about me anymore," Anthony said.

"Until you're in the grave, you'll always be a worry to me. Get the woman." The connection broke with a soft click.

That had been thirty minutes earlier, and now they were shooting toward Brussels at more than 150 miles per hour. It was fast enough to get there, find the address and set up a reception for Maggie and that bastard—one that she would never forget, and he would never survive.

34   II 1165 III I ■ I 5911 II ■I III ■ I■

Kate studied the screens floating in virtual reality around her. The largest one was keeping real-time tabs on her single Midnight Team member in France—the only link they had to the girl and the stolen data. Other monitors showed possible routes the runner could take, based on her travel so far and the statistical probability of her destinations. And on each of them were travel lines and estimated intercept times for Room 59 operatives to apprehend them.

The last screen— to which she paid only peripheral attention—was CNN. The news channel was covering the recent incident in Paris with the most aplomb, although the anchors couldn't help speculating about whether it was some kind of foiled terrorist incident or a crime gone wrong. They hadn't posted any photos of suspects yet, but Kate kept glancing over, expecting to see them as soon as the French police held a conference about it. She knew the next few hours would be critical.

At least they got out of the city, even if he hasn't been able to contact us, she told herself.

That last part was the most worrisome. An operative wasn't supposed to lose his or her phone, period. Kate had spoken to the woman who had answered David's—and who had no doubt ditched the device soon after so it couldn't be traced. She's no dummy, that's for sure. But if she'd been able to take the phone from David, why was she still taking him with her? Kate had rather expected that her operative would have been thrown out along with the phone, but instead his dot was still traveling steadily toward Belgium. Why?

A chime alerted her to more news. It was Autom8 again, looking as haggard as Kate felt. "Got a line on the car they're in. It's an '08 silver Peugeot 407. Here's the license plate number."

"Fantastic. Have you been checking the road cameras for a description?"

A small frown appeared on his face. "I was getting to that. The computers are scanning for it now. We found them about twenty miles out of Paris, and once more after that at fifty miles, then they seem to have pulled off the highway at a place called Valenciennes. Do you want to order an intercept?"

Kate scanned through her screens, bringing up a map of the area around the town. She continued her conversation while issuing orders to Judy after patching her in. "No, she's with an operative right now, and I'm assuming he is still in control of the situation at the moment. However, a surveillance team could meet them on the road into Brussels, which is her likeliest destination. But I'll assign a team to cover Calais, as well, in case she thinks she's clever—or crazy—enough to double back to England. Give the team the specs on the car, and update them every time you have a positive ID from a road camera. If Louis has a team that can get there from Paris, fine. Otherwise, scramble whoever is closest to them."

"Affirmative. Anything else?" Judy asked.

"Yes. Send Louis a request that he sanitize the bodies of the Midnight Team members killed during the incident. They must be removed from the French law enforcement and any records pertaining to them erased."

"Don't take this the wrong way, but are you sure? We just got a message suspending all French directorate activities—" Judy began.

Kate gritted her teeth in annoyance at the bureaucracy that Judy insisted upon interfering with her cleanup operation. "Put it through, and tell them this is straight from the director, and priority one—they'll get it done."

"I'll send the message, and assign someone to back-door the French mainframe."

"Thanks, and keep me updated, of course."

"Of course," Judy said.

No sooner had she disconnected than her computer chimed again. "Go for Primary."

A girl's lilting voice, accent colored with equal parts Middle Eastern and British prep school answered. "This is B2S. I have good news for a change."

Born2Slyde was the handle of the new caller, and Kate's top hacker. Like the others, she was a freelancer, although a very well paid one on permanent retainer with Room 59. When Kate had taken over as director, she had made it clear she wanted the best of the best for the electronic surveillance and infiltration department, no matter where or who they were. She knew B2S was the third daughter of a prominent oil sheikh—and just about everything else there was to know about her—Room 59's vettors being no slouches on the job themselves. In the end, it all came down to what she could do—everything but make computers stand up and dance, and Kate was pretty sure she was working on that, as well—and if she was committed to the same goals that the other operatives were, which she most certainly was. Kate often thought B2S would do what Room 59 assigned her for free, since it combined the two things she was most passionate about—hacking, and making a difference in the world.

"That would be a refreshing change of pace. What have you got?"

"Your mystery woman's name, record, basically everything I could find on her, which wasn't much. I'm posting it to you now."

Kate bolted upright, her weariness forgotten over this revelation. "B, if you were here, I'd kiss you, and never mind what anyone else would say about it."

"A simple thank-you will suffice. It's pretty standard stuff, but it was hidden mega deep. Either she's been very good at living off the grid, or she's done a fantastic job of erasing her tracks."

"Most likely the latter." A locked folder popped up on Kate's monitor, and she unlocked it and spread out the virtual pages. "Margaret Britaine, eh? You're right about not much being here—shuttled around foster homes for much of her childhood…reunited with her brother at age twelve. They've been close ever since. Awarded a full scholarship to MIT when she was sixteen, dropped out three months before graduation, then nothing for the past eleven years—until this."

"Yup. I can do some snooping around on some sites I know, see if anyone knows anything."

"Pursue anything that would help us get a lead on what she's been up to in the last decade—besides getting people killed all around her. I'm going to take a close look at what you found here and see if anything pops up. Great work, B."

"As always. I'll text you if I get a line on anything solid."

"Sounds good. Primary out." Kate took a minute to get up and stretch her cramped muscles, working out the kinks and tension from the past several hours in the chair. Walking to the minifridge, she removed a diet ginger ale from inside, glanced longingly at the tiny bottle of Jack Daniel's on the door and shook her head, popping the soda open and pouring it into a glass before returning to her chair and sitting back down and slipping her VR glasses back on.

"All right, Ms. Britaine, let's see who you really are."

35

Maggie walked out of what passed for a small strip mall in rural France, a row of shops designed to ensnare tourists that also carried enough items to serve her purposes, as well. Quick visits to a clothing store, then a grocery with a bathroom allowed her to alter her appearance yet again, leaving the old clothes in the trash and changing into comfortable jeans, a black blouse and tennis shoes. Pulling her hair back from her face, she secured it with a spiraled blue headband with a small butterfly on it. Using a bit of foundation to mask the dark circles under her eyes, she examined herself in the mirror.

Not bad. *I could pass as a young mother on vacation, or a rich girl slumming across France with my boyfriend—maybe.* She knew she had a problem, though. What was she to do with David? She certainly couldn't take him to Brussels. Leaving him here was good enough. He could get the medical attention he no doubt needed, and those other guys had to be well off their trail by now; otherwise they would have tried something already while she was stopped. Yeah, best to break this off sooner rather than later, before he tries to figure out a way to mess up my next rendezvous.

Making sure the clothes were hidden deep in the covered wastebasket, Maggie shouldered her laptop and walked out of the bathroom. Leaving the store, she slipped on a large pair of sunglasses that covered her eyes and then some as she headed for the car.

She caught David staring as she got in. "Yes?"

"Nothing, just—you clean up well."

She tossed him the extralarge light gray pullover sweatshirt, with the word Provence embroidered across the front in large blue-and-plaid letters, that she had purchased in the clothing store.

"This is certainly inconspicuous," he said.

"It fits with our new disguise of a tourist couple driving across France. I couldn't find a zip-up, sorry." Another white lie, but Maggie had told so many in the past hour, she was sure another wouldn't matter.

He gave her an odd look. "Couple, eh? I think you got the better wardrobe."

"But of course." She watched as he tried to maneuver into the garment in the cramped space. "Why don't you just step outside and slip it on? I won't go anywhere, I promise."

He nodded. Opening the door, he levered himself out with difficulty, holding the sweatshirt with his good arm. Leaving the door ajar, he began working his way into the sweatshirt.

As soon as his face disappeared into the shirt, Maggie shifted the car into gear and pulled away, careful not to hit him. Fifty feet away, she stopped, reached over and pulled the passenger's door closed, then sped away, trying not to look into the rearview mirror but unable to help herself. She saw David standing there in the parking lot, staring after her.

It's for his own good, she told herself as she found the on-ramp to the highway and took it, making sure she was headed to Brussels.

Dividing her attention between her mirrors and the speedometer, Maggie accelerated to seventy miles per hour and drove, enjoying the fact that she wasn't under anyone's thumb for the moment. It was tempting to just keep driving, to bypass Brussels and head into Germany, or Switzerland, or anywhere else, to get away from all of this violence and killing. With a weary sigh, she banished the daydream and concentrated on the task ahead of her. There was still a way to go, and there was also the matter of payment. Aragorn wasn't going to be thrilled that she couldn't give him his cut right away. But she could lead him on with a promise of riches to come once she had delivered her package. It might mean a slight renegotiation again, but for the amount she planned to make those bastards at Mercury pay, she could cut the hacker in and still have plenty left over for a long, long vacation.

The miles rolled by under the Peugeot's humming wheels, and before Maggie knew it she was nearing Brussels. Pulling off at a rest stop on the side of the road, she fired up her laptop again, and called Aragorn.

"Hello, lass. Where are you?"

"I'm about ten minutes from the city, and I wanted the directions sooner rather than later, so I can get an idea of where I'm going."

"No problem. I'm sending them right now." A

moment later, a set of directions flashed on her computer. "Follow those, and we should see you in about thirty minutes."

"Thanks, Aragorn—I won't forget this. See you soon."

"I'll be waiting for you."

Maggie closed her laptop and pulled onto the road again, leaning forward in the leather seat in her eagerness to be among friends again, and out of reach of her pursuers once and for all.

36

David watched the silver car disappear into the distance, shaking his head. I should have known not to trust her, he thought. But even more, he was disappointed that he hadn't convinced her that he really could protect her, that the men after her at the hospital would keep trying until they had caught her once and for all.

With a sigh, he walked into the nearest store and asked, in halting French and flashing a twenty-Euro note, if he could use their phone.

"This is Primary, the lock word is 'alpine.'"

"This is M-Two, the key word is 'evergreen.'" It was a risk using an unsecured line like this, but David had to report what had happened and get reinforcements after Maggie while there was still time. While he could have stolen a car and continued the chase, he was in no shape to do that, or face an unknown number of potential hostiles alone.

"One moment."

David waited for the transfer. If he had given a different word, it would have meant he was under duress, either captured or that he just couldn't talk freely. If a word was given that didn't match any of the codes for the mission, the connection would be broken, and an immediate trace would be put out to discover where the call was placed from and who had done it.

He heard a slight click. "This is Primary. Report everything that occurred after the hospital."

He kept it short, turning his back to the store clerk and keeping his voice low. "After leaving the hospital in an acquired car, subject and I proceeded north-northeast. My wounds, which the subject field-dressed, caused me to pass out for a short time, during which she discarded my cell phone. We reached the town of Valenciennes, where she eluded me and has now left the city. I'm requesting backup to continue to her target city and apprehend her."

"You're injured, and therefore not fully capable of continuing the mission. Procedure mandates that you be deactivated and called in," the voice told him.

David gritted his teeth at the standard plan, but kept his voice calm as he replied. "Primary, I'm the only one on our side who knows what she looks like, or her name, for that matter. Also, I'm the only one who knows where she's going at the moment—well, except for the hostiles."

"Her name is Margaret Britaine, but no doubt you already knew that. Are you attempting to blackmail me into letting you continue this mission?" Rather than sounding angry, David thought he detected a faint note of humor in the woman's voice, and tried to play to it.

"With respect, Primary, I prefer to think of it as laying out the reasons why I should continue the mission, even if it is in an advisory capacity."

"And?"

David frowned. "I'm sorry?"

"You have another reason for wanting to continue."

Revenge? David shook his head. "It's not what you think. This target is so important to this other team that they are willing to kill anyone who gets in their way—including the rest of my team. I want to know she's out of their hands myself, not be stuck back at HQ watching while she lives or dies."

"I can understand that. You're not personally involved with this subject, are you, M-Two?"

"Primary, the only thing I'm involved with at the moment is completing my mission, not just for myself, but for my team, as well. I don't want them to go out with a failure on the books."

"An admirable sentiment—that has absolutely no place in clandestine operations. However, your other mission-oriented points are valid. A team should be arriving to pick you up in the next three minutes. You will follow the leader's directions to the letter. Is that understood?"

"Affirmative, Primary."

"Get her back, M-Two. Good luck." With that sign-off, the connection was broken.

David hung up the phone, thanked the clerk and walked outside to wait for his pickup. He settled on a bench and idly watched people go by, coming in and out of the store, laughing chattering, living their lives, with no idea what he did to keep them safe, to let them live their lives without worry, without fear.

And now my team is gone, he thought. David knew he couldn't allow himself the luxury of wallowing in guilt at the moment. He couldn't even blame himself for Kanelo's or Cody's death. Both of them had been beyond his control. But Tara's, that had been another matter entirely.

Looking back, he knew he hadn't had a choice. If he had shot the man holding her, David would have been shot himself, and Tara would have died right after him anyway. His only chance had been to take out his own attacker, then shoot hers, except that he hadn't been fast enough. And now he never would be.

Feeling his anger growing, David took a few calming breaths just as a dark gray Range Rover pulled up in front of him. Its windshield and windows were tinted to obscure whomever was inside. The driver's door opened, and a man got out and walked up to sit next to him. He looked to be in his early fifties, with salt-and-pepper hair cropped close to his scalp, and pale blue hooded eyes that regarded him from under a heavy brow. He was dressed casually, in khakis, a button-down shirt with the sleeves rolled up to his elbows, and casual leather slip-on shoes. David was also sure he was ex-military, and even with a quarter century on him, David was pretty sure he wouldn't want to tangle with the guy—he looked as if he knew all the tricks, and wouldn't hesitate to use anything in his bag when necessary.

"Excuse me. My brothers and I are traveling to Paris, and we're wondering if there was a quicker way to get there besides the highway?" His voice was quiet and precise, with a slight, guttural German accent stressing the vowels.

David made sure he was in control of himself before he replied. "Besides the high-speed train, a car is the best mode of transportation to get to the City of Lights."

The man extended his hand. "For now, you can call me Jay. How are you, Mr. Vert?"

David smiled at the play on words—his cover name was the French word for "green." "I've been better, Jay. I'm missing something very important to me. Are you here to help me get it back?"

"That's exactly what we're here for. Come on, we can fill each other in on the way."

David rose and walked slowly to the SUV, feeling his injuries flare with each step. He was grateful for the sweatshirt he had forced himself into. It would hide his wounds quite well, as long as neither of them reopened in the next couple of hours. As he approached the vehicle, the front passenger's door opened, and a man with coal-black hair, swarthy skin and a gleaming white smile slipped out, gesturing to the front seat with a flourish. "My name is Julio. Please, Mr. Vert, you and Jay will want to talk more, I'm sure."

"Thanks." David got into the seat and closed the door, trying not to sigh with relief as he sank into the butter-soft leather. Julio got in the back, sitting next to another man, this one a nondescript Caucasian with a buzz cut and deep brown eyes who looked far too young to be in this line of work. Julio introduced him as Fritz.

Jay slid behind the wheel, started the Range Rover up, and pulled out of the parking lot. "Where's she headed?" he asked immediately.

"I'm sure she's going to Brussels. It's the nearest large city with a transportation hub. There's a bug in her car, from the other team, that I left inside the vehicle for our use."

"Good. Julio, see what you can find on the standard frequencies. Of course, since we know the make and model of her car, we can also use the GPS tracking unit on it, as well."

David turned away so his flush wouldn't be as noticeable; he should have thought of that. "I thought they'd send someone from Paris to handle this."

"You haven't heard, then?" Jay continued as David frowned. "All activity at the Paris bureau has been halted pending an investigation of the incident earlier today. It seems that the backup operatives for your team were incapacitated at the station before the firefight broke out. That, and how the situation escalated, is going to cause some harsh questions up and down the line before this is all over."

"Are the operatives all right?" David asked.

"They're fine, but there were several civilians injured or killed in the standoff between the police and one of the hostile team members. Apparently he killed himself rather than be taken alive."

David nodded. "We didn't have any choice—"

Jay held up his hand. "At this point, I don't really care what happened back there. My goal—and yours, too—is to get the subject back in our control before they find her again. Put all the second-guessing and evaluation away. There will be plenty of time for it later. Now, tell me everything you know about our target, followed by everything you know about the hostiles."

David took a moment, mentally gathering what scattered bits of information he had observed over the past twelve hours, and started talking. "The woman's name is Maggie—Margaret Britaine. She's a data thief…."

As he spoke, he felt the man known as Jay absorbing every word he said, measuring it, sifting his comments for the useful data and discarding the rest. I only hope this helps us when the time comes, he thought as he told them everything he knew about her and the men they were almost sure to be going up against.

37

The directions Aragorn had given Maggie were perfect, taking her up the A7 to the outskirts of Brussels. On her left, Maggie saw a large hospital complex, but she was driving past it, out into the countryside. The road turned to a narrower two-lane street known only as Postweg, and Maggie slowed when she saw the first sign, scanning the right side of the road intently. She drove past what looked like a huge manufacturing plant, then saw green fields next to it, and a short row of tile-roofed, plain one- and two-story houses on her left.

On the other side of the road, just beyond where that row ended, was the building she was searching for. It sat alone, a larger dark gray house with what looked like a low stone fence marking its perimeter. As she approached, she saw a large hedgerow stretch off to the north, obviously the demarcation of an ample yard. There was a broad parking lot stretching the full length of the building's front side, and Maggie wondered if this was some kind of bed-and-breakfast for the area, even though there were no signs advertising it as such.

Maybe I can get something to eat before we go, she thought. Although she had eaten on the train, it seemed as if that hurried meal had been ages ago, and now that she would be safe as soon as she walked through that front door, her stomach growled in anticipation.

Parking the car, she engaged the emergency brake, then realized she had no way of turning off the Peugeot. There was no key, or key card, as many European cars used, and David's phone was probably in a junkyard by now. With a shrug, she left it running and got out, carrying her laptop. If anyone comes along, they can have it, she thought wearily. She climbed the wide concrete steps, and tried the heavy, dark brown, wooden door, pleased when it swung open toward her.

Inside, Maggie was greeted by the odors of must and rot. She stood in a small foyer that opened into a common area, with a small desk built into the wall to her right. What had once been a cozy, furnished living room years ago was now taken over by neglect and decay. The matching wingback chairs were faded, with large water spots on the arms and seat from the leaking ceiling. The small table in the middle of the room was also dilapidated, its once smooth finish now bumpy and cracked. A narrow hallway led to the back half of the house, but Maggie stayed where she was, unwilling to explore the unfamiliar surroundings any further. The air was as cold as it was outside, and Maggie wrapped her arms around herself as she walked farther into the room.

She felt a sudden chill at being there. Her overtaxed mind raced, thinking up horrible things that might have happened to the occupants of the house before it was deserted. Then she got a firm mental grip on herself. *Stop jumping at shadows. It's the perfect place to meet without anyone else taking an interest in what's going on.*

"Aragorn? It's me, Mags. You can come out anytime now." Her voice sounded loud in the silence, and Maggie kept looking around, wondering where he was. *If this is his idea of a joke, it's in pretty fuckin' poor taste—*

"Hey, you." She recognized Aragorn's voice before he stepped out of the shadows in the hallway, his tall, lean body clad in a long, dark brown, leather trench coat. On most other people it would have seemed like an affectation, but he wore it well, and the garment suited his shock of unruly dark blond hair and hazel eyes. Once, Maggie had been attracted to him, but she had soon realized that Aragorn was nothing like his fictional namesake—he was a vain hedonist, a hacker who loved to be the center of attention, and often would go to outlandish lengths to put the spotlight on himself. He also had a powerful attraction to money, which, of course, was why he was here for her. Still, at that moment, he looked like a divine vision, and Maggie ran to him and hugged him hard.

"Damn, it's good to see you. You have no idea what I've gone through just to get here—"

Maggie trailed off, aware that something was wrong. Aragorn wasn't returning her hug, in fact, he had stiffened at her touch. "Hey, Gorn, what's wrong?"

"I'm afraid you're not out of the woods yet, Maggie." He disentangled himself from her embrace and stepped around her into the foyer, revealing another man who'd been standing behind him, now coming forward into the gray afternoon light.

"Hello again, Ms. Britaine. You certainly have a knack for getting yourself out of unpleasant situations. But that all ends now." The grim, unsmiling face of the man who had tried to kidnap her at the train station—a face she had hoped never to see again except in her nightmares—was right in front of her again.

"Aragorn, why?" She looked to him, hoping that there was a reasonable answer for all of this, hoping he would say they had forced him to do this. The expression on his face, however, said such things.

"Sorry, Mags, but you should have been more honest with me in the first place. You got me curious about just who you had crossed, so I did some poking around. A friend of a friend told me there was a PMC spending a lot of time looking for someone who had done a huge hack job in London, where you had just been. Well, I put two and two together, and made them an offer they couldn't refuse."

"You son of a bitch!" Aragorn hadn't moved that far off, and Maggie's roundhouse slap caught him completely by surprise, the sharp crack resounding in the squalid room. Aragorn reeled away, his hand going to his reddening cheek in shock. The other man said nothing, didn't even shake his head or crack a smile.

"You fucking bitch!" Aragorn had regained his composure, and now glared at her, his eyes blazing. "Always lording over the rest of us, thinking you were better than everyone else. How's it feel now? How high-and-mighty do you feel now, you arrogant ass?"

"There were times I didn't like you very much, but I never would have sold you out, you fucking, betraying bastard—" Maggie's legs wobbled, and she stumbled to the nearest chair. "Oh God, I'm going to be sick." She hunched over, clutching her stomach with both arms while trying to figure a way out of this mess. The car! If she could just reach the still running car, she had a chance.

Aragorn gloated over her distress. "You're going to feel a whole lot worse when they're done with you, my dear." He turned to the silent man. "Well, there she is. Once your people have transferred the agreed amount to my Swiss account, she's all yours."

"Yes, you've done exactly what was asked of you, and you shall receive the price that is due." The man pulled out a small cell phone, and Aragorn, visions of his payoff dancing behind his eyes, turned back to Maggie, a fatuous smirk on his face. He didn't see the silenced pistol the man drew with his other hand. Before Maggie could say anything, he placed the muzzle an inch from the back of Aragorn's head and pulled the trigger.

A gout of blood and brains spurted from the hacker's eye socket as his short-circuiting body crashed to the floor, arms and legs twitching in shocked response to the assassination. Maggie stared in shock, but realized that if she had any chance of escaping, it had to be right now, as the man was still checking the dead body.

She forced her leaden limbs to move, rising from the chair and grabbing the table. With all her remaining strength, she threw the sagging piece of furniture at him, the veneered top spinning through the air toward the hired killer. Maggie didn't wait to see if it hit him, but ran for the front exit. Rebounding off the desk, she scrambled toward the door, fingers questing for the handle, knowing she only had one chance to get it open and get out before he caught her. She grabbed, pushed and almost fell out onto the concrete steps.

Outside, everything was as she had left it—the idling car, the quiet cluster of houses down the road, the leaden sky overhead. Sobbing with fear, Maggie flew down the steps to the car, wrenched the driver's door open and threw herself behind the wheel. She fumbled for the gearshift with fingers numbed by fright, and had just jammed the car into Reverse when the hood of the Peugeot seemed to flex and groan as something thudded into it. Maggie watched in dumbfounded fascination as a neat row of holes appeared in the front of the car, causing the engine to sputter and hiss. With the realization she was being shot at, she pressed the gas pedal to the floor, but the once pristine car only shook and jerked, rolling a few yards, then wheezing to a halt as its engine died.

Maggie knew that her attempt to escape was not going to go unpunished. All she could do was watch in helpless, frozen terror as the man strode down the steps of the house toward the car. Without pausing, he raised his arm and hammered the butt of his pistol on the window glass, shattering it into hundreds of pieces that sprayed across her. Reaching in, he grabbed her neck and dragged her out of the car.

Maggie's hands pried at the fingers clamped around her neck like bands of steel, trying to dislodge them, but to no avail. He hauled her out of the dead vehicle, then raised his pistol again and slammed the butt across her mouth, sending her sprawling to the ground. Through the shocking pain, as Maggie spit out thick, red blood and a broken tooth, she was dimly aware that her captor was speaking. Suddenly her head was wrenched back, and she stared into the dark, black hole of the man's pistol, still smoking from when he had shot Aragorn. Is this the last thing my brother saw before he died? she wondered.

"I'm through being nice. The next time you try to escape, I will shoot you in the wrist. If you try again, I will shoot you in the elbow and keep moving up your arm. Do you understand?"

Holding her mouth, Maggie nodded, a dim part of her brain aware that she had no fight left in her.

"All right. Get up." He waved to another man, who had been positioned in the second-story window, a sub-machine gun in his grasp. "Do exactly as I say, and I won't have to do that again—"

His attention was drawn to the road, where a speeding gray SUV was heading right for them. He grabbed Maggie's arm and yanked her to her feet. "Into the house, now!"

38

"There she is!" David could only watch as the brown-haired man pulled Maggie toward the building. His arm extended, pistol aimed at them, rounds spitting from it to strike the SUV's bulletproof windshield.

"Hang on." Jay cranked the wheel over, sending the SUV skidding into the parking lot. "Julio, Fritz, there's a shooter on the second story."

"I see him." The two men in the backseat had produced two compact HK MP-7 A-1 submachine guns, inserting magazines and pulling back the cocking levers with practiced efficiency.

"I'll pull up to block the front. Once we're inside, take the upstairs man out or force him to cover, then head round back to cut them off. Mr. Vert and I will take the front." He nodded at David. "Open the glove compartment."

David did so, finding an HK USP 4.6 mm pistol resting in a special compartment, its butt protruding toward him. Next to it were two full magazines. He drew it and checked the load, keeping the gun near his waist to not aggravate his injured arm, and slipped the spare magazines into his back pocket. "I'm ready," he said.

"Okay, here we go." Jay hit the brakes, stopping the vehicle right in front of the door, cutting off most of the avenue of fire the second-story man had enjoyed until now. It did not stop the hail of bullets that were still thudding into the roof, however.

"David, give me covering fire," Julio said.

David and Julio both rolled down their windows and pointed their guns toward the upper window, triggering several rounds from each weapon. Glass shattered and wood splinters rained down on them as the bullets chewed up the front facade.

"Fire in the hole!" Julio held the live flash-bang grenade for a second after he had pulled the pin, then launched it toward the window. His timing was perfect.

The flash-bang went off in the window frame with a bright burst of light and a loud bang, even outside. As soon as it did, David ran around the front of the SUV, following Jay, who was at the top of the steps. He looked back to see Julio and Fritz checking around the front corners of the house before progressing down the sides.

"Go!" he told Jay, who pulled the door open and covered the right side, while David held his pistol steady and watched the left. No gunfire answered their preliminary recon, so Jay motioned David inside, holding the door open and covering him.

Pistol out in front, David crept inside, walking heel-toe and making sure of each step before placing his foot down. The entryway was a prime ambush site, with a built-in counter to his right, and what appeared to be a living room to his left. Ahead, a dark hallway stretched a few yards to open into another room, but he couldn't see any details.

He took another cautious step into the house, and what did leap out at him immediately was the smoking object that skittered along the floor toward him, his mind recognizing what it was even as he dived into the living room.

"Grenade!" he shouted.

David landed on the thin carpet with an impact that sent pain shooting through his body. He tried to protect his injured shoulder as much as possible, but the injury still hurt with new agony. Mouth open, ears covered, he drew his legs up and had just enough time to hope the wall between him and the grenade would be solid enough to protect him.

The detonation burst through the room in a clap of thunder, the pressure wave pushing over him as plaster and smoke billowed out of the hallway. David grabbed his pistol from the floor and covered the hallway, expecting an attacker to come charging in at any second. He heard the door creak open again, and Jay's low voice calling out.

"Vert?"

David spit plaster dust out and called back. "On your left." He rose to his feet, aware of warm stickiness that had penetrated the bandage on his side. Creeping to the edge of the now pockmarked wall, he saw Jay near the counter, uninjured. He pointed at the hallway. "It came from back there."

"You okay?" Jay's eyes dropped to David's left side. He glanced down to see a dark blotch staining his sweatshirt. "Yeah, just a flesh wound. I'm fine." His words were interrupted by a sound like a long strip of cloth being torn coming from somewhere outside. David peered into the gloom, trying to make out anything. "Did they get out?"

An answering burst came from above them, shells rattling on the floor over their heads. "There's your answer. Let's take him out and secure the high ground. The boys will keep anyone at the back door pinned down until we can reinforce them."

They leapfrogged down the hallway, each one taking a step forward, then covering the other as he advanced. At the entrance to what looked like a kitchen, Jay indicated for David to head left, and he would go right, both of them sweeping and clearing the room in approved procedure. David nodded, and they burst into the space, weapons up and tracking any movement that might be hostile.

Silence and emptiness greeted them. Light green cabinets and avocado countertops ringed the kitchen, with a dusty Formica table on its side against the far right wall. A stairway headed up, next to a door that might have been a pantry, or it might have led to a basement. Evidence of movement was everywhere on the dirty linoleum floor, but before David could make sense of it, Jay was at the stairs, submachine gun leading, listening for any movement above them. He pointed at David and himself, then up the stairs.

David nodded, walking to the right side and covering the stairway, then motioning for Jay to go up. The older man was noiseless as he ascended the staircase, ghosting up what should have normally been a creaky set of wooden steps. They didn't make a sound under his feet.

Another burst of silenced submachine gun fire came from above them, the noise allowing Jay to reach the top of the stairs. He checked the landing, then waved David up.

Sticking to the edge of the stairs so he wouldn't alert their quarry to their presence—David sneaked up to stand behind Jay, who had readied another flash-bang grenade. The room beyond had fallen completely silent. Jay pointed at himself, then straight out along the nearest wall of the room, then at David, motioning for him to go around the corner and clear the right. David nodded, feeling the familiar adrenaline surge he always felt before entering a hostile, unknown room.

Holstering his pistol, Jay made sure David was ready, counting down from three before pulling the pin, tossing the flash-bang into the next room, then clapping his hands over his ears. David did the same, opening his mouth again to equalize the pressure as the grenade detonated.

The moment it went off, Jay drew and rushed along the far wall, covering the left side. David rounded the corner and swept his area of the small room, ducking to avoid hitting his head on the sloped ceiling. This room had been cleared out, leaving no furniture behind. Except for the smoldering remains of the grenade in the middle of the room, and a few dozen shell casings on the floor, it was empty.

"Clear!" David whispered, not wanting to alert the gunman in the event he was hiding somewhere nearby. The window that opened out to the back had been smashed out completely, a weak breeze stirring the light blue curtains framing it. David pointed at the opening, then up on the roof. Jay nodded and crept over to the left side of the window. Just as he hit the wall, a burst of fire stitched through the ceiling, bullets thudding into the middle of the floor in small clouds of dust, sending wood splinters flying. David turned away, not wanting to catch a fragment in the eye. It was followed by another burst, this one only a yard or so away from David, then a third one that tore the roof open near Jay's head. No sooner had the submachine gun fire died away than the roar of an SUV engine sounded from the backyard.

David stepped beside the window, pressing his back against the frame to steady himself as he peeked out over the yard and saw a black van accelerating toward the left side of the house. Gunfire flashed from the corner, then David heard a surprised shout, three shots, then a loud thud.

Grabbing the top of the window frame, he pulled himself up onto the ledge, feeling the sharp burn of his injured shoulder and warm, sticky blood flowing as the wound reopened. He stood, peeking his head out and looking up.

The shooter, a very tall man with short black hair, stood at the edge of the roof on the left side of the house, his head down, poised as if to jump. Holding on to the roof edge with his wounded arm, the pain throbbing through his upper body, David managed to get his pistol up and aimed at the man.

Lining up the three-dot sights, he was about to squeeze the trigger when the tall man looked in his direction, his eyes widening at the sight. He swiveled at the hips, bringing his short-barreled submachine gun around to fire. Before he could, however, David squeezed the trigger of his pistol three times, the small bullets punching into the guy's chest.

At the same time, a burst from the other window hit

the gunman in the back, making him stagger and step off the roof, pitching over without a sound. David glanced over to see Jay, who'd apparently had the same idea, propped up on the other side, subgun held in both hands. A second later, there was a meaty thump, as if someone had pitched a pig carcass off the side. Jay's head disappeared as David heard automatic fire from the parking lot out front.

"Shit!" Sweating and shaking, David slowly lowered himself back inside, mindful that he could easily take the same route to the ground the shooter had if he wasn't careful. Only when his feet touched the floor did he breathe easier.

Jay stood at the other window, firing at an unseen target. "Damn, they're armored, as well." He whirled and headed for the stairway. "Julio's down—come on!" He pounded down the stairs in huge steps, with David behind him, struggling to catch up. On the main level, he followed Jay out the door and around the corner, where Fritz was already tending to Julio, who lay on the ground, clutching his side and groaning. The roof shooter lay unmoving a few feet away, his legs twisted beneath his body, a submachine gun in the dirt near his limp hand. His open, sightless eyes confirmed his death.

Fritz looked up, his unlined face furrowed as David and Jay ran over. "That bastard nailed him pretty good, threw him hard into the wall. He's got broken ribs, maybe a punctured lung—I'm not sure."

Indeed, Julio didn't look well at all, gasping for breath as his normally caramel-colored face turned a flushed pink. His voice still worked, however. "Get—that—motherfucker—" he gasped in between breaths.

Jay produced a small medical kit and tossed it to

Fritz. "Call the local hospital. They can send an ambulance. Use the Good Samaritan cover. We'll grab the SUV and go."

Fritz had pulled open Julio's shirt and was gently probing his abdomen, eliciting small gasps of pain when his fingers touched the other man's skin. "We'll be all right. Get after them, before they get away," he said.

Jay slapped David's shoulder. "Let's go."

David followed him to the SUV, which bore plenty of evidence that their enemy had tried to take it out. The grille was punctured and broken from multiple bullet hits, but Jay barely glanced at it as he ran to the driver's side. "Come on!"

David scrambled for the passenger's seat, getting in as Jay fired the engine and took off, rocketing onto the road in a squeal of tires.

"How's your side?" Jay asked.

David grimaced when he saw how far the bloodstain had spread. "It hurts—a lot."

"Are you good to keep going?"

David probed his side, and gritted his teeth. "I'm okay, but I could use a pick-me-up."

"There's a case in the back—get what you need there."

David turned in his seat and saw a small case, similar to the one Jay had tossed Fritz, on the seat behind him. Grabbing it, he pushing it open and found the stimulant he needed, popping the small red pill out of its foil and swallowing it dry. Tucking his pistol away for the moment, he leaned back in the seat and buckled up as Jay pushed the SUV harder after the fleeing van.

39

Anthony cursed as he saw Gregor fall off the roof. Pressing on the gas, he headed for the road, but stopped when he saw the SUV parked outside the front of the house. Rolling his window down, he sent a burst of bullets into the front of the vehicle, hoping to disable it, but no sooner had he started firing than the van shook from the impact of bullets hitting its roof and side. Growling, he hit the gas again and roared onto the road, the vehicle slewing back and forth as he headed due west.

In the passenger's seat, Maggie was huddled against the far door, curled in on herself. The blood on her face had clotted and caked, making her look as if she had smeared dark, reddish-brown lipstick all over her mouth and chin. She didn't move, didn't look at Anthony, which was just fine with him. Having broken her, he was concentrating on one thing only—getting to the helicopter and getting the hell out of there.

It had been a near enough thing already. Despite

hitting the back door right after throwing that frag grenade into the front room, they had nearly been caught in the ambush by the other two shooters. If Gregor hadn't been able to drive the one on the right corner back under cover for a moment, allowing Anthony to keep the left one's head down, he never would have made it to the van. The thump as he had rammed the guy on the left had been most satisfying, but not at the cost of Gregor's life. Unfortunately, there was nothing to be done about that now—not when he had what he had come here for, risked his life for and would now deliver safely to his company, no matter what the cost. Anthony had the girl and her computer, and no one was going to prevent him from getting her back to Mercury headquarters.

In the passenger's seat, the girl's head rose a fraction, and she seemed to be looking at something other than the floor. Anthony checked his rearview mirror.

"Goddamn it!"

Coming up behind them was the same dark gray SUV, with the old man and that fucking guy again, and it was gaining fast.

In the heavy, slower van, Anthony had no hope of outrunning them. But he had another trick up his sleeve. "Okay, boys, come on—just a little bit closer." Opening the glove compartment, he pressed two buttons, then gripped the joystick that popped up when he activated the defense system. His lips peeled back from his teeth in a feral grin as the SUV grew larger and larger in his mirror. Just a little closer, he thought. Then you're gonna get the surprise of the rest of your very short lives.

40

"Pop the storage compartment in the cargo area. We're going to need something bigger to take this thing out," Jay said as he leaned forward in his seat, as if he could somehow help the SUV go faster.

David reclined his seat and scrambled into the rear passenger's compartment. The pill was already working, reducing the aches in his side and shoulder to mere twinges. He felt energized, wide-awake and ready to take on anyone. He knew that was also a notorious side effect of the medication, and tried to keep his mind clear so that he wouldn't go charging off into certain death. Reaching down to the floor of the cargo area, he pulled up the rough cloth covering, revealing the cross-hatch-stamped metal covering of a secret compartment.

"Standard code?" he called out.

"Yeah," Jay replied.

The codes to unlock certain parts of a Room 59 vehicle varied, depending on what day of the month it was. David ran the equation in his head and punched in the numbers. The panel recessed and slid away. "Yeah, this'll definitely help." He bypassed the submachine guns and rifles in favor of a drab green-and-black weapon that looked like a bulky, futuristic automatic shotgun. Grabbing a magazine, he slammed it into the empty well in the weapon's stock, then primed it.

"I just heard from Fritz. The Brussels police are on-site, and so is an ambulance. They're radioing the surrounding towns to be on the lookout for us, so—*Gott in himmel.*"

Jay's abrupt utterance made David turn to look out the window. What he saw made his jaw drop, the XM25 grenade launcher almost forgotten in his hands.

Jay had approached to within twenty yards of the van, which would have been almost too close to use the launcher in the first place. However, a large panel had opened up on the top of the van, and David saw something he hadn't expected to see outside of armored personnel carriers in Third World countries.

A large machine gun, mounted on an independently moving pintle and frame, had popped out of the roof, its perforated, air-cooled barrel pointing directly at them. Jay swerved the SUV to the right just as the automatic weapon roared, releasing a burst of bullets that slammed into the road next to them, blowing chunks of asphalt into the air.

"Jesus Christ, is that a Ma Deuce?" Still holding the grenade launcher, David turned around in the backseat and opened the door, locking it in place. He flipped down the platform that would enable him to stand behind the door to use it as cover while he fired at the van. Even though the SUV was covered in Level 4 armor, he also knew that if a .50-caliber shell hit the door, it would punch right through it, and him, as well.

"Yes, it most certainly is." Even with this new development, Jay's voice remained calm. "Good thing he doesn't have a copilot in there, or we'd be dead already—he must be aiming it himself." The German cursed and wrenched the wheel over, nearly dislodging David, who had just managed to buckle himself in to the safety strap on the reinforced door. "You better take that gun out quick—I don't know how long I can keep playing hide-and-seek."

"Can you get alongside? Better chance of trying for a tire." The wind rushing around the door whipped past David's head, making him squint as he focused on his target weaving back and forth on the road ahead, trying to line them up in his sights.

"He's blocking both lanes. I can't risk putting the SUV in the ditch. Besides, that .50-caliber has a good arc of fire—he might be able to tag us anyway. Hold on!"

Jay tried to swerve out of the way of another burst. This time he wasn't so lucky. The bullets chewed into the front driver's-side panel of the SUV, piercing the rolled steel–lined body panel and hitting the tire, which burst, sending the SUV's corner lurching down for a moment before the run-flat propped it up.

Jay hunched over the steering wheel, trying to minimize his profile in the driver's seat. "We can't take another hit like that—you ready?"

"Just give me three seconds!" David snugged the butt of the XM25 into his shoulder and put his eye to the built-in targeting scope, which used a laser rangefinder to give the exact distance between the launcher and the target and adjust the fuse on the grenade itself, making it detonate at the most optimal time, allowing for increased lethality. The only problem was whether the system could compensate for a moving target, not to mention that David was not exactly on a stable platform himself. "Hold it steady!" he shouted.

"Easier said than done!" To his credit, Jay did his best, jinking left, then right, then left again and falling back suddenly. "Hit it!"

The deceleration caught David by surprise, but he adjusted and set the sight on the heavy machine gun that was already tracking toward them. He got a firm tone, then squeezed the trigger just as the .50-caliber spit another long burst at them. The SUV's windshield exploded, the bulletproof glass fragmenting under the ball ammunition's onslaught. David huddled behind his armored door, praying that he wasn't going to die from either the SUV rolling over or a bullet punching through his gut.

The clamor of the rounds piercing the upper part of the Range Rover's roof was almost immediately drowned out by the blast of the 25 mm grenade exploding within a yard of the machine gun. The gun immediately stopped firing, its barrel sagging toward the ground.

Jay poked his head up from underneath the dashboard. "You okay?"

David clung to his moving barricade, checking to see if all of his body parts were still intact. "Yeah, so far so good. Give me another shot at that SOB, will you?"

"Sure, if I can drive a straight line!" The Range Rover was wobbling severely, throwing David's aim off each time he tried to draw a bead.

"Stop the vehicle!" he shouted, slamming into the door barrier as the SUV screeched to a halt. David put his eye to the scope again and aimed at the back of the fleeing van. He waited until he got lock on again, then pumped two rounds at the back of his target.

The van's cargo area might have survived one detonation, but two were beyond even its reinforced capability. The first round impacted on the rear doors, punching one in and tearing the other off completely. The second one hit low, and blew out both rear tires, sending the back of the van crashing to the ground in a spray of sparks as it ground to a halt about two hundred yards away.

Through the sight, David saw the brown-haired man stagger out of the van, dragging Maggie with him into a nearby field, where a helicopter was waiting, its rotor already whirling lazily around. He swung over and got a lock on the chopper, but stopped. "They're heading for the helicopter—I don't want to hit it, the shrapnel might take them out, too!"

"Hold on!" Jay floored the gas pedal again, sending the limping, shuddering SUV off-road. David wrestled himself back into the backseat, leaving the door open in case he needed to get out quickly.

Although they closed the distance quickly, their targets reached the helicopter first, and David watched the man shove Maggie aboard. "Get closer!" he urged.

Jay obeyed, gunning the engine, and sending the crippled Range Rover hurtling over the grassy field. David dropped the launcher and jammed the HK pistol into his waistband. They were only about fifty yards away, but the helicopter's blades were whirling even faster now, as the man climbed in and pulled the door closed behind him. Through the window, he grinned wickedly at them, and shook his head as he tapped the pilot on the shoulder.

"Faster, Jay!"

"This is all she's got!"

The chopper's rotor sliced through the air, straining to haul the aircraft aloft. David knew there was only one chance left. "Drive underneath it!" Opening the door again, he climbed onto the roof, spread-eagled to maintain his position. A wrong jolt or bump at this speed would send him flying, and probably kill him on impact.

The helicopter had gotten enough lift, and slowly rose off the ground. Somehow, Jay managed to coax an extra burst of speed out of the laboring SUV, and brought the vehicle right below the rising aircraft. The downdraft from the rotor flattened David against the roof, but he got to his knees in time to wrap his arms around the landing skid just as the helicopter cleared the Range Rover's roof and accelerated into the air.

41

Kate rubbed her eyes, trying to clear the graininess out of them. Her palms weren't much help. Now up for more than thirty-four hours, the world had taken on that slightly surreal aspect that she had never liked with sleep deprivation. It was as if everything around her were one tenth of a second off—just enough lag to notice, but not enough to be able to focus on and fix. Blinking, she considered mainlining another shot of espresso, but decided to hold off for now.

An insistent beep from her computer slowly drew her attention. Answering it brought another young hacker on-screen. Automa8 had logged off after a full day of demanding duty, but only at Kate's direct order. He would have much rather stayed on until the mission was completed, but she had insisted, wanting her people as fresh and alert as possible. Unlike myself, she admitted.

Still, at least her avatar projected the composed, confident aura that Kate usually wore like invisible armor. "Yes."

"I've got Jay on the line for you. He's already passed our security check."

"Put him through." The man called Jay was, in actuality, Jonas Schrader, Room 59's Eastern European director. While normally his attention would have been directed on the reemerging, post–Cold War Russia and other former Soviet Bloc countries, Kate had needed someone she could absolutely trust to get the job done in Brussels, and had tapped him. Although almost sixty years old, he had the body of a man fifteen years younger, and was still incredibly capable. A founding member of GSG-9, Jonas was also an accomplished sniper. That skill probably wouldn't come in handy on this mission—at least, not as far as she knew, but from what had happened up to this point, who could tell anymore. However, he had many other talents that had probably already come into play. Kate's fatigue fell away as she heard his calm voice.

"Primary, this is Jay. There have been some complications on this end."

Kate sighed. "Jay, that is not how I expect your reports to begin."

"There was little choice in the matter. We moved to reacquire the target at a meeting house, but encountered the other hostiles there, who tried to set up an a ambush. We took out one, and had one of our own injured. I think he'll be all right, but we'll have to get him and Julio out of the country."

"That's the least of our worries right now. Go on."

"Mr. Vert and I pursued the hostile into the countryside—no doubt there will be a report on the local news about it shortly—where they pulled a heavy machine gun on us. It was built into their vehicle."

"Jesus—are you okay?"

"*Ja,* I'm still breathing. Mr. Vert disabled the gun with a well-placed grenade and then stopped their vehicle, but they managed to make it to their escape helicopter. Mr. Vert decided to follow."

Kate nodded in relief. "So he's aboard, as well."

"In a manner of speaking—he grabbed on to the landing gear as they took off."

"Oh, God." Headlines sprang unbidden into her mind: Secret Agent Splattered Over Belgian Countryside. "Where are they headed?"

"Toward the coast. I expect the hostile is headed back to his base of operations, once he shakes off his unwanted passenger."

"What about you?" Kate asked.

"I set the SUV to self-destruct. It was too heavily damaged to keep using. I proceeded on foot into the nearby fields. I'm about a quarter-mile away from where I last saw Mr. Vert on the helicopter. They were traveling north-northwest on a heading of 295. I'm still moving, and will circle back around into Brussels and withdraw from there."

Kate rubbed her temples and checked the virtual screen for David's locator chip. It still glowed a steady green. "Well, he's still alive, I can tell you that, so I can only assume he's trying to gain control of the aircraft. We'll try to get a fix on him, but you just concentrate on getting out of the country right now. We'll assist your other team members immediately. If Julio can be moved, we should have him back in our care as soon as this evening."

"Thanks, Primary. Anything else at this time?"

Only my wish that you were up there assisting

David, Kate thought. "No, Jay, we'll get your full debriefing later. Keep moving, and good luck."

"One last thing, Primary."

About to log off, Kate paused. "Yes?"

"Don't count Mr. Vert out. From what I've seen of him, if there is a way to get this job done, I believe he'll find it."

"I hope you're right, Jay, I really do. Primary out." Kate disconnected the call and brought up the VR ops room again, bringing the screen with David's chip on it, which, knowing the circumstances, was currently moving much faster than she would have liked over the Belgian-French border.

42

Okay, maybe this wasn't such a good idea, David thought.

He had managed to pull himself up to where the skid met with the strut that attached to the underside of the aircraft. At the moment, however, that was about all he could do. The buffeting wind stream felt as if it were clawing at him with a thousand icy fingers. His hands were already turning numb in the frigid atmosphere, and every second he stayed outside was one more that he risked falling to his death.

It was at that moment that the door above him opened, and David saw the now familiar face of the brown-haired man as he extended a leg to kick him off the skid. He quickly scooted backward down to the rear strut and out of range. However, the man brought a pistol up in his hand and took aim at David, who had nowhere to go.

His fingers scrabbled for his own pistol, yanking it from his waistband and bringing it up as he hooked his leg around the strut and swung under the fuselage, only exposing a small part of himself. His injured arm quivered with the strain, feeling the pain even through the numbing stimulant. David waited, knowing that the man would either blow off his kneecap or come out to try to shoot him face-to-face. He hoped it would be the latter, as unlikely as that seemed.

A spark flashed off the metal of the strut as a bullet came within inches of his leg. The bastard's toying with me! David looked down to make sure he hadn't been grazed by a ricochet, as the drug he'd taken could block nerve impulses enough that he might have been injured and not know it. Not only was he unhurt, but he also saw the safety strap from the SUV, with its sturdy buckle, was still around his waist.

Wrapping his uninjured arm around the strut, David aimed his gun near the passenger's compartment, but not into it or near the rotor. He fired several rounds to keep his opponent's head down. He tried to see if the man was still outside, but didn't want to risk leaning out far enough to expose himself again.

Tucking his pistol into his pants, he turned around so that he was sitting facing the strut. Using his injured arm, he ran the strap between his body and the skid to hold it in place in the energy-sapping wind. Once it was around the thick metal tube, he clicked it back in place, securing himself to the metal bar. Far below, the Belgian landscape, a patchwork of fields, trees and small towns, seemed so very far away. David figured they had to be at least five thousand feet high, give or take a few hundred. More than enough to kill him from sudden deceleration trauma, as his Marine buddies had joked more than once about falling out of helicopters back in Afghanistan.

The passenger's door opened again as the helicopter turned right and dived steeply, the pilot obviously trying to shake him off. Ignoring the flare of pain in his side, David drew his legs up and turned around so that his back was to the strut. He managed to wrap his legs around the skid as the helicopter leveled off. The sudden altitude changes, dips and swerves were making his head spin. Groping for his pistol, he drew it as the man leaned out the door again, his own gun in hand, and now secured to something inside the helicopter, as there was a safety harness visible around his chest. Even with that, he kept a tight grip on the helicopter's door frame.

Their eyes met. In that second, David knew it was likely he was going to die. It was only a matter of whether he would get his shot off first. He lined up the pistol and brought pressure down on the trigger with his numb fingers, praying he could fire before taking the bullet he knew would be coming for him.

HUDDLED IN THE CORNER of the helicopter's seat, Maggie wavered on the edge of near catatonic shock. The events of the past few minutes had rushed over her in a frightening blur—Aragorn's betrayal and his almost casual execution, the assault on the house, their subsequent flight. She still saw that man's face in her mind's eye as her captor had run him down like a stray dog, with bullets chipping at the windshield, and her screams stuck in her throat…. During the hurried chase down the road, whatever weapon he had been firing made such an earsplitting racket that all she could do was cover her ears and try to shrink even further from the emotionless, unstoppable killer holding her prisoner.

When the back of the van had blown up, a part of

Maggie had almost cried with relief, because she'd figured they would stop running, that they had finally been caught. She almost didn't believe it when he'd pulled her out of the wrecked vehicle and dragged her to the helicopter. By that time, she was too far gone to even try to resist, couldn't muster up the will to attempt to escape, couldn't do anything but go along with him since the alternative would have been far worse. She had stumbled to the aircraft and collapsed into her seat as they took off, registering the thump of something hitting the aircraft's underside, but not really caring.

Her captor did, however, muttering under his breath and opening the door to step outside for a moment, then coming back in and rummaging under the seat for something.

The pilot got the man's attention, and they had a hurried, shouted conversation over the roar of the engine, most likely, Maggie thought, about why the man had stepped out of the helicopter. It was apparently resolved to their satisfaction, as the pilot suddenly put the helicopter into a steep dive that threw her against her seat belt, which she didn't even remember buckling around her waist. The man came back to his seat and found the thing he was looking for, an orange woven-nylon harness that he buckled around his chest. When he glanced at her, Maggie looked away, even as a thought rose in her head, one that she hadn't allowed herself to think, but which now cut through the fog of terror and shock to focus her mind.

That man killed my brother.

It was an inescapable fact. She hadn't seen the face of the man who had coldly placed three bullets into her only living relative, the one person she had relied on for the past thirteen years. But she was sure it was him. It was in the way he moved, with a singular, ruthless efficiency. It was in his eyes, his stance, his casual brutality. He was a man who used violence like other people used a spoon—as an effective tool to get the results he wanted, and one of the casualties had been Ray.

He was preparing to open the door again, having secured the safety harness to a metal ring that he had raised from its recess in the floor. While seeming to stare at the floor in front of her, Maggie watched him out of the corner of her eye, that one thought looming larger and larger in her mind.

That man killed my brother.

Her fingers went to her bruised and tender jaw, gingerly exploring the swelling there, feeling the cracked bone and the space where her tooth had been. She felt the flash of pain that accompanied her touch. Instead of impeding her, the sting did the opposite, clearing her brain of the numbing cloud that had settled over it, and letting her think clearly for the first time since she had left the house where her brother had died.

The man opened the door. The wind filled the cabin, rippling Maggie's clothes and making her squint her eyes at the sudden force buffeting her.

She had been running from him for the past thirty-six hours, but wherever she tried to go, he was there. St. Pancras, Paris, Belgium. I'll never be free of him, Maggie thought, until one of us is dead.

Almost without realizing it, her hands stole to the seat belt buckle, and she slowly unlocked it, careful not to make a sound, even though there was little chance she'd be heard over the helicopter's engine. The man's back was to her as he leaned out the door, about to shoot something outside. Maggie placed the two pieces of the seat belt next to her, her gaze alternating between the man and the ring his harness was locked into.

She edged out of her seat, crouching on the floor, only three feet from the ring. She reached out for it, her hand creeping closer and closer. She touched the smooth, cold metal, her fingers unfastening it from the metal circle.

The scream burst from her lips as she leaped forward, hands reaching out to shove him through the door, every synapse, every fiber of her being wanting to push him out into the cold air and watch him fall, helpless, until he hit the ground.

Her hands contacted his back, and she pushed with all her might, throwing him off balance and down toward the lip of the door frame. Even in the buffeting wind outside, Maggie was aware of something blurring past her head, then, before she could follow up and heave him the rest of the way out, the man reared up, throwing her off like a rag doll.

Staggering across the passenger's compartment, Maggie cracked her head on the roof and fell back into her seat. Blinking back tears of pain, she looked up to see the man standing over her, his face a mask of raw fury. Then he was upon her, and she could only curl up and try to cover her face with her arms as the merciless blows rained down.

43

David wasn't exactly sure what had happened. As if in slow motion, the man had leaned out, raised his pistol and put a bullet into David's shoulder, the already injured one, making him shout and drop his pistol even as he had fired. The man had smiled grimly and aimed at David's face, about to put a bullet between his eyes, when he had suddenly lurched off balance. His second shot had gone wild. Then he was gone, vanishing inside the helicopter with a roar of rage. The door slammed shut behind him in the wind turbulence.

Clutching his injured shoulder, blood oozing between his fingers, David leaned against the skid and gasped for breath in the tempest under the helicopter blades. He was trying to get his battered body under control again. He wanted to rest, to close his eyes for just a moment. It was overwhelming, but he knew he couldn't give in. Instead, he unbuckled the strap around his waist and tied it to the skid, forming a slipknotted loop on the other end that he could put his leg through.

Holding on to the cold fuselage, he eased along the helicopter's side until he was at the door, tensed to react to it opening again. He wasn't sure what he would do if it did. He slowly reached for the handle, straining against the wind, and got his good hand on it. He yanked the metal release and pulled the door out with all of his remaining strength, forcing it open enough to wedge his body inside.

The brown-haired man was hunched over something, his right arm rising and falling with powerful regularity. Drops of some liquid spattered against the cabin's ceiling, and it took him a moment to register that blood was spraying with each blow. The man was savagely beating someone.

Maggie.

David crawled inside and lunged at the man, ready to put him down once and for all.

As he did, however, the man whirled to meet his charge, bringing up his pistol and going for David's throat with his other hand. Stopped in midstep, David was forced back against the closed door, with the man choking the life out of him until he could bring his pistol over to shoot him. David got his free hand up to stop the pistol before it was aimed at his head, but he was exhausted after everything he had gone through, and the muzzle came closer and closer to the side of his head.

Stars swam in his vision as the man's choke hold intensified, cutting off the flow of blood and oxygen to his brain. Something had to give, and David knew what it was. The only question was whether he could do it before he either was strangled to death or took a bullet in the brain.

Grasping for whatever gasps of oxygen he could suck down, he moved his wounded arm to the door handle. His opponent, hearing him wheeze, snarled and squeezed even tighter.

"You just don't know when to fucking die, do you?"

"Afraid not…despite your…best…efforts…" As he had hoped, the retort made his attacker more furious, and he redoubled his efforts to kill David, smashing him into the door. At the same time, David pulled on the handle and pushed back with all his strength, leaning out into the airstream. He shoved the pistol away and grabbed the man's jacket with his hand as he arced backward, pulling the mercenary out of the helicopter with him.

David tumbled head over heels, and felt a peculiar, weightless sensation as the earth and sky tumbled crazily about him. Then reality reasserted itself, and the nylon strap connecting his leg to the skid tightened around his thigh with a painful jerk as it stopped him cold, leaving him suspended in midair. The momentum of his fall shot him completely under the helicopter, making him swing back and forth, all of his limbs flailing wildly.

The plan should have been more or less foolproof, except that something had gone terribly wrong. A heavy weight was wrapped around David's torso, crushing him, dragging him down. Something blocked his vision and David heard panicked, ragged breathing in his ear that he was sure wasn't his own.

The bastard's hanging on to me! Hanging more or less upside down, David's injured arm dangled uselessly below his head, and for a moment he thought his other one might be broken or injured, as well, since he couldn't seem to locate it as he whirled and spun in the downdraft. The other man's arms and legs seemed to be everywhere at once, crawling on and clawing at him as he tried to improve his hold. David's uninjured arm smacked into something, and he grabbed on and held on tightly.

The other man shouted, but David couldn't make out what he was saying. He realized he was holding on to the back of the man's jacket, and that his enemy was trying to climb up David's body to reach the nylon strap. Using his hold on the cloth, David pulled him back with all his strength. The man tried to wriggle free, but David brought his free leg up into the man's face, feeling the crunch of cartilage as it met his nose. The man's grip slackened, and David did it again, and again. He pulled at the man's back, trying to peel him off.

David felt fingers scrabbling at his torn and bloody sweatshirt as the stunned man slipped farther down. He helped him along by grabbing his wrist and twisting it. Finding the other hand near his mouth, David sank his teeth into the back of it, biting as hard as he could. His opponent shouted in pain, and David tore at the slick, bloody flesh until the fingers released. The hand clawed at his face, but David swung his head so that it couldn't find any purchase. His sweatshirt was peeling away from his body as it came apart under the pressure.

As a last-ditch effort to save himself, the man tried to bring his legs up to wrap around David's waist, but David jackknifed backward to prevent him from cinching around his lower abdomen. The last threads of the sweatshirt tore apart, and the man fell away from David.

David hung there for long seconds, completely exhausted. Now that he had gotten the man off him, there was the complicated matter of trying to get back up into the helicopter. The pressure on his leg was excruciating, the nylon biting deep into his thigh, cutting off the blood supply. If he didn't do something about it quickly, he would end up permanently crippled. Taking a deep breath, David arced up, his fingers straining for the strap. His hand just brushed it, then he fell back again, sending a fresh jolt of pain through his leg and shoulder.

Long seconds passed before he gathered the energy to try again. This time he attempted to get himself rocking back and forth, building up the momentum to make that one desperate lunge to grab the strap. David swung back and forth, going just a bit higher each time. But he tended to swing around in the helicopter's downdraft, which could put him into a dizzying spin and make him miss the grab or, even worse, black out completely. But if he didn't try, David knew he was dead anyway.

He kept going, arcing himself up higher and higher, until with one final burst of energy, he hooked the strap with a white, wind-chilled claw of a finger. He hung there, unsure of what to do next. There was no way he'd be able to haul himself up with one hand—

David looked down, wondering if it might be better to fall rather than succumb to hypothermia, when he saw something very odd indeed. The ground seemed to be rising to meet him.

For a second he thought it was a trick of his vision, some kind of optical illusion, but the landscape below kept growing closer. We're going down, he thought. Sure enough, the helicopter descended to a field near the coast, slowing enough and hovering until it was only a few feet from the ground, then slowly settling to the earth. David managed to avoid the skids of the helicopter, landing and rolling out of the way as it settled into the grass, whipping twigs and debris up all around him. David lay on the ground, trying to claw the strap off his leg, when a shadow fell over him.

"Let me!" The voice sounded odd, clenched somehow, as if the words were spoken through gritted teeth. Someone bent over him, and with a few quick movements, the strap was off his leg. "Come on, let's get you inside!"

He allowed himself to be helped up and into the helicopter, which revved up and took off again. David lay on the floor, looking in disbelief at the orange strap that ran from around the pilot's neck to Maggie's wrist, held taut by her. Her face was a mask of bruised, torn flesh and blood, with one eye swollen completely shut, and her nose squashed into itself, crushed under the pounding she had taken. The way she held her jaw suggested that it had been fractured at the very least.

"Thanks…" he gasped, massaging the numb flesh of his leg with his good arm as he lay on the floor. He thought she might have grinned in response, but it turned into a grimace of pain instead.

"I had to pay you back for saving my life—again." She leaned back against the bench seat, slipped on a pair of headphones and addressed the pilot. "Now, take us to Heathrow, and you get to keep breathing normally."

David tore a strip of his shirt off to make a compress and tried to apply pressure to his arm wound, but he couldn't make his fingers hold on. His vision kept graying out, but he knew he had to stay awake, to make sure she was taken into custody.

"Oh, you're bleeding bad. Here, let me do that." David felt a warm hand on his skin, and firm pressure was applied to his shoulder wound, making him grit his teeth with the pain, and causing the grayness at the edges of his vision to swell into black as he passed out.

44

The next several hours were a blur for David. He remembered bits and glimpses—being carried from the helicopter…the roof of a fast-moving ambulance…hearing a squeaky, rattling wheel as he was carted through bland, sterile hallways…searing pain as something was done to his shoulder…then merciful blackness again.

He came to with a grunt, half-sitting up in his hospital bed, only to fall back as pain racked his body. His left arm was in a heavy, immobilizing cast, and he felt a thick bandage covering his left side, as well.

Before he could move or speak, a doctor was at his bedside to check on him, along with a nurse.

"Water," he croaked from a dry mouth, which was quickly supplied, the coldest, freshest liquid he ever remembered sliding down his throat. They monitored his vital signs, adjusted the flow of two IVs stuck into his arms and nodded to a short, chestnut-haired, intense-looking woman with gray circles under her piercing gold-green eyes. "You've got a minute, maybe two, then the morphine will kick in again. He needs to rest anyway," the doctor said.

She nodded, the simple action appearing to take more effort than it should. "Leave us."

David stared at her for long seconds, wondering if he should somehow know her, but unsure from where. "Hello."

"Good evening, Mr. Southerland. Glad to see you're still with us."

Regardless of her appearance, her voice was certainly familiar. "Nowhere else I'd rather be—even if I don't know where that is," he said.

She smiled, the simple expression transforming her face. "Rest assured that you're with friends. My name is Donna Massen, from Primary."

David's brow wrinkled. "Really? The lock word is 'alpine.'"

Her grin turned sly, as she nodded. "Very good. The key word is 'evergreen.' Glad to hear that your training still comes through, even in your current circumstances."

"Which are what and where, exactly?"

"You're in a private hospital that Room 59 keeps available in western England for just such occasions. You've earned a fairly lengthy stay here, due to that shoulder, but they'll have you right and fixed up as soon as possible."

"What about Maggie?"

"We found her with you at the airport. She could have left, although I'm not sure how far she would have gotten, looking as she did. But she didn't. She said she wanted to make sure you were all right. We've taken her in, as well. It's best to keep her out of sight for now, for both the obvious and more subtle reasons. She's going to be fine, even with the number that was done on her."

"Well, if she doesn't know, tell her that the man who did that to her won't ever come after her again. He's splattered over a half acre of Belgium right now."

"I'm sure she'll sleep easier hearing that. They wired her jaw, but she still tries to speak, even while asleep. She mentioned two names—one is Ray, does that mean anything to you?"

David shook his head, the motion making him dizzy, and he leaned back against his pillow. "Maybe a relative?"

"The other name is yours."

He shrugged, wincing at the movement. "We've been through a good deal together. What about the package?"

"It's been recovered. MI-6 are going through it, just to make sure that all is as it should be. Still, we'll keep our Web crawlers busy for the next couple of weeks, just to make sure that nothing was leaked."

"Glad to hear the mission was a success," he said.

"I know about the losses your team took. It was a terrible thing."

"I let my team down. I couldn't save them. I don't know why I lived and they didn't," he said.

She frowned. "I think you do know the reason why, even if you don't want to admit it. If you had been killed, Mr. Southerland, then the enemy would have that information, and from there who knows where it would have gone and how many more lives would have been lost. You did the right thing. You kept going, even though it must have been very hard to do."

A pleasant heaviness was spreading over David's limbs, and his eyes drooped to half-mast. "Not that difficult. Had to continue the mission…"

"Yes, the director mentioned something about your stubbornness. Apparently you don't like to lose."

"Not if I can help it. What about the…rest of the team. Were they brought back?"

An odd look crossed her face, but Donna recovered quickly. "Their bodies are being flown back from France as we speak." She smoothed the blanket at the edge of the bed, a gesture David found oddly maternal. "You just get some rest now, and we'll begin your debriefing in a few days, when you're feeling better. After that will be several weeks of intense physical therapy, since we'll want you back in tip-top shape. Sleep well, Mr. Southerland."

David barely heard Donna Massen's goodbye or her quiet exit from the room, as he was already drifting off into sleep….

EPILOGUE

Outside David's room, Kate resisted the urge to tear the brown wig off her head, striding instead through the quiet halls until she had left the hospital part behind as she headed back to the small manor house on the grounds, now divided into several apartments for visiting personnel and recovering operatives.

As she walked, she punched an autodial number on her cell, then slipped her earpiece on.

"Kate, you're right on time."

"Have I missed anything?"

"No, just inconsequential small talk." She heard the quiet sounds of chewing. "Jake, are you eating while talking to me?"

"My roasted Cornish scallops with white truffle and white chocolate risotto is best eaten while hot." Although Jake was usually under strict orders to never leave Kate's side, the hospital, between the Snowdon Forest and Lake Te Anau in Wales, was guarded by a rotating schedule of Midnight Team members. Kate felt quite secure there, even with Jake a few hundred miles away.

She trotted up the refurbished nineteenth-century home's front steps and through the doors into the main suite. It was as well appointed as her hotel room back in London. Making for her laptop, Kate brought up the screen. "And here I thought you'd be an Angus-beef-and-Yorkshire-pudding sort," she said laughing.

"Not while on duty. All that heavy meat can make a man slow to react," Jake said.

Kate sat at the desk and brought up what Jake was looking at through his spyglasses at the moment—a stunning redhead in an off-the-shoulder black velvet dress. "And I'm sure you have no designs on impressing the young lady across from you," she said.

"That *young lady,* as you so casually describe her, is Darlene Thomason, who, I think, has done as many missions for MI-5 as I did for the army, perhaps more. But enough shop talk for now, darling," he said, raising his voice and taking his dinner companion's hand. In a lower tone, he spoke to Kate. "The show's about to start. You sure you don't want to get some rest and read Samantha's report in the morning?"

Even though Kate's eyes felt as if bits of ground glass had been sprinkled in them, she said no. "This guy works for the bastards who casually murdered four of our operatives, and nearly brought MI-6 to its knees. I wouldn't miss this for the world."

"Then switch over, because Samantha's claws are about to come out."

"Switching over to Samantha now. Enjoy the rest of your evening, Jake."

"I will. Oh, and Kate—I wouldn't wait up."

"I have absolutely no intention of doing so. Kate out." She switched over to Samantha's spyglasses in time to see her glance about the room, taking in Jake's chatting up of his companion. He was alert enough to catch her gaze out of the corner of his eye and nod subtly at her.

I have to admit, the room is something else, Kate thought. The Grill Room at the Dorchester was decorated in an unusual blend of baroque and modern elegance. Gilded gold chandeliers dangled from the recessed ceiling, casting their intimate light around the room and onto the classical figures painted right onto the walls. Dark-green-and-bright-red-plaid patterns on the casually mismatched chairs accented the red tartan pattern on the carpeted floor. Tall wine cabinets dotted the walls, and the whole place looked as if serious money flowed into and out of it. Kate would have bet a year's salary that the food no doubt tasted like it, as well.

She tuned in to the conversation. "More wine, Terrence?" Samantha asked.

"Thank you, but please—allow me." He poured what looked like a chardonnay into her glass, then refilled his own. Terrence Weatherby looked like a man who was slowly coming apart, but doing his best to hold himself together. Although he was impeccably dressed in a dark, worsted-wool suit that draped his tall frame well, Kate saw small beads of perspiration dotting his hairline, and noted the small tremble in his hand as he replaced the wine bottle in its ice bucket. He's nervous about something, she thought, watching him polish off half his wine in one large swallow. It might be just that he's sitting across from Samantha, or it might be something else entirely.

Regardless of how he looked, Terrence was still trying to project a nonchalant air. "It is so refreshing to relax in a fine restaurant, with such attractive company, for a change."

"Terrence, you're too kind. I suppose your work keeps you busy, especially nowadays," Samantha said.

"Well, you know how it is in the global security market—good business is where you find it."

Oh, Terrence, you really shouldn't set yourself up like that, Kate mused.

Apparently Samantha had the same thought, for she leaned forward a bit, making Terrence grow larger in her view. "And how is business in Europe for Mercury—say, in France, particularly?"

Terrence had been about to take a forkful of what looked like some sort of fish in a cream sauce, and he barely paused as he ate it, chewed and swallowed. Not bad, taking a moment while he tries to figure out exactly what she means, Kate thought.

"France? I'm not sure I follow. There isn't any reason for us to be in France at this time."

"Oh, excuse me, I must have been too vague. How about your business in Paris, in particular, at the Gare du Nord train station earlier today?"

Terrence tried to chuckle, but the sound died in his throat. "I heard something about a shootout there on the news. Are you insinuating that my company had something to do with that?"

Samantha dabbed at her lips with her napkin, then laid it across her plate. "Terrence, you should know me better than that by now. I don't have to insinuate anything. We have the bodies of two of your mercenaries. And we also have one of your pilots, taken alive from Belgium, where he was sent to pick up a certain young woman who had carried out a very nasty mission on your company's behalf."

His face turning as pale as his fish entrée, Terrence rose to his feet with such force that he overturned his chair, attracting startled stares from nearby patrons. "I don't have to sit here and listen to these ridiculous accusations—"

"Actually, Terrence, if you'll look to your left, you'll see two very good reasons why you're going to do exactly that." Samantha's gaze followed Terrence's as he glanced over to see Jake and Darlene, both of them staring back at him with their best dead-eyed, covert-government-assassin gazes.

"They are my operatives. And if I give the word, they will follow you out of here, wait until the proper time and place and spirit you away to one of our little hiding places." Samantha's voice, which had still been light and jovial, turned ice-cold. "And I can guarantee you that the setting, and the conversation therein, will not be nearly as pleasant."

"Sir, is everything all right?" A solicitous waiter, unaware of what he had walked into, addressed Terrence, who was looking as if he might keel over at any moment.

"My dinner companion just had a slight shock, but I'm sure he's all right now, aren't you?" Samantha's tone hid honed steel under velvet.

"Yes, I'm just fine, thank you. Terribly sorry about the disturbance, everyone. Please, enjoy your meals." The mercenary didn't so much fall as collapse into his chair, which had been righted by the waiter.

"There, isn't that better, Terrence? Perhaps you should take some water," Samantha said.

"To hell with that." Terrence grabbed for his wineglass and knocked back the rest of the chardonnay, then poured himself another. "I could really use a double Scotch."

"Perhaps later, after we've concluded out business."

He stopped with the glass still raised. "Business? What business? You've caught us dead to rights. We're finished. After this breaks, Mercury Security is over. You've ruined my company and me, you heartless bitch."

"No, that you did all by yourself. However, I have a solution for you. Let's say that I'm not representing MI-6 or the British government right now."

Terrence's sweating brow frowned in annoyance. "I don't understand—"

"That's fine, but just go with it. I'm not here to arrest you or to dismantle your company, Terrence. In fact, I'm here to offer the opposite. I can make this all go away, for you, and for Mercury. No one outside of you, me and a small, select group of people ever need know that it happened at all."

"Why would you do that?" he asked.

"Because your company is worth more to us intact than torn apart. Mercury Security has its fingers in some very nasty pies, and the people I work with want to know what's happening in those kitchens, to extend the metaphor."

"You want me to be a double agent—spy on my own people?"

Samantha picked up her glass and sipped the chardonnay, then set it down again. "Again, an excellent recommendation. It's either that or you stand trial for treason, of which you will most assuredly be found guilty. Your choice, of course."

Terrence visibly deflated, any semblance of the

polished, refined gentleman disappearing as he hunched over in his seat.

There was a long silence before he mumbled the words that Kate wanted to hear: "I accept your terms."

"Excellent." Samantha rose from the table. "So glad to have reached such an amicable solution, Terrence. My people will set up the details. Oh, and it was *wonderful* to see you again." She strode out of the restaurant, drawing stares from both men and women as she passed their tables.

Kate hit a button on her phone.

Samantha's voice answered. "Yes?"

"That was marvelously done," she said.

"I must admit it gave me a small amount of pleasure. However, I would have given it all up if our team had survived instead."

"You and I both. Still, a masterful job. I have a feeling that this is going to pay off huge in time."

"Yes, I do, as well. Who knows—we may even subcontract with them for some of our messier jobs."

"I'm not sure I'd go that far. Take the rest of the night off," Kate said.

"I'll be drawing a bath and rewarding myself with a good, long soak. What about you?"

"Believe me, there's a bed calling my name this very minute. Thanks again, Samantha."

"No problem at all, Kate. Get some rest yourself—and that's an order."

"Message received. Good night."

Kate set her phone down, turned it off and took out her earpiece. She'd need at least six hours of rest, then the whole thing would start over again.

As she undressed and walked into the tiled bathroom,

she pondered Samantha's words. While she also would have given up the chance to turn Terrence in exchange for her Midnight Team's survival, those decisions always had to be made sooner or later, or else very bad things would happen. And Kate knew that, no matter what the consequences, the responsibility for those decisions rested squarely on her shoulders.

And I would make them again if I had to, if it meant accomplishing what we have tonight, she thought as she stepped into the shower. I would make the same one every single time. But even though she made the water as hot as she could stand it, Kate never truly felt warm, not then, nor under the thick blankets on the bed. Her sleep, however, was relatively untroubled and in the end, that was all she ever could ask for.